"I appreciate your helping us," Sabrina said.

"No problem," Malcolm said as she handed him a wrench.

When their fingers touched, a jolt burned right through Sabrina's spine. *Had he felt it, too? What was wrong with her?* Just being in this stranger's presence was causing her to stutter and get weak in the knees.

"Do you always stop and help strangers?" she asked.

Malcolm raised a brow. "I always stop for a beautiful lady in distress."

"How very gallant of you," Sabrina said.

It took fifteen minutes for Malcolm to fix the tire. "All done," he said when he was through.

"Thanks," Sabrina gushed. "You saved my life."

"Lucky for you I happened by," he replied. Then, grasping one of Sabrina's hands in his, Malcolm lightly brushed his lips across it. "Until we meet again, fair maiden...."

Malcolm bowed gallantly and sauntered back to his car. An instant later, he roared away in his Jag, leaving a starstruck Sabrina standing on the side of the road.

Books by Yahrah St. John

Kimani Press Arabesque

One Magic Moment
Dare To Love

YAHRAH ST. JOHN

lives in Orlando, but was born in the Windy City, Chicago. A graduate of Hyde Park Career Academy, she earned a B.A. in English from Northwestern University. At present, she is an assistant property manager for a commercial real estate company.

Yahrah first began writing at the age of twelve and since that time she has written over twenty short stories. Her first book, *One Magic Moment*, a contemporary romance, was released in December 2004 and was followed by the connecting story *Dare To Love* in July 2005. She was rewarded for her hard work when she was nominated for an Emma Award for Favorite New Author of the Year in 2005.

A member of Romance Writers of America, Yahrah is an avid reader. She enjoys the arts, cooking, travel and adventure sports, but her true passion remains writing. She likes creating romantic stories about that first spark a couple experiences and their journey toward an enduring and lasting love. Currently, Yahrah is working on her fourth novel.

Yahrah St. John

NEVER *Say* NEVER

KIMANI
ROMANCE

 KIMANI PRESS™

ISBN-13: 978-0-373-86003-6
ISBN-10:   0-373-86003-X

NEVER SAY NEVER

Copyright © 2007 by Yahrah Yisrael

www.kimanipress.com

Printed in U.S.A.

Dear Reader,

Thank you so much for spending your time with me. I hope that you enjoyed reading Sabrina and Malcolm's story, just as much as I loved writing their incredibly moving tale. My aim was to create a second-chance-at-love story featuring a tortured hero and a reluctant divorcée. Seeing the characters move forward and heal the wounds of the past while falling madly in love was truly magical. We've all had a failed relationship a time or two, but if you're as lucky as Sabrina and Malcolm, love could be waiting for you around the corner.

For more information about me, please visit my Web site at www.yhrahstjohn.com or please feel free to drop me a note at Yahrah@yahrahstjohn.com. And stay tuned as I bring you more great stories filled with love, sizzling passion and romance.

This book is dedicated in loving memory to my mother and best friend, Naariah Yisrael.

Acknowledgment:

These acknowledgments are for the special people in my life who've always been wonderfully supportive.

First and foremost, I acknowledge my mother Naariah Yisrael, one of the most important and influential people in my life. She steadfastly believed in my talent and instilled in me great confidence and values. Not a day goes by that I don't think of her and the close bond that we shared. I miss her terrible.

I thank my father Austin Mitchell for his word of encouragement and for holding me up throughout this difficult period. To The Mitchell family for being the best fans a writer could have by showing up to every one of my book signings.

Much love to my cousin Gita Bishop and uncle Marvin Smith for reminding me of the joy and comfort I find in writing.

Special thanks to my sister Cassandra Mitchell and best gals, Dimitra Astwood and Tonya Mitchell, for reading my drafts and offering valuable critiques.

Tons of love to my dear longtime friends: Therolyn Rodgers and Tiffany Harris.

I wouldn't be where I am today without all of your support.

Chapter 1

"**I**'m never going to fall in love again," Sabrina Parker vowed to her best friend, Deanna Griffin, as they packed up the five-bedroom stucco house she'd once shared with her ex-husband, Tre Matthews, and eight-year-old daughter, Jasmine. Now that her divorce was finalized, Sabrina was free to leave Baltimore for good.

"Never say never," Deanna replied. "You have no idea what life has in store for you."

"You have met my lying, cheating ex-husband, Tre, haven't you?" Sabrina asked. The words sounded funny coming out of her mouth. It was hard to believe that after ten years of marriage, she was a single woman again.

"Of course, I have," Deanna said. "But there's no reason to give up on men altogether. There are some good ones out there."

"I wish I believed that," Sabrina responded, "but I don't anymore. I no longer believe in fairy-tale endings."

"You may feel that way now, but are you sure *this* is what you want?" asked Deanna, extending her tape for the linen they were packing in the upstairs hall closet. "To leave your home and your friends?"

Sabrina was sad, too, at the prospect of saying goodbye to her dear friend. She had known Deanna and her husband Aaron since she and Tre had first moved to Baltimore for Tre's new job as a labor attorney with Dean and Vickers. They'd often been at tae kwon do matches, dance classes or PTA meetings together. Deanna had been a real lifesaver when Sabrina's marriage had begun to fall apart, but Sabrina had to get out of Dodge quick before she turned into a vengeful man-hater.

"Trust me, Deanna. I have to do this."

"I don't understand, Sabrina. With Tre's infidelity, you could have easily gotten the house and a whole lot more. Why are you running away to Savannah with your tail between your legs?"

"I'm not running away," Sabrina replied testily, snatching the tape out of Deanna'a hand and taping the box herself. "After all the lies Tre's told, I don't want anything from him."

"Why?" Deanna bent down and stared at Sabrina.

"You earned it. You've taken care of him and Jasmine for the last ten years. He owes you."

True enough, Sabrina had sacrificed a lot over the years to become the perfect housewife and mother. She'd given up finishing college and having a career all in the name of fulfilling Tre's idea of what a good wife meant. And what did it get her? A cheating husband. Thank God she'd found that hotel receipt or Lord knows how long she would have continued in the dark.

"He owes me nothing except child support," Sabrina said, as she went downstairs for a cool drink. "I won't let him forget his obligation to provide Jasmine with the best life possible, but as for me, I'm quite capable of looking after myself."

Deanna followed close behind her. "I have to hand it to you, Sabrina. If the shoe was on the other foot, I most certainly would have taken Aaron to the cleaners."

Sabrina opened the fridge and pulled out a Pepsi can and cracked it open. Spinning around, she replied, "I could have done that. And don't get me wrong. I thought about revenge, but then that would be giving Tre too much power over me. And those days are over." Sabrina handed Deanna a soda.

"Good for you!" Deanna replied, setting down the soda on the ceramic-tile counter and clapping her hands. "Hell, I've never seen you like this. So… so…" Deanna searched for those words. "So self-assured and confident. Tre didn't know how good he had it."

Sabrina laughed to herself. Clearly, she had done a good job of convincing Deanna that she'd moved on.

"Thank you, sweetheart." Sabrina feigned a smile. "Even I didn't realize how much I allowed Tre to control my life, our life. I don't know if that was the beginning or the end of us. But mind you, I do have a heart and I can't bear to live in the same town and watch him and Melanie start a life together. It's hard enough just making it through the day."

Deanna patted her shoulder and smoothed Sabrina's straight ebony locks. Deanna adored Sabrina's long, thick hair that fell so generously below her shoulders. She often wished her short mousy-brown hair would grow that long, but it never did. She envied Sabrina's petite five-foot-two frame. Deanna had to content herself with the fact that at thirty-eight, she still had a size-eight figure.

"I loved him, you know." Sabrina's voice caught in her throat.

"I know, Sabrina." Deanna rubbed her back. "So, what's next?"

"Home to Savannah."

"How does Jasmine feel about that?"

Sabrina rolled her eyes. "She absolutely hates the idea. You know how much of a daddy's girl she is. I think she thinks I'm doing this to punish him."

"Aren't you?" Deanna smiled devilishly.

"No!" Sabrina denied the truth.

"Are you sure?" Deanna inquired.

"Of course," said Sabrina emphatically. "No

matter how much I hate Tre, I would never deprive my daughter of her father. But I have to make a fresh start." The only reason she'd stayed in Baltimore this long was so Jasmine could finish out the school year.

"Well, Aaron and I are going to miss you terribly. You've been such an important part of our lives."

"We'll keep in touch," Sabrina offered.

"Yes, of course, but it won't be the same."

"How 'bout I promise to call every week, how's that?"

"I would love that." Deanna hugged her dear friend. "I wish you all the best in Georgia. I know that you'll do well, Sabrina. You may not even realize it, but you're much stronger than you think."

Sabrina squeezed her back in return. "Thanks Deanna, you're a peach."

"Well, what do you think, Dr. Winters?" the excited real-estate agent asked, eager to make a sale on the two-story five-bedroom home that had stood empty on the outskirts of town for well over a year. No one had been able to sell it, but now it looked like this wealthy Boston doctor was ready to make an offer.

Spacious with plenty of sunlight and noisy neighbors a discreet distance apart, the Tybee Island house was exactly what Malcolm was looking for. There was a fireplace in the master suite, a kitchen with an island and a laundry room. The carport was perfect for his Jag. And it came complete with a white picket fence, big front porch and lots of wide open space. Sure, it needed a lot of work, but Malcolm looked forward to getting back to basics and working with his hands rather than having his life revolve around his medical career.

Glancing out of the large bay windows in the front parlor, Malcolm thought back on his former lifestyle. As a cardiologist for Boston Medical, he'd rarely had time to eat or sleep, let alone take on a large project such as renovating an old house. If he wasn't in surgery performing a coronary artery bypass or in the catheterization lab, he was consulting and evaluating cardiac cases under his jurisdiction at the hospital.

But that was then and this was now. He was determined to make a go of his new life. "I'll take it," he replied brusquely.

"Great!" the agent replied enthusiastically. "Let's fill out the contract and I'll present your offer to the sellers."

"How long do you think it'll be?" Malcolm asked as they continued walking through the large, rambling old house. From what he could see, the plumbing was shot, the electrical wiring had gone to hell in a basket and the fireplace was backed up to holy heaven.

"Not long. I'm sure it won't be a problem. The owners are quite eager to make a sell."

He could see why. "Excellent. You can have the

papers sent to me at Parker House." He was staying at the bed-and-breakfast Michael had once said was one of the best in Savannah. The location was ideal because it was convenient to the clinic. It was less than ten minutes away.

Now, he could try and begin building a life here in Savannah and forget the deadly mistake that had cost his twin, Michael, his life.

Locking up the two-story stucco house she'd called home for more than five years was difficult. Sabrina could remember the first time she'd ever seen the two-acre estate. From the very first moment she'd seen it, she'd known that she, Tre and Jasmine would be happy there. A huge backyard with a swing, a built-in deck for grilling and socializing; it had been absolutely perfect for their growing family.

Or so she'd thought. Unfortunately, Tre had had other ideas and decided that one child was all they'd have. "What do we need another child for? Things are perfect the way they are. And one child, we can give her the best in life," he'd said. So as much as she'd wanted another baby, Sabrina had desperately wanted to make Tre happy, so she had agreed. She'd given up her dream of having more children, all to please Tre. And so the other three bedrooms remained empty until Tre finally turned one of them into a study.

Tre had been controlling her for so long. Why hadn't she seen it back then?

"Mom, when are we stopping for something to eat?" asked Jasmine, fidgeting in the passenger seat.

Sabrina shook her head in amazement. Before they'd left, she'd made sure Jasmine had gone to the bathroom and had breakfast. "We just got on the road, Jazzy. We won't be making any stops for some time. Didn't you have cereal this morning?"

"Cold cereal isn't much of a breakfast. When Daddy was here, you always made sure I had a hot breakfast." Jasmine pouted from beside Sabrina.

At the stoplight, Sabrina turned to face her daughter. "Well, Daddy's not with us anymore, Jasmine. So we might be having cold cereals for a while."

"Why, Mom? Why did Daddy go away and leave us?"

Glancing at the road, Sabrina patted her upset daughter's thigh. "Daddy didn't leave *you*, Jasmine. He left me. You still have him. And you'll visit him on holidays and during the summer. Daddy and I just won't be living together anymore."

No matter how much she hated Tre, she would not let her feelings interfere with her daughter's relationship with her father. That wouldn't be right. Though why she even bothered, she didn't know. Tre hadn't bothered to ask for joint custody. She'd obtained sole custody, while he'd been content with visitation rights. One month in the summer and every other Christmas.

"Why? What did you do?"

"Enough with the questions, okay?" Sabrina replied testily. She couldn't take driving the next ten hours if Jasmine was going to whine the entire time. Then again, it wasn't Jasmine's fault that Sabrina was angry. Taking a deep breath, Sabrina calmed herself. "Listen, Jazzy, it's just me and you from now on. And that's how it has to be, okay?"

"If you say so." Jasmine jerked away, folded her arms and proceeded to ignore Sabrina by staring out of the car window.

"Why do we have to leave our home anyway?" Jasmine murmured underneath her breath. "I like it here. All my friends are here. Daddy's here."

Sabrina hated to see her daughter so distraught but it was inevitable. Tre barely found the time to spare from his latest conquest to remember his daughter. Tre was never around that much, yet Jasmine absolutely adored her father. Why? Sabrina would never know. Sabrina would have to be both a father and a mother to Jasmine.

"C'mon, Jazzy. Can't you be open and look at this as an adventure?" Sabrina inquired, but Jasmine didn't respond. Instead, she sulked in the far corner of the passenger side.

That was okay. Sabrina would give her time to heal. And pretty soon Jasmine would see that Savannah was exactly what they both needed. Clean air and good living. A place where you could depend on family and friends, and where people's word meant something, where you could leave your door open and not have to worry about someone robbing you blind.

There would be no more kowtowing to Tre's every whim or letting him run her life. Those days were over. She was taking back her life.

As they made their way out of Baltimore, land of vipers, to sweet-as-a-peach Savannah, Sabrina adjusted her seat and prepared for the long ride ahead.

"Nurse Turner, can you please hand me that chart?" requested Malcolm as he leaned down over her desk in the front reception area of his new clinic. He'd returned from his meeting with his agent, excited about his new purchase.

"Sure thing, Dr. Winters."

Malcolm hazarded a smile. Thank God for Nurse Turner, he thought as he glanced over the patient's chart. She was a godsend. Fifty-two years old, Grace Turner was a RN with over twenty-five years experience. When he'd originally asked the employment agency to send over qualified nurses, he'd received babes in the woods. Straight out of nursing school with no formal experience. He'd quickly had a word with the owner and had made it clear that they needn't bother with anyone under thirty.

That was when they'd sent seasoned RN, Grace Turner. Steadfast and dependable, he could rely on her to handle the patient load without any messy complications.

At Boston Medical, he'd encountered many an intern or resident who'd thought they could slide their seductive fannies into his view and earn themselves a different rotation or an attending physician's position. Little did they know that he was not for sale.

"What's on our slate for this morning?" Malcolm inquired, looking up at the chalkboard that held the day's patient list.

"A broken arm, an upset stomach, a prenatal checkup."

Good, thought Malcolm. Life as a family practitioner was much simpler. Gone were rounds and consultations first thing in the morning. Or a triple bypass surgery at 1:00 a.m. Accepting this position was the best thing he'd ever done.

Now he would have time to enjoy the finer things in life without being interrupted by a page from the hospital, without trying to battle death day in and day out and maybe one day even start a family.

Life as a cardiologist was never easy. You learned to live with the fact that someday your patients wouldn't always make it. Someday you couldn't save everyone. But he'd sure tried.

Head of his class at Dartmouth, he'd specialized in cardiology. A successful internship at Boston Medical, followed up by a prestigious surgical fellowship, had left little doubt that his career was on the right path. Too bad it had left little room for a social life. He'd dated rarely. And sex? Well, any number of females would certainly oblige a physician's needs. But none had ever thrilled him, except Halle Davis, a beautiful statuesque BAP, born into wealth but determined to prove she was more than a pretty face. They'd met in undergrad at Dartmouth and had continued dating throughout his internship, but once his residency came, their once solid relationship had hit rocky waters. The long hours had taken their toll on Malcolm physically, as well as emotionally, so much so that Halle had enough and ended their five-year courtship abruptly and married a financier.

But Malcolm had never looked back. His career had prospered when he'd successfully treated Senator Andrews's heart condition and performed a triple bypass, catapulting his surgical career.

Why hadn't he seen that he was doing too much? Trying too hard to win the respect of his colleagues, who'd thought a thirty-six-year-old black man could never be a good surgeon. He'd been so quick to prove them all wrong. How could he have been so self-involved?

"Dr. Winters?" Grace asked, looking up at him. "Are you ready for your next patient?"

"Certainly. I'll be there in a moment."

And the clinic, it had fallen into his lap when Dr. Baker, Cuyler-Brownsville's oldest family practitioner had retired. He'd handed his entire client roster over to Malcolm, including allowing Malcolm to rent the property until he could buy Dr. Baker out.

The clinic came complete with three exam rooms, office, storage room and a reception/waiting area.

Malcolm wrote some notes down in the chart. He'd had quite a few non-existent cases recently. He could only hope they eased up once the town's curiosity was cured.

"So, who else do we have?"

"We have a former patient of Dr. Baker's presenting with pre-heart attack symptoms."

"Show him into my office immediately."

Malcolm wasted no time getting right down to brass tacks. After reviewing his chart, he didn't see any need to beat around the bush. "Mr. Gibson, I see here that you're a smoker."

"Yes, Dr. Winters. I've tried giving up the habit, honest I have, but I haven't had any luck," Mr. Gibson chuckled.

Malcolm did not share his amusement. "Your luck may be running out, Mr. Gibson, if you continue to abuse your heart in this fashion. The heart is not meant to take this sort of abuse." He leaned back in his chair and regarded Mr. Gibson for a long moment.

His patient was not easily embarrassed and did not look away. "That may be the case, but who's to say it's the smoking? Couldn't it be something else?"

"Yes, indeed, you are correct," Malcolm answered, sitting upright again, "which is why I want to do a complete blood workup. I also want to do a cardiac stress test."

"Isn't that one of those treadmill tests I've seen on TV?" Mrs. Gibson queried, speaking up for the first time. Mrs. Gibson was a timid-looking Caucasian woman. Short, petite with mousy-brown hair, she was rather unassuming. Malcolm had almost forgotten she was in the room, she was so shy. Mrs. Gibson was the sort of woman who lived in the shadow of her husband. He wondered what she would do if she had to live without him. Hopefully, she wouldn't get that chance.

"Yes, it is. And what it does is detect the heart rate, rhythm and blood pressure. It helps us better determine coronary artery disease and it's less invasive than an angiography. I'd also like a stress echocardiography done, as well—this will show me images of your heart at rest and during the peak of the exercise."

"Sounds like a whole lot of mumbo jumbo to me, Doc Winters." Mr. Gibson wasn't sure he believed in all this medical hocus-pocus. If it's your time to go, it's your time to go. But he did this for his wife. She wouldn't know what to do on her own without him in the world.

"I know it sounds like a lot, but all these tests are needed to make an accurate diagnosis," Malcolm replied, writing out a script and handing it to Mr. Gibson. "Speak with my nurse at the front desk and she will set up the tests at the hospital. Then we'll reconvene in a few weeks and review the results."

"Sounds good to me," Mr. Gibson replied, standing up and shaking Malcolm's hand. "You know, Dr. Winters, you really are a nice man. You need to find yourself a wife to settle down with."

Malcolm didn't comment. He merely smiled kindly at the man. A wife and kids. He wasn't ready for that kind of life-changing commitment. Maybe one day soon. *Then why,* an inner voice rang out in his head, *did you by a house complete with a white picket fence and five bedrooms if you don't want a family?* That was a good question, Malcolm thought as the Gibson's left.

Malcolm blew out a sigh of relief, when they'd gone. Just what he needed starting off his new life in Savannah, his first heart patient in a year!

Driving into Savannah was cathartic as the sweet smell of magnolia blossoms and azaleas filled the air, reminding Sabrina that she had indeed come home. The moss-laden two-story homes and large oak trees that lined the brick-paved historic district and park squares were just as fragrant as she remembered since she'd last visited with Tre.

Sabrina remembered that visit. It had been an uphill battle to convince Tre to come, but her family hadn't seen baby Jasmine. Tre had considered anything south of DC hick country and had steadfastly refused to come. She'd finally pressed him until he'd had no choice but to give in.

Though once they'd arrived, Sabrina had wished he'd stayed home. He'd complained about the long ride and the accommodations. He'd even complained about the food, claiming that Southerners ate so much fatback no wonder the majority were overweight. One time was all it took for Tre to vow never to come back to that "ho bunk town." She'd returned alone with Jasmine when she was three, but Tre had complained so much about their absence that she had never dared try it again.

Sighing, Sabrina realized that she should have known then that something wasn't quite right in Denver.

Sabrina caught Jasmine's yawn as she emerged from her two-hour slumber. Stretching out her arms, Jasmine perked up at her new surroundings. "Are we there yet?"

"Yup, this is my hometown, baby doll. This is where your mama was raised." Sabrina brushed back some hair off Jasmine's forehead.

Jasmine glanced out of the window in wonder. "Can I have some ice cream?" Jasmine pointed to the ice cream shop at the corner of the block.

"You may certainly not. You haven't even had dinner."

"But I'm hungry. And we've been driving all day."

Sabrina breathed in deeply. Jasmine was severely testing her nerves. They'd already stopped off at Denny's.

"I promise I'll get you something to eat when we get to my parents' house, okay?"

"I don't even remember what they look like," Jasmine commented aloud.

A hot tear trickled down Sabrina's cheek, nearly blinding her as she drove. It was her fault that Jasmine didn't have a relationship with her own grandparents. She should never have let Tre insist on their not visiting, but all that was about to change. Savannah was filled with lots of aunts, uncles and cousins. Sabrina was thinking that Jasmine was about to get more family than she knew what to do with when the unthinkable happened. She got a flat.

Chapter 2

Malcolm sighed heavily as he drove his vehicle down the road. He should never have taken that side street. Now, he was lost *again*. For such a small town, he'd gotten lost nearly a dozen times since his arrival.

This latest debacle was going to cause him to miss dinner at Parker House. The cook served dinner promptly at six and if you weren't there, you were out of luck. The food the last several nights had been divine and Malcolm did not want to miss out, which was why his getting lost was so frustrating.

It was definitely time to invest in a map of the area, Malcolm thought. It was the first item on his agenda after supper until he saw a woman along the side of the road.

* * *

Sabrina slowly decreased her speed and moved to a safe place on the side of the road. After setting the parking brake and turning on her hazards, Sabrina called AAA. That's when the dispatcher informed her it would be nearly an hour before someone could arrive. Apparently there was an accident on Highway 95 and everyone had been dispatched to that site.

"Great!" Sabrina muttered as she exited the vehicle and walked around to the passenger side. Sure enough, the tire was as flat as a pancake. What was she going to do now? It was sweltering outside and she had to keep the air on, which meant that she'd most likely run out of gas.

"Mom, can't you change it?" Jasmine asked, leaning out of the window.

"Sorry, baby. That was Daddy's department," Sabrina replied. And now it was going to be hers, but she didn't know how. Tre had tried teaching her once, but when she hadn't picked it up right away, he'd given up on her.

And now she had a child in the car and it was getting dark. She had no choice but to try and change it herself. She couldn't wait on AAA; it would take them hours to get here. Did she even have a spare?

Opening the glove compartment, Sabrina pulled out the owner's manual and was thumbing through it when she heard the roar of another engine coming down the road.

Thank God, thought Sabrina. Maybe she could flag down some help.

"Stay inside the car, Jazzy," Sabrina ordered. "And lock the door. Keep this—" Sabrina handed her the cell phone "—while I check out who this is."

A red Jaguar pulled in front of her and the engine shut off. From where Sabrina was standing, she could tell it was a man, but she couldn't clearly see his features because the windows were tinted. For a moment, Sabrina wondered if she was safe. There was still a little daylight; hopefully she had nothing to worry about, but just to be on the safe side, Jasmine would remain in the car.

When the stranger disembarked, he towered over her and Sabrina instinctively took a step backward. He had to be at least six foot three, with a slender frame and an all-around fine build. Whoever he was, he sure kept himself in excellent shape.

"Are you all right, ma'am?" a smooth tenor voice asked.

Sabrina heard the words, but was too caught up in his mystique to speak. Were all rescuers as good-looking as this one?

Nutmeg-colored skin, well-groomed mustache and coal-black hair clipped short to reveal nice wavy lines, made for a dashing demeanor. Clearly the man prided himself on his appearance if the pressed navy trousers and crisp white shirt underneath a beige cardigan were anything to go by. Sabrina couldn't put her finger on it, but his presence and features were almost regal. She did her best to ignore the pair of white irises and onyx eyes with curly lashes that were watching her so intently.

"Are you hurt?" he asked, moving swiftly towards her.

"Ummm, no," Sabrina said with a slight catch in her throat. "But I do have a flat," she said, pointing to her left rear tire.

"You most certainly do," the mysterious stranger said, smiling back at her.

Malcolm was in awe when he stepped out of his vehicle and found the most beautiful woman he'd ever seen. She was absolutely breathtaking.

Throughout their exchange, he was mesmerized by this exotic creature. She was wearing a pair of ripped jeans and a tank top revealing what he estimated to be B-cup breasts and the derriere…well, that was small, but curvy. He wondered though how she could have even given birth with such a petite frame. What did she weigh? A buck and a quarter, if that. And from his view, she was barely over five feet.

But what drew him to her the most was the hair. Long, thick and luminous, it hung generously past her delicate shoulders. Oh and the rich honey-brown face was even more impressive and those expressive copper eyes only added to her allure.

"Uh, hum." Sabrina coughed to regain the stranger's attention. He'd been staring at her very intently. "So what do you think? Can you help me out? Because I have no idea how to change a tire."

Malcolm shook himself out of his daydreaming. "Oh yes, of course," he replied. "Pop your trunk."

Sabrina unlocked the trunk while the stranger returned to his car, removed his cardigan and rolled up his sleeves.

Once he'd returned, Sabrina watched him pull out the spare tire and jack and start to work. "I sure do appreciate your helping us," Sabrina said, nodding to Jasmine who was still staring openly at them from the back seat.

"No problem, miss." Malcolm grinned as Sabrina handed him a lug nut wrench to remove the hubcaps.

When their fingers touched, a jolt went straight up Sabrina's spine and she jumped away from Malcolm as if she'd been burned.

Did he feel that? What was wrong with her? Just being in this stranger's presence was causing her to stutter and get weak in the knees. She couldn't remember the last time she'd felt this way. It had certainly not been with Tre.

Sabrina was curious about something though. "Do you always stop and help strangers?" she asked.

Malcolm raised a brow. He seemed surprised at the question. As if the thought had never crossed his mind not to. "I saw a lady in distress," he answered, looking over her seductively. "Who needed my assistance, so the answer would be an emphatic yes," Malcolm replied, looking up at her. She was so amazingly beautiful. He wondered why she was alone along the side of the road with her daughter. What had happened to her? Someone else's loss was his gain. He hadn't missed the sensuous tingle that had passed between them a moment ago.

"How very gallant of you," Sabrina replied as he lowered himself to the asphalt and jacked up the car. It took Malcolm all of fifteen minutes to remove the flat and put on the spare. He didn't say much while he worked; he just finished the task at hand. When he was done, he announced it was ready to drive and Sabrina was thrilled.

"All done," he said, wiping his hands on a towel Sabrina supplied from her trunk.

"Thank you so much," Sabrina gushed. "You saved my life. I'd still be waiting here for AAA to come."

"Then it's lucky I stopped by," Malcolm replied. Grasping one of Sabrina's hands in his, he lightly brushed his lips across it. "Until we meet again, fair maiden."

Malcolm bowed gallantly and sauntered back to his car. An instant later, he roared away in his Jag, leaving Sabrina standing on the side of the road, starstruck. When she finally started her engine, she realized she didn't even know the stranger's name!

When she arrived on her parents' block, the driveway was already packed with cars. A party looked as if it was already in full swing. Sabrina parked alongside the side curb with the rest of the vehicles.

Her parents had no idea that she was coming, but Sabrina knew her family and the entire community would welcome her back with open arms because that's how Georgians were.

"We're here!" Sabrina announced cheerily as she unbuckled her seat belt and disembarked from the vehicle.

Hauling several suitcases out of the trunk, Sabrina set them on the sidewalk and took a moment to look around the neighborhood. Built in the sixties, the Cape Cod-style house was still holding up, even though it could use a new coat of paint and some siding, but all in all, it still looked good. Her mom and dad's favorite rockers were sitting out on the wooden porch, next to her mother's crocheting basket.

It brought a smile to Sabrina's face knowing that Savannah was still a place she could be proud to raise her daughter.

"Is that where we're going to live?" Jasmine inquired, looking up at the two-story house.

Sabrina didn't miss the disdainful tone that escaped her eight-year-old daughter's lips. It was a far cry from their five-bedroom estate in Baltimore. And Jasmine's disdain was all Sabrina's fault, too. She and Tre had raised a snob.

"Yes, it is, sweetie." Sabrina leaned down to her daughter for a tight squeeze. "C'mon. It's time you meet your family." Sabrina held out her hand, but Jasmine ignored it and walked ahead of her up the porch stairs. Sabrina sighed, then picked up the suit-cases and headed for the house.

Now that she was here, Sabrina was scared to ring the doorbell, but she'd sold her house and most of her belongings. There was no turning back now.

Exhaling, Sabrina prepared herself for the endless questions that would befall her this evening. Her family wasn't known for being shy or tactful.

Depressing the buzzer, Sabrina waited with bated breath.

Her mother answered on the second ring and screamed in delight. "Oh…James, come quick."

At the sight of her portly, five-foot-five mother in roller-set hair, Sabrina's eyes shone bright with tears. All this time, she'd thought she hadn't needed her. How wrong she'd been!

"Oh, Mama," Sabrina cried and was immediately enveloped in the safety of her mother's arms.

"Oh, baby, let me look at you." Her mother's small hands grasped either side of her face. "You're all grown up. Give your mama another hug." Sabrina was all too obliging and gave her mother another gentle squeeze. How was it that being near your parents made you feel six years old again?

"And who is this delightful creature behind you?" her mother asked, openly staring at Jasmine. Surely this couldn't be her eight-year-old granddaughter? Time somehow had flown when she wasn't looking.

Sabrina walked over to Jasmine, who stood frozen

at the doorway. "There's no need to be scared," Sabrina whispered in her ear and grabbed Jasmine's hand.

"Mom, this is your grandbaby," Sabrina replied and pushed Jasmine toward her grandmother.

Beverly Parker bent down and looked at the beautiful child staring back at her. Jasmine had no idea who she was and it broke her heart.

"Sweet heavens." Her mother clutched her chest. "My prayers have been answered." When her mother reached for Jasmine, she stepped backward.

Beverly saw the fear lying in her granddaughter's eyes. She was a stranger to her. It tugged at Beverly's heartstrings. She stood up, swallowed hard, biting back the tears.

"Woman, what's with all the screaming? Who was at the door?" her father asked, finally emerging inside the foyer.

James Parker was a sight to behold. No one could ever say that her father wouldn't go down fighting. He looked as fit as a fiddle. No middle-age spread for him. Her father was tough and lean. A powerful set of shoulders, set off by a massive chest. He could probably be a linebacker for the Green Bay Packers.

Her father's inherent strength could be seen on the few lines that marked his African features. James Parker carried himself with a commanding air of self-confidence that many recognized, but few could imitate.

"Little Bit!"

Sabrina's heart filled with joy at seeing her father.

Sure he was older than she remembered, but he was her pops. "Yes, it's me, Daddy. Your baby girl has come home."

"Well, come here and give ya old man a hug," James Parker replied with a grin on his face from ear to ear.

"Oh, Daddy. I've missed you so much."

"So have I, Little Bit."

"It's good to be home. You don't know how much I've needed you."

"Come on in then and get out of the street." Her mother pushed the front door closed. "No need for everyone to know our business."

But as soon as the door was closed, Beverly yelled out to the family already assembled in the living room. "Alton, Felicia. Come quick."

Sabrina inhaled deeply. So much for easing back into town. Sabrina had hoped to catch a quick shower and change her clothes before facing the crowd in a pair of ripped jeans, tank top and flip-flops.

Unfortunately, Felicia arrived first with her three children, Destiny, Chynna and Lucas, in tow.

"So, the prodigal daughter has returned," her sister sneered, with Chynna on her hip.

Sabrina caught the hostile tone in Felicia's voice and rolled her eyes heavenward. Obviously nothing had changed in the six years since they'd last seen one another. Her older sister was still holding on to a grudge, and for what? Sabrina couldn't fathom why.

She appeared to be in good health. Although a few extra pounds had crept up on her five-foot-nine frame, Felicia was still the picture of youth. There were no fine lines around her thirty-three-year-old smooth chestnut complexion. So, why was she still giving her grief after all these years?

"It's good to see you, too," Sabrina returned evenly. "My nieces and nephew are as gorgeous as ever." Her nine-year-old niece Destiny was a little angel with small features, a slender shape and a head full of hair, while her baby sister Chynna was equally irresistible. A little chubbier than her sister, Chynna was a head shorter with pigtails and barrettes. Sabrina didn't know what to make of her six-year-old bespectacled nephew Lucas who carried around a pet frog. He didn't seem to come from the same family. "How's Sean? Is he here?" Sabrina looked over Felicia's shoulder.

"No," Felicia replied through pursed lips. "I came alone. He's holding down the fort at the resort on Tybee Island. Someone has to, you know? Since some people went off and left the rest of the family to deal with the fallout."

Sabrina ignored the dig. She refused to let her sister bait her into an argument when she'd only just arrived. "Glad to hear it."

"Is that my little sis?"

Sabrina distinguished the voice, but didn't see the owner until her brother peeked out from over their father's head.

"Alton." Sabrina's eyes shone bright with tears at the sight of her big brother. He was exactly what she needed. At thirty-five, her brother was tall, handsome and athletic. Alton prided himself on his male physique and had maintained it for years by playing sports. His smooth honey coloring favored her buttery-brown tone. When people saw them they easily passed for sister and brother. Sabrina wondered if that's why Felicia always gave her such a hard time. Was she envious of her and Alton's closeness?

Alton gave Sabrina a massive hug, giving Sabrina the opportunity to feel the muscles rippling under his white shirt. "Wow! Someone's really beefed up."

Alton patted his chest. "Yes, well, my job does require some muscle. But forget about me. How long are you planning on staying?"

Sabrina paused before saying, "Indefinitely. I've decided to move back home."

"Pardon? Did I hear correctly, Little Bit?" her father asked. "Because you haven't called this house home for sometime."

"You are?" her mother said. "That's fantastic!"

"You lost the right to call this home when you left ten years ago and never looked back," Felicia commented, narrowing her eyes at Sabrina.

Sabrina spun around and glared at Felicia. She couldn't believe Felicia would speak this way in front of the children. "Jasmine, why don't you and your cousins go play in the other room while we grown folks talk?"

"I don't know anyone here, Mom," Jasmine complained.

"I know, sweetheart," Sabrina bent down to look in her daughter's eyes. "But wouldn't you like to get to know them? You've always complained that you were an only child. And now you've got this whole extended family with lots of aunts, uncles and cousins. Aren't you the least bit excited?"

"I just wanna go home and see Daddy."

"I'm afraid that's not going to happen, Jasmine. We are not going back to Baltimore," Sabrina stated vehemently.

Reluctantly, Jasmine took her cousins to the living room.

"Well? We're still waiting to hear what happened," her father said from her side. "Just spit it out. What happened between you and Tre? Better to pull off a bandage quick than to play around at it."

"Fine. I know how you feel about marriage, Daddy, but Tre and I are divorced," Sabrina replied, tossing her head. She eyed her father, waiting for his reaction.

"What?" Her father stepped back. A devout Baptist, her father was a religious man and believed in the sanctity of marriage. He and her mother had been married for thirty-six years and were still going strong. "What went wrong? Couldn't the two of you have worked it out?"

"Afraid not."

"Oh my Lord!" her mother said. "When did this happen?"

"Six months ago," Sabrina responded. "They hopped a plane to the Dominican Republic and ended it."

"Why didn't you call us? Why are we just hearing about this now?" Alton jumped in before their father could get a word out.

"I couldn't." Sabrina bowed her head in shame. In all her years married to Tre, she'd always portrayed them as the perfect family. How could she say it had all been a lie?

"Why? What happened, Little Bit?" her father asked.

"He…he…" Sabrina could hardly get the words out. She'd thought she was over the pain of Tre's betrayal. How could it still hurt after all this time? "He cheated on me, Daddy," Sabrina plunged on. "For months, he lied to my face while he went to bed with another woman."

"Oh, baby girl." Her father pulled her close to his chest. "I despise that man. Any man who could cheat on my baby girl… God, I want to strangle him with my bare hands."

"I'm not far behind you, Pops." Alton puffed out his chest. "Just point me to the nearest map and I'll scour Baltimore looking for that scoundrel and beat some sense into him."

"No need to go and get yourself arrested," replied Felicia. "You are sheriff."

"Sheriff? Wow! I'm impressed," Sabrina remarked. "How long have you been in office?"

"Oh, about three years now."

"That long?" Sabrina asked.

"Enough with the welcome backs," her father said, stepping in the middle of their circle. "You should have called us, Sabrina. Maybe we could have helped."

"What could you do, Daddy? It wouldn't change anything. My marriage would still be over."

"Well, you can dry your eyes, girl. You're not alone anymore."

"Yes," her mother replied, "Your family will get you through this awful time." Her mother stretched out her arms and pulled Sabrina close. "You're home now. And you don't have to worry; you always have a home here. Isn't that right, James?"

"Of course, woman!" her father said gruffly. "That goes without saying."

"Well, there are other guests who I'm sure are eager to see you." Her mother pulled her toward the living room with her siblings following behind her, Alton with a smile and Felicia with a scowl. She was silent for now, but Sabrina had a sinking feeling that wasn't the end of her sister's hostility.

Her family welcomed her back with open arms and was truly excited to see Jasmine after all these years. Her happiness was short-lived, however, because Felicia wasted no time telling everyone of her single status. Instead of making her feel better about coming home, she was plagued with self-doubt. Was it her imagination or did she see pity in some of their faces?

Poor Sabrina. Not only was she a single mother now, but she was jobless and homeless.

Turning away, she found a quiet spot in the kitchen and found her mother icing a German chocolate cake, her favorite. Beside it sat a sweet potato pie.

"Mom, did you cook all this?"

"Of course, baby." Her mother placed the knife down on the table and took a seat. "I love to cook and you know how much I love to dote on the family. And now I have you to work on."

"I'm sorry, Mama. I should have never distanced myself from the family."

"Let's not worry about the past, let's just enjoy the present," her mother said, handing her a paper plate.

"Still catering to you, I see," Felicia retorted underneath her breath from the door before spinning on her heels and storming away.

Later, the family stood around the table and bowed their heads while her father said grace over the fried chicken, red beans and rice, green beans, potato salad and homemade biscuits. After the prayer, everyone dug in.

Sabrina smiled; now this, she remembered. Everyone gathered around eating good soul food. She was filling her plate when her father started in.

"So have you thought about what you're going to do for work?" her father asked in front of everyone.

Sabrina groaned inwardly. Exactly the topic she wanted to avoid at dinner with a table full of family.

Several curious pairs of eyes fixated on hers, waiting for an answer.

A lump formed in Sabrina's throat and she found it hard to speak. There was nothing like being interrogated by one's own father. He intimidated easily. Even when she'd been a little girl, Sabrina could never keep a secret, which had irritated Alton and Felicia to no end.

"No, Daddy, I really hadn't gotten that far yet. I've only been home *one* day," she emphasized. "I was hoping Jasmine and I could stay here for awhile until I figure things out."

"That may be so, but it's best not to let the dust to settle under your feet. And as for a job, I'm sure Felicia and Sean could use some help at the hotel or at Parker House. Not sure if you know, but they're mainly running things now. Your mom and I have retired."

Of course, working at the family business went hand-in-hand with living in the Parker residence. "I would be more than happy to help out, Dad. Give me a few days first, okay? And then I'll find out where Felicia and Sean need help."

"What do Felicia and Sean need?" Felicia snapped, butting in.

"Help with the hotel and Parker House," her father answered.

"Listen, Sabrina," Felicia cocked her head to one side and a pair of furious brown eyes settled on Sabrina. "Sean and I have been doing just fine handling things. We don't need the likes of you coming back to tell us how to run it."

"Felicia, I've only been back for a New York minute, so I'm not sure where all this hostility is coming from. But I am a part of this family, too."

Felicia rolled her eyes. "You could have fooled me, *sista.* I don't recall seeing you over the last ten years working twelve-hour shifts and entertaining the tourists. Making sure their beds were clean or that the breakfast buffet was on. So don't tell me about family."

"And am I supposed to bow at your feet because you did?" Sabrina returned. "'Cause it'll be a cold day in hell, *sista!*"

"Wait a minute!" Her father's voice rose over their bickering. "That is my hotel and don't the two of you ever forget it."

"Of course, Daddy." Felicia lowered her head. Her father was the one person that Felicia respected and didn't dare raise her voice to. Everyone else was fair game. "But you have to realize that the business has been my baby and I won't have her—" she pointed to Sabrina "—coming back and usurping my position."

Sabrina spoke up on her own behalf. "Why do you always think the worst of me?"

"Why not? You've always been nothing but a thorn in my side since the day you were born!" A deafening silence fell across the room.

"Leave my mom alone," Jasmine yelled running in and charging at Felicia. "You leave her alone, you hear me. You're nothing but an evil witch!"

It hurt Sabrina to see Jasmine's beautiful face nearly red and curled in anger and her mouth down-turned in an ugly snarl. Was this her precious baby that had spit such venom? What had happened to her little girl?

"Jasmine, that's enough. I've had enough of your behavior, young lady. I will not have you disrespecting your aunt. You will show her some respect. Even if she doesn't deserve it," Sabrina countered, turning a contemptuous look on her older sister. She was sick of her twisted jealousy. It had gone on for years and she wouldn't let her evil poison her daughter.

"I don't care!" Jasmine yelled back at her. "I hate these people and I hate it here," Jasmine retorted, running out of the house.

"Why should I be surprised? Like mother, like daughter," Felicia spat out.

The family hushed, expecting a fight, but Sabrina didn't have time for one. Noting the embarrassment on her mother's face at Jasmine's outburst, Sabrina turned on her heel and stormed out the front door. She wouldn't give Felicia the satisfaction by stooping to her level. What she needed was to have a word with her angry daughter.

When she stepped onto the porch, Sabrina expected to find Jasmine outside sulking. Instead, the porch was empty. Sabrina searched around the house calling out to Jasmine, but no one answered. Five minutes later, she ran back inside the house.

"It's Jasmine," Sabrina choked out. "She's gone!"

Chapter 3

"Are you sure? Maybe she's outside hiding?" Her mother rushed forward.

"No!" Sabrina muttered, running her fingers through her hair. "I looked around the house. And she's nowhere to be found."

"Sounds like she's run away," Felicia stated unceremoniously from the other side of the room with a glint in her eye.

"Ohmigod!" Sabrina covered her mouth with her hand.

"Felicia!" her mother reproached her older daughter.

"Not for long." Alton pulled out his walkie-talkie from his waist. "I'll get on the horn and get some deputies out there looking for her. Don't worry, sis. We'll find her." Alton squeezed her shoulders before walking outside to radio his men.

"I'm going after her," Sabrina replied, running out of the house and brushing past Alton.

"Wait!" she heard her mother say, but she was out the door.

Sabrina couldn't stand still and wait for news. She had to find her baby girl. This was all her fault. She knew Jasmine was unhappy. Had been for months since the separation, but what else could she do? She couldn't stay in that house and relive the life she'd once shared with Tre. It just wasn't healthy. And it hurt way too much to think of what might have been.

Running down the street, Sabrina cried out her daughter's name. "Jasmine! Jasmine! Jasmine, honey where are you?"

Tears blinded her eyes and glistened on her cheeks. How did she let things get this far? Why hadn't she seen that Jasmine's acting out was a cry for help? What if something happened? If it did, she would never forgive herself.

The cool breeze felt good against Malcolm's nutmeg skin. After the long day he'd had, the fresh air was a relief. Who said that dealing with pre-schoolers, hormonal pregnant women and elderly flirts was any better than heart patients?

His first week at the clinic had been maddening.

It had become common knowledge that he was the new doctor and a bachelor. So, every widow in town was lining up at his exam table. He'd politely let each and every one of them down gently. The last thing he wanted was a relationship.

Then there was Mr. Gibson. A habitual smoker on the verge of a heart attack who refused to listen to reason. The man should know better. He'd already suffered one heart attack, but still continued to smoke. Did he want to make it two? Malcolm had tried to get through to him, explaining the stress effects of nicotine on his heart. That it could increase his heart rate, causing irregular rhythms, or constrict the blood vessels in the heart and increase his risk of cancer. None of that seemed to penetrate his thick skull. He insisted that he had lived this long and he intended to live even longer.

Malcolm had come to Savannah to avoid cardiology, figuring heart patients would be few and far between. Why after only one week on the job did his first major patient have to have a heart condition?

Now all he wanted to do was sit on a bench and throw bread at the little ducks in the pond. But when he arrived at his favorite spot in Forsyth Park after a hard day's work, he found a young girl crying her eyes out on the wooden bench.

A mop of curls and big brown eyes, she was the cutest thing he'd ever seen. As he approached, he noticed something oddly familiar about her. That was when he recognized her as the little girl from inside the car earlier this afternoon. But why was she sitting alone when it was getting dark outside? Where was her mother?

Turning his shoulder, Malcolm looked around the park, but didn't see the gorgeous siren that had wandered into his thoughts throughout the evening. Should he approach? His first instinct was to help, but he had a funny feeling that he was walking into the middle of a lion's den.

Brushing off the bench beside her with his hand, Malcolm sat down. He let her cry until she was ready to speak.

When she didn't right away, Malcolm pulled out a handkerchief and handed it to her.

Sniffling, Jasmine looked up at him suspiciously before finally accepting it, but she still didn't say a word. She dabbed at her eyes and blew her nose before returning the handkerchief.

After a while, Malcolm finally spoke. "Okay now?"

Jasmine nodded, but she didn't look up from her lap.

"Want to tell me what's wrong?"

Jasmine shook her head.

"Like why are you sitting here all by yourself? What's your name, little girl?"

She wanted to answer. This one didn't look so bad, but her mama didn't raise no fool. Never talk to strangers, she'd always told Jasmine.

"You can trust me, you know." He smiled when Jasmine's eyes finally rested on his. "Okay, how about I go first? My name is Malcolm Winters, and I'm the new doctor here in Savannah. I recently moved here from Boston where I was a cardiologist."

Apparently, he sparked her interest because Jasmine's round saucer eyes perked up. "What's a cardiologist?"

"It's a doctor who treats people with heart problems."

"Wow! That sounds cool."

Malcolm laughed heartily. That was the first time someone had ever thought his former specialty was cool. Most people thought it was grueling and gut-wrenching.

"So? Now it's your turn."

Glancing sideways, Jasmine figured she could trust him. He was a doctor after all, and weren't they supposed to help people?

"My name is Jasmine. And I moved here today with my mom from Baltimore and I already hate it. Everyone is yelling at each other. But most of all, I miss my dad."

When Malcolm noticed her mouth start to upturn as if she was about to cry again, Malcolm lightly patted her knee to soothe her.

"It's okay, you know. We all miss our parents sometime."

"You do?" Jasmine asked, surprised. She thought that once you became an adult you didn't need your parents anymore.

"Yes." After Malcolm's father left when he and Michael were five years old, things went horribly wrong for the Winters family. That's when his mother, Dinah, changed from being a warm, caring wife and mother to a cold, calculating... No, no, no, he wasn't going there.

Shaking himself, he found a pair of eyes watching him. "Are you okay?" asked Jasmine. "You look kinda sad, too."

"I'm okay, Jasmine. And trust me, I understand that parents can sometimes upset you, but don't you think you should have told your mother where you were going?"

Jasmine hung her head low. "Why should I?" she asked, arms folded across her chest. Her mom was the one who decided to move to this horrible town with mean relatives thousands of miles from her father. Why didn't kids get a choice?

"Because your mom loves you and is probably worried sick."

"I suppose you're right. But do I have to go now? My grandparents' house is so loud and noisy," Jasmine commented on the adult's complete lack of manners. "Everyone is yelling and screaming at each other. Can't we sit here for a little bit?"

"Sure we can." Malcolm relented. What could it hurt? The child was obviously upset. "But what do you say we give your mom a call, first?" Malcolm asked, pulling his cell phone out of his cardigan pocket. "So she doesn't worry."

"I suppose I could do that," Jasmine replied.

Malcolm rose to stand and that's when Sabrina came charging at him.

Sabrina didn't know how long she walked the neighborhood. Dusk had long since past and Sabrina was terrified that she hadn't found Jasmine yet. What if someone abducted her?

It finally occurred to her to walk through the park. Jazzy loved the swings; maybe she'd gone there.

It didn't take long for Sabrina to recognize Jasmine sitting on the bench as she walked up the concrete path to the swings and monkey bars. Then she realized Jasmine was not alone. Instead she was sitting next to a stranger, who could easily be trying to persuade her daughter into his car nearby.

Sabrina's heart pounded. She'd heard the stories. Seen the news. Kids turned up missing every day. Their bodies found in the woods or washed up along the shore of some beach. Sabrina ran toward them as fast as she could. Her daughter would not be a statistic or a picture on a milk carton. She had to prevent a kidnapping. His back was to her, so he would never see her coming.

"Get away from my daughter!" Sabrina yelled at the predator's back, catching him off guard.

The man rose from the bench and Sabrina was startled to discover that he was none other than the mystery man who'd helped her change her flat.

But at the moment, Sabrina redirected her attention on the little head hiding behind Malcolm. "Come here, Jasmine!" Sabrina ordered.

Jasmine heard the tone in her mother's voice and obeyed, taking the space beside her. "Mom, I'm sorry," Jasmine began, walking toward her.

"It's okay," Sabrina tightly hugged Jasmine to her side and gave her a quick peck on the forehead before letting her have it. "I'm just glad you're okay. But don't you ever pull a stunt like that again. Do you hear me? You scared me half to death."

"I'm sorry, Mom, but I—"

"Not another word, Jasmine." Sabrina pointed her finger in her daughter's direction. "We will talk more about this when we get home."

Malcolm watched Sabrina, and while she scolded her daughter, his eyes traveled along her delicate frame. From his view, she looked even lovelier than she had the last time he saw her.

When she was through reading Jasmine the riot act, Sabrina turned her attention to the mystery man. "And you," she said, spinning around to face him. "What are you doing here? Are you following us?"

Maybe he'd been planning something sinister and she'd caught him in the act. This afternoon he'd appeared trustworthy, but maybe her radar was off. It wouldn't be the first time.

At her hostile glare, Malcolm stood firm. He was not backing down from this emotional but very beguiling creature. His intentions were honorable.

"Of course not," Malcolm returned evenly. "I just

happened to be in the right place at the right time." At Sabrina's raised brow, he continued, "Look at her," Malcolm said, inclining his head toward Jasmine. "Does she appear to be hurt?"

Sabrina took a long hard look at her daughter. Jasmine didn't appear to be harmed. Not a hair was out of place and her clothes were in the same condition as when she'd left. "Well…no," Sabrina replied reluctantly.

"Then you can see that your daughter was in no harm from me. I was just about to dial your number when you arrived breathing fire. And it's a good thing, too, because you never know what predators lurk in the dark," Malcolm replied.

"You're so right," Sabrina said, fumbling over her words. She felt foolish standing next to him, especially when her senses were going haywire. "I'm sorry for overreacting. It's just when I saw you with Jasmine, I got so scared."

"Understandably," Malcolm replied.

"Then you've just saved me and my daughter for the second time today and I don't even know your name," Sabrina commented. "My, my, for such a small town, you do get around."

"What's the old saying? Once you save someone's life you're responsible for them. I guess today is your lucky day," he replied, his eyes alight with amusement.

"It must be. Though you must think I'm a terrible mother for letting Jasmine run off."

"Why would I think that?" Malcolm replied. "I'm sure there's a logical explanation."

"You don't know the half of it," Sabrina muttered underneath her breath.

"Well, I have an ear to listen, if you want to talk," Malcolm said. "It would be nice to hear about someone else's troubles instead of my own."

So, he had troubles? What could possibly be bothering *him*. From where she was standing, he had it made in the shade. He had sex appeal, good looks and a really hot car. She was sure he wasn't like her, jobless and homeless.

"Well, I would love to commiserate woes with you, but I must really get Jasmine to bed."

Malcolm's mouth formed into a frown. "Oh, of course. I'm sorry. I didn't mean to detain you."

"You didn't," Sabrina said, bending down and zipping up Jasmine's jacket. "Another time?"

"Certainly, but first take this." Malcolm pulled his wallet out of his pocket and handed Sabrina a business card.

The card read Dr. Malcolm Winters. "What's this?" she asked.

"My business card," Malcolm replied, "in case you're ever in need of my white-knight services again."

Sabrina blushed a thousand shades of red. Was he flirting with her? Because if so, she was a tad bit rusty. "I'm Sabrina Matthews, by the way." She extended her hand. "I…I mean, Sabrina Parker," she corrected herself.

"Nice to meet you, too, Ms. Sabrina Matthews Parker," Malcolm replied, bemused at her confusion.

"Please, call me Sabrina."

"All right, Sabrina it is. Remember to keep that card handy."

"I'll keep you in mind, Dr. Winters. Don't be surprised if you get a call from me one day," she teased.

"Oh, I most certainly hope so," Malcolm replied underneath his breath as Sabrina and Jasmine walked away.

Once they'd finally arrived back at the house, Sabrina found it nearly empty. Most of the family had long since dispersed in search of Jasmine while her mother stood vigil at home. When they'd come through the door, her mother had hugged them close not wanting to let go.

Sabrina made sure Jasmine called each and every one to inform them that she was home safely and that she was sorry to have caused them any trouble. Then she waited in Jasmine's room for her to return from brushing her teeth and changing into her pajamas before really laying it onto her daughter.

"Do you have any idea how you scared us, Jasmine?" Sabrina lectured.

"I'm sorry," Jasmine replied in that little girl voice of hers. Sabrina knew what was about to come. Crocodile tears. Those might work with Tre, but they weren't going to work with her.

"You'd better be. 'Cause if you ever do that again, you'll get more than just a time-out. Do you hear me?"

"Yes, ma'am."

"Now, give your mom a hug," Sabrina ordered.

Jasmine scooted over to the edge of the bed and gave Sabrina a huge bear hug. Sabrina didn't realize just how much she needed it. She was beginning to think Jasmine didn't love her anymore.

"I love you, sweetie. And we'll talk more in the morning."

"Can I call Daddy?"

"It's past your bedtime." Sabrina didn't miss the downtrodden look on Jasmine's face. "But I promise we'll call him in the morning." At this, Jasmine perked up.

"G'night, Mom."

Sabrina turned off the light and solemnly walked downstairs. They had dodged a bullet tonight and she was thankful. Who knows what would have happened if she hadn't arrived when she had. If Dr. Winters hadn't found her, a predator could easily have walked away with her daughter.

If Tre ever found out, it would give him fodder to think that Jasmine wasn't better off with her. At that moment, Sabrina determined that she wouldn't let anyone, including Jasmine or Dr. Winters, shake her off course ever again. Somehow she was going to make a better life for her and Jasmine in Savannah. Sabrina stayed with Jasmine until she finally drifted off to sleep.

When she made it downstairs, all the lights were out. So Sabrina stepped outside onto the front porch for some much needed fresh air to clear her head. She was surprised to discover her mother already seated in one of the wooden rockers. Sabrina didn't speak; instead she joined her in the adjacent chair. Her mother glanced her way and smiled.

Silence ensued while they both rocked back and forth. It was several minutes before Sabrina finally let out the pain deep inside her heart.

Although the night was clear and quiet with many stars in the sky, a dark cloud surrounded her. Sabrina's head fell to her chest and she allowed the numbness to wash over. She felt drained having used all her energy just to get through the waking hours of the last six months. It was replaced instead with grief.

"Oh, Mom, how did I get here?" she cried, a loud moan escaping her lips. "How did it all go wrong?"

She'd never thought that she'd be back home in her parents' house at twenty-eight.

"I don't know, baby doll," answered her mother as she scooted closer to her and grabbed her hands.

"I feel like such a failure," Sabrina cried. "Tre was lying to my face, day after day, and I didn't see it. Why didn't I see it, Mom?" Tears streamed down Sabrina's cheek.

"Maybe you didn't want to see it?" her mother replied honestly.

"I knew things weren't right between us. That

we'd become distant…but I had no idea there was another woman." Sabrina shook her head in amazement that she could have been so trusting. So naive. Tre must have had one helluva laugh at her expense.

"How did you find out?"

"I found a hotel receipt in his suit pocket and followed him there. If I hadn't, I would have never known. He would have continued to lie to me day after day. How could I have been such a fool?" Sabrina stood abruptly and stared at their quiet tree-lined street.

"Believing in someone, trusting someone, does not make you a fool, Sabrina. It just makes you human." Her mother rose to stand beside her and squeezed her shoulders.

"I hate him so much, Mama." Sabrina's voice shook with anger. "I hate him for what he did to Jasmine. To me. To us. He ripped our lives to shreds and now I'm left to pick up the pieces." Sabrina ran her fingers through her long ebony hair.

"And you will, Sabrina. Look at me, girl." Her mother grabbed her by the chin. "You're a Parker and if nothing else, this family is resilient."

At Sabrina's raised brow, her mother continued.

"You remember when that hurricane came along the coast when you were twelve and damaged the hotel? When it seemed like this family's heritage was sunk in the mire, what did we do? We prayed to the Lord, dug our heels in the sand and banded together to rebuild that hotel. And right now that's what you have to do. It's all about faith, Sabrina. You have to believe in yourself."

"I don't know if I can, Mom," Sabrina replied. "I don't know if I have what it takes."

Her mother grabbed her by the shoulders. "What's wrong with you child? What happened to my fearless daughter? The one who flew off to Georgetown on a scholarship without ever looking back. Where's that girl?"

"I don't, Mama. I just don't know. Somehow I've lost my way."

"You'll find it again, dear girl. Because you're home," her mother predicted.

Sabrina was still in her pajamas when she finally made it down to breakfast the following morning. Her parents were seated at the kitchen table and Jasmine was already dressed. Sabrina caught the worried expressions on their faces, but feigned ignorance. Jasmine was eating Cocoa Pebbles and reading the back of the box, oblivious to the older folks.

Opening the cupboard, Sabrina took a mug down and poured herself a cup of coffee. Over the steaming Colombian brew, Sabrina watched her parents glance back and forth at one another, neither knowing where to begin.

It was her mother who finally spoke. "So, what are you going to do today?" her mother asked, trying to sound chipper. She saw the dark circles around her daughter's eyes and in the morning light weight loss was evident as the pajamas hung off Sabrina's frail shoulders. Beverly was heartbroken to see her daughter's devastation. She wished she could help make it all better, but this was one lesson that her daughter would have to learn: life doesn't turn out the way you planned.

"Not sure, Mom," Sabrina replied listlessly, staring out of the back window.

"Why don't you come out with Jasmine and I?" her mother suggested. "I promised her that I would show her around town. Introduce my grandbaby around so she can make some new friends before I go to my picnic committee meeting. Why don't you get dressed and join us?" Beverly hoped to get her daughter out of her funk.

"Mom, do you mind if I stay in?" Sabrina asked, sipping the hot liquid. "You know, get my head together. I'm not really in the mood for company."

"Sure, baby. If that's the way you want it. And what are you going to do all day, dear?" Beverly Parker turned her attention to her husband, who sat quietly throughout the exchange.

James sat stoically beside his wife. He couldn't understand why Beverly was catering to the girl. So, her marriage failed. Marriages fail. Hers wasn't the first and most certainly wouldn't be the last. Sighing, he replied. "Oh, I don't know. I figured I'd sit here and enjoy my breakfast first, woman. And then, maybe join the fellas at the diner for a card game or two."

Retired, he often went to the City diner to play

cards with his buddies: Caleb Williams, minister of First Baptist Church, Corey Johnson, a handyman at Ace Hardware and Raymond Brown, his best friend and the community barber, and have some of Karen's peach cobbler.

"You don't need to be doing no gambling, James," her mother admonished.

"Oh, woman, it's only cards."

"Well, don't go spending all your money. You remember what happened the last time," her mother warned.

Her father rolled his eyes. Beverly wasn't going to let him forget that he'd bet over two hundred dollars and had lost every penny. Now, although they led a middle-class lifestyle, Beverly was none too pleased at his extravagance and for months had steadfastly refused to let him go near the monthly game.

"Of course, I do. You never let me forget it," James replied, pushing his chair back and walking to the stove to add some ham, eggs and an extra biscuit on his plate. "Now go on and show Jasmine Savannah. Let her experience firsthand the land of the peach."

"All right, well, have a good day," Beverly replied, standing up and kissing her husband goodbye. "Jasmine, are you ready?"

"My mom calls me Jazzy," Jasmine replied, looking up from her empty bowl of cereal and joining the conversation for the first time.

"All right then, Jazzy it is." Grabbing her purse

and keys off the Formica counter, Beverly opened the back door and held it open for Jasmine.

As Jasmine scooted from the table and followed her grandmother, Sabrina called after her. "Don't I get a hug and a kiss?"

"That's for kids," Jasmine replied and walked out the door without a backward glance at her mother.

Sabrina felt as if a knife had been stuck in her heart. Where was her sweet little girl? The one who adored her mother. The one who begged her to be Den mother for her Girl Scout's troop.

"We'll see you both later on this evening." her mother replied, closing the door quietly.

The moment her mother and Jasmine were out the door, her father offered some advice. "Now, listen up, baby girl," her father began. Sabrina loved her father's endearments for her. "Now that your mama's gone, we can talk."

"Dad…" Sabrina started, but James held up one hand.

"Don't get your panties in a twist—what I have to say is short and sweet." He scooted his high-backed oak chair toward Sabrina's. "Sometimes life gives you lemons, but it's up to you to make lemonade. Understand my drift? So, this man has hurt you… I understand all that, but your life, Sabrina, is more than this one event."

"I suppose you're right, but moving on is easier said than done."

"I guess you've got to figure out if this event will define your life or make you stronger. I hope that the latter is true." Her father shrugged and rose from his chair. His youngest was determined to wallow in her despair and he didn't have the heart to watch her do it. "It's all up to you, Sabrina," he said before leaving.

Sabrina was so deep in thought, she didn't hear her father creep out of the kitchen.

Chapter 4

Malcolm paused before going inside the exam room. He didn't relish giving bad news but it had to be done. Mr. and Mrs. Gibson both looked up at him as he came in and walked over to his desk.

"From the look on your face, I guess I can assume that the test results are not positive," Mr. Gibson commented.

"I'm afraid so," Malcolm replied. "Your blood pressure is elevated. Now while I can give you medication to bring that down, at this juncture it's irrelevant. The blood work revealed that your cardiac enzymes are high and more importantly the ECG showed blockage to the coronary arteries."

"What does that mean, Dr. Winters?" Mrs.

Gibson clutched at her husband's arm. "In plain English, please."

"Well, first I'd like to try medication. There are several clot-dissolving medications we can use to correct blocked arteries."

"And if the clot medication doesn't work?" Mr. Gibson asked.

"Then a coronary angiography will be necessary."

Mrs. Gibson looked fearful of all the big words that Malcolm was using, so he moved from behind his large maple desk and bent down beside her. "I know this sounds frightening, but all of this is necessary to save your husband's life."

Mrs. Gibson nodded. "It is very much so."

"If an angiography is needed, I can perform the test. I'm a licensed cardiologist and have done hundreds of these procedures."

"Then why are you down here in some clinic in Savannah," Mr. Gibson asked, "instead of some fancy hospital up north?"

It was a fair question, so Malcolm answered it as honestly as he could. "I decided that I needed a slower pace."

"And that's all there is to it?" Mr. Gibson asked, suspicious of Malcolm's background.

"I assure you, Mr. and Mrs. Gibson—" Malcolm stood up and patted Mrs. Gibson's knee "—my no longer practicing cardiology full-time was not due to anything sinister. I merely felt that I was missing out on life and felt it was necessary to make a change."

"Then, let's get on with it."

"Great." Malcolm returned to his desk and scribbled a prescription.

"Thank you, doctor." Mrs. Gibson attempted a halfhearted smile.

"Don't thank me, yet," Malcolm replied. "Thank me when your husband is well." As he turned away, Malcolm could only hope that the medication would solve the problem; if not, open-heart surgery would be the only viable option. Malcolm prayed that wasn't necessary.

Sabrina took her father's advice and entered the land of the living. Her first stop was City diner for lunch, but when she arrived the small diner was packed to capacity. She had to wait several minutes for a seat. Looking around, she saw several regulars and pillars of the Cuyler-Brownsville community seated at plastic booths drinking coffee and talking politics, sports and religion. There was the Reverend Caleb Williams, Raymond Brown, the town barber and Jacob Young, who owned a small grocery mart.

Sabrina stood frozen to the spot, transported to another time and place when she and Dorian, her first love, had cuddled up in one of those plastic booths, holding hands or sharing a milkshake and fries. Why couldn't things stay that simple?

When she brought herself back to the present, Sabrina noticed an empty single seat open up at the counter and made a beeline for it before anyone else noticed the empty chair.

Pulling a menu from the napkin holder, she surveyed the menu for the day's special. Now she could get down to business because she was famished. A healthy portion of turkey meat loaf, mashed potatoes and home-style gravy would do her just fine. But first she'd start with a piece of Ms. Jackson's homemade sweet corn bread.

Sabrina was deep in her menu when she looked up and noticed the waitress staring at her. Recognition took several moments.

The hair was different—cut into a stylish short layered bob. The clothes were similar: formfitting low-rider jeans, sexy black lace top and loud red lipstick. But the café au lait face with the brilliant brown eyes, she would remember anywhere.

"Monique, how are you? How's your mom? It's so good to see you. How long has it been?" Sabrina fired off a slew of questions.

"Humph," Monique murmured underneath her breath before turning on her heel and stomping off towards the kitchen.

She hadn't seen Monique in over seven years, but it was obvious Monique was upset with her, too… Sabrina had a mind to go in there after her, but thought better of it. She'd let her cool off first and try again later.

"We meet again, fair Sabrina," a tenor voice said from behind her.

Whirling around, Sabrina glanced up and saw Dr. Winters smiling at her. "Yes, we do. You have an uncanny knack for showing up when I'm having a really bad day," she huffed and swirled back around in her stool. Why was the devilishly handsome doc in her business? His face was reserved, yet Sabrina found him deliciously appealing. Why was that? He surely wasn't her type being such a stuffed shirt. Perhaps it was the touches of human kindness he'd shown her or the glint in his eye or that strong jaw. Stop it, stop it, Sabrina scolded herself.

Malcolm joined her at the counter where an empty seat had suddenly materialized beside her. Despite her lack of makeup and casual look, Sabrina was a real stunner. Something about her drew him to her and he couldn't quite put in his finger on it.

Sabrina yelled down to a waitress at the far end of the counter. "Can we get some service or what?"

Annoyed, the waitress turned her head. "Just a minute. I'll be right with you."

What was with this town? Why was everyone against her? She'd allowed Tre to rule her life, but must she constantly be punished for it? What was done was done and there was no turning back.

"Do you ever have a good day?" Malcolm inquired.

Sabrina chuckled. "I suppose you might think that, given the last few times you've seen me. But I'm hoping my luck is about to change."

"How so?"

"Well, I've moved back home."

"To make a fresh start, I presume?" He understood her reasoning. He came to Savannah for the same thing. Perhaps that's why he found her so intriguing. They had a certain kinship. Perhaps she, too, was trying to escape the past.

Sabrina nodded. "For me and for Jazzy. Maybe I'll even go back to school."

"Good choice. Education is very important," Malcolm said. "You can't go wrong."

"Thanks. It's nice to have someone on my side. Especially since my return hasn't been well received."

"I'm sorry to hear that," Malcolm said. "I, for one, am very happy to see you again." Since he'd met Sabrina and her daughter, he'd felt the best he had in a year. He'd even smiled more often.

Sabrina was touched by Malcolm's comment and took the opportunity to study his profile. She didn't know what it was about Dr. Winters, but he had a calming presence, which was exactly what she needed given the upheaval in her life. "I must admit it is funny how fate keeps throwing us together," Sabrina replied, after the waitress had finally come and taken their order. Sabrina ordered an open-faced meatloaf sandwich, while Malcolm stayed healthy with a grilled chicken Caesar salad.

"Maybe it's trying to tell us something?"

"Hmmm…and what do you think that might be?" Sabrina wondered aloud.

"I don't know." Malcolm paused. "But how about

we find out over dinner?" Malcolm was surprised when the words tumbled out of his mouth. It was just that when he was around Sabrina the deep fog that had surrounded him for a year would lift.

"Pardon?" asked Sabrina. Did he just ask her out on a date? If so, she was nowhere near ready to join the dating pool. The ink was barely dry on her divorce papers. "I couldn't possibly."

"Why not?" Malcolm asked, picking up her left hand. "I don't see any rings on your finger."

"I'm divorced and…" Sabrina hesitated.

"And what?" Malcolm asked. "Is there something wrong with me? Do I smell?" He sniffed his armpits.

"No," Sabrina laughed. "It's just a little soon for me. Perhaps you should try hanging out with the boys down at Mimi's after work. That might get you some companionship."

"I prefer the female variety or to be alone," Malcolm replied.

"Sounds a little rigid," Sabrina commented.

"That's the way I like it," Malcolm replied. "Listen, how about I make it easy for you, dinner and a movie. As friends," he threw in at the last moment, hoping to sell her on the idea. The more time he spent in Sabrina Parker's company, the more he wanted to know.

"I don't know." Sabrina argued with herself in her head. Here a good-looking man was asking her out and her heart said yes, take a chance and enjoy life. But her mind said no way. Don't risk it. "I'm sorry, Malcolm. I appreciate the offer, but I can't." Sabrina stood up to leave. "I'm just not ready to start dating again. It's just too soon."

"I take it it was a bad breakup."

"You have no idea," Sabrina responded. "But mostly I need time. Malcolm, I need time to find out who I am outside of Tre. For years, I'd been altruistic. Catering to Tre and Jasmine's needs before my own. And now, I'm finally at a point in my life that I feel free to be me. And to find out what *I* want in life. Can you understand that?"

"Of course." Malcolm understood. He'd made a gross miscalculation in pushing too soon. He was attracted to Sabrina, but she wasn't ready for him yet. A casual flirtation was all the lady was ready to handle. But one day soon, when she let her guard down long enough, he'd try again.

"I don't want to get in the way of your self-discovery, Sabrina. Listen, I understand that you're still getting over your ex-husband and are not looking for a relationship. And to be quite honest, neither am I. I'm getting over a traumatic event myself and my head isn't right, either. So if all we're meant to be is friends, then that's what we'll be," he stated, completely out of breath.

"Do you mean that?" Sabrina searched his face for a sign that he wasn't completely above board. "Do you really mean it? Because I'm not sure I can offer you much more than friendship."

"And I'd be a lucky man to have that," Malcolm replied.

Sabrina's brow rose. Had she indeed found a man worthy of her, but who had impeccably bad timing? "Then consider Jasmine and I your friends," Sabrina replied.

"Excellent," Malcolm said underneath his breath. He wanted more, but for now he wasn't going to get it. And that was unusual for him. He was used to getting exactly what he wanted out of life. Used to the tide turning his way, but not this time. Maybe his romancing needed a little work.

Chapter 5

As Sabrina walked back to her car from the diner, she noticed how awful she looked in a store window. How could anyone, including Dr. Winters, find her attractive? Sabrina gave herself a long hard look. She saw a round face devoid of makeup and in a severe need of an eyebrow wax, and her usually long and straight ebony hair was in bad need of a style and cut. But maybe it was time for something drastic to shake things up. Suddenly she knew exactly what to do and where to go.

She walked into Curl and Weaves determined to free herself of some hair, but when she arrived, her hairdresser, an old high school girlfriend had other ideas.

"So you want to cut off all your hair because you're upset over some trifling man?" Stacy had asked. "I think not," she said, snapping her fingers. "Sabrina, this is not *Waiting to Exhale* and you most certainly are not Angela Bassett. You've got some beautiful thick hair," Stacy J had told her. "I'll give you a good condition, add a straw set and you'll look and feel like a brand new woman."

Sabrina thought about for it a moment. Her hair was naturally curly. *When had she stopped wearing her natural hair?* The reason suddenly came rushing back to her. She'd stopped wearing her hair au naturel because Tre hadn't liked it that way. He'd told her it made her look like some bush woman or something, so he'd asked her to get a relaxer, but she'd steadfastly refused putting any chemicals in her hair. Her hair was a part of her African and French heritage and she wasn't about to change that, not even for him, but she'd acquiesced and started going to the hairdresser and having her hair blow-dried out and had been doing so ever since.

"That sounds fabulous," Sabrina said, turning back around and leaning back in her seat. "Hook me up, Stacy J."

Afterward, Sabrina emerged looking hipper than she had looked in a long time. Stacy J hadn't lied when she said she'd give her a fresh look. Sabrina's natural curly hair had been stylishly set with straw rods before she sat her under a dryer. When the dryer shut off, Stacy unfastened the rods and her normally thick curls were replaced with ringlets that reached her neck. Sabrina absolutely loved the new look and tipped Stacy J twenty bucks to prove it.

Strutting up Main Boulevard, Sabrina swung her purse in abandon. On the way to her car, she couldn't resist passing by a window and admiring herself. The new hairdo was definitely a thumbs-up.

After her new hairstyle, it was off to Dixon Elementary School to enroll her daughter Jasmine in the fourth grade. She'd made an appointment with the school principal to find out the necessary requirements to get Jasmine prepared for September classes.

The parking lot was surprisingly full when she pulled into a spot later that afternoon. Teachers must be preparing for summer school, thought Sabrina as she smoothly parked her car. A gift from Tre, the silver luxury roadster was one of Sabrina's most prized possessions and one she'd fought for during the divorce when Tre had wanted to sell it, maintaining that she'd needed a reliable vehicle to get Jasmine to and from school. Tre had always been into appearance and the convertible befitted the wife of a rising star in his firm.

Sabrina found the architecture surprisingly modern as she opened the school's front door and walked the long corridor to the principal's office. When she arrived, his assistant informed her that he was running behind schedule.

Sabrina took a seat and was flipping through *Essence,* when the door swung open and Monique

Jackson and her two kids walked in. Sabrina was none too happy to see the little diva, after their last encounter. Monique had treated her with such contempt that Sabrina hung her head low and got deep into her *Essence*. She could only hope that she didn't see her.

No such luck! While the assistant went to check on the principal, Monique turned around to survey the room and discovered Sabrina hiding behind a magazine.

Annoyed, she walked toward her chair and snatched the magazine right out of Sabrina's hands. "Trying to avoid me," Monique asked huffily.

"Excuse you," Sabrina replied, rising to her feet.

Monique raised one thin arched eyebrow. "Touchy, touchy."

"Why wouldn't I be, Monique?" Sabrina inquired, boldly meeting her gaze. "From the way you ignored me, I can only assume you want nothing to do with me."

"Are you trying to provoke another argument?" Monique asked, standing up straight and putting her hands on her hips.

"Enough okay, Monique. You don't wish to rekindle our former friendship, so let's leave it at that. If we happen to see each other at school engagements, I'll be sure to turn the other cheek."

"Ahhh," Monique stomped her foot in frustration. "Don't you know why I'm hopping mad? I'm mad that you left Savannah without a backward glance.

I'm mad that when you came back for the summer after meeting your husband that you'd changed. And I'm mad that you never came back to visit. And I'm even more mad that when I should be angry with you, all I want to do is give you a big fat hug and welcome back one of the best friends I've ever had."

Sabrina's eyes welled and she rushed into Monique's open arms. "Monique, I'm so sorry, ya hear?" Sabrina said. Her southern accent came back as she squeezed her old friend. "I was wrong for forgetting about my family and friends all to please Tre. Look what it cost me. Look at where I am now."

Monique stepped away and wiped away the tears that were streaming down Sabrina's honey-brown cheeks. "It's so good to have you back, Binks."

A smile formed on Sabrina's lips as Monique used her old nickname.

"Let's have a seat." Monique gave Sabrina a reassuring touch to sit before taking the adjoining chair beside her. "I want to know everything that's happened in the last what...seven years?"

"More like ten," Sabrina replied. "How about I fill you in over a cup of coffee? I noticed that new Starbucks next to the dry cleaners."

"You like those fancy coffees?"

"Girl, you will, too. I promise."

"Ms. Jackson," the principal's assistant interrupted them, from across the counter. "I have Brandon's summer school schedule for you." She held out an envelope to Monique.

Rising, Monique walked over to take the manila envelope. "I swear," she said upon her return. "If that boy fails one more class, I'm going to strangle him."

"You ready for that coffee?" Sabrina asked, reaching for her Dooney & Burke purse on the counter.

"I would love some," Monique laughed.

After picking up some groceries for her mother at the Winn-Dixie up the street, Sabrina returned home with her findings later that evening. She'd truly enjoyed catching up with Monique over coffee.

"I'm home," Sabrina yelled as she entered her parent's kitchen loaded down with several bags. After depositing them on the counter, nothing could have prepared her for the sight that greeted her.

Jasmine was standing in the middle of the living room, dressed in the frilliest pink outfit her mother could find for church on Sunday, while her mother and father sat center stage. Complete with bows and ribbons, it was the most extravagant and hideous creation Sabrina had ever seen. And to make matters worse, her mother had done Jasmine's hair up in a bunch of pigtails and curls and now her poor baby girl looked like something out of the Land of Oz!

Bless her heart, her mother had gone cuckoo!

At the sound of her mother's voice, Jasmine rushed over, but stopped dead in her tracks. "What did you do to your hair?" Jasmine asked, stunned.

"I changed it," Sabrina stated matter-of-factly.

Kneeling down, Sabrina attempted a happy face when she really wanted to burst out in laughter. Her mother had no idea that Jasmine was the exact opposite. She hated all that girly stuff. Sabrina had long since accepted that Jasmine was a bonafide tomboy. No Barbies and dress-up for her. Her daughter liked to climb trees and play sports.

"Come here, Jazzy," Sabrina held out her arms, but she stayed away.

"Daddy liked it straight," Jasmine said, folding her arms across her chest. "It was his favorite. I guess that's why you changed it, right?"

"Young lady, you hush," her grandmother ordered. "You need to stay out of grown folks business, ya hear?"

"Yes, Grandma." Jasmine hung her head low, but Sabrina doubted the warning had sunk in.

"I, for one, love it. I'm so glad you're wearing your natural hair again, Sabrina. I thought it was a travesty when you went for the straight look. It felt like you were trying not to be you. This is much more befitting," her mother commented. "James, don't you agree?" her mother asked, turning to her husband.

Deep into his television program, and sitting in his favorite La-Z-Boy, her father shrugged his shoulders. "I like it either way. Anyway, it's Sabrina's choice. Let her decide."

"I couldn't agree with you more," Sabrina replied.

"Well, it looks fabulous. I'm so glad to see the old you emerging," her mother said.

"Thanks, Mama." Sabrina gave her mother a quick squeeze and a kiss on the cheek.

"No problem, sweetie. I'll tell you as many times as you need if it'll help keep that smile on your face." Her mother pulled away and went to check on supper.

"Mom, can I go change?" Jasmine asked, tugging at her mother's shirt while plastering a fake smile across her face. After the hour-long lecture on how to speak to one's elders over breakfast, all Jasmine wanted was to go to her room.

"Sure, baby," Sabrina replied as she watched Jasmine roll her eyes and stomp up the stairs to the guest bedroom. It took every ounce of Sabrina's strength not to let it hurt her.

"Mom, I hate it," Jasmine uttered the second Sabrina made it up the stairs to her room. "Look at it." Jasmine pointed to the hated garment lying in a puddle on the carpet.

"And do you know Grandma made me put on ten others like it?" she asked in frustration. "Mom, I know she means well but do we have to stay here? I miss Dad and Baltimore so much. Can't we go back?"

Sighing, Sabrina took a seat on Jasmine's frilly pink bed. Her mother was trying so hard to make Jasmine feel at home and not like a guest. The problem, thought Sabrina, was that's exactly how Jasmine felt. And there was only one person to blame. She and Tre had never come down to

Savannah and allowed Jazzy and her grandmother the opportunity to become acquainted. So, her mother still thought of Jazzy as a two-year-old, when in fact she was one bright cookie. She was the smartest kid in her class and excelled in all her studies. She was a straight-A student.

"No, we can't," Sabrina replied emphatically. "This place, as you call it, just so happens to be my home. It's where I grew up."

"I know, but our life is back in Baltimore, that's where all my friends are. And it's summer now. We were all planning to hang out. And go to the movies, to dance lessons or swimming at Suzie's house. And now…" Jasmine's voice trailed off.

"I'm sorry your summer plans were ruined, Jasmine," Sabrina took a firm tone. "But it couldn't be helped. Our life is going in a different path."

"Great! You get what you want!" Jasmine threw back at her. "And Dad gets what he wants, but what about what I want? And you…you just don't care." Jasmine flung herself across her pillow.

"I'm sorry it seems that way, Jazzy—" Sabrina switched tactics and softened her voice "—but I do care about you and your needs. It's why I moved us here." Sabrina leaned down to rub Jasmine's back as she lay crying into her pillow. "Don't you know that you're the most important thing in this world to me?"

Sabrina lifted her daughter up under her arms, to sit up straight, but Jasmine wouldn't hear a word. "I want Daddy," she cried.

Hurt by her daughter's rejection, Sabrina moved away and stood up. "Well, he's not here. And I'm all you've got," Sabrina replied testily.

On the other side of town, Malcolm sat listening to the pianist while he ate a solitary dinner at the bed-and-breakfast where he was staying. Parker House had a small jazz band every Thursday, which had appealed to him tremendously when he'd made his initial reservation. The blackened chicken, sautéed vegetables and garden salad, however, remained untouched on his plate. It wasn't that the food wasn't superb; he just didn't have an appetite. The waiter had long stopped catering to him, retiring to the kitchen and leaving him to enjoy his glass of red wine.

He wanted to drink enough to make him forget, but somehow he couldn't because his mind kept wandering to saucy Sabrina Parker. Fate had propelled them to meet, first on the side of the road, then at the park and today again at the diner. She'd surely been taking some heat from the waitress when he'd arrived and was none too pleased about it. Yet, something within her compelling eyes spoke to something deep inside his core. He sensed that she, too, was haunted by a sadness that took over your whole inner being.

He knew the kind of pain that enveloped you at every turn, so much so that it was hard to breathe and it stayed with you through the waking hours and in the darkness. The nights were the worst, though, because when the uncontrollable memories haunted him, they gave him insomnia.

Malcolm didn't know how he made it up to his room several hours later, but he arrived at his room on the third floor in just enough time to hear the telephone ringing from inside. Pulling the key out of his breast pocket, he quickly inserted it into the cylinder.

Stumbling into the room, he patted the wall. Finding the light switch, he flicked it on, flooding his room with muted lighting. He rushed across the room and caught it on the last ring. "Hello," he said breathlessly.

"There you are," his mother's voice came over the line.

"What do you want, Mother?" Malcolm fell unceremoniously across the bed, but landed on the floor instead with a loud thud. *Did she hear that?* he thought as he rose from the floor.

"Is that any way to greet your mother?" Dinah Armstrong asked from the other end, ignorant to Malcolm's current state as she applied moisturizer to her hands.

At his silence, Dinah continued, "I called to check on you, that's what. It's been weeks since any of us heard from you. I've even been thinking of coming down for a visit. I have something very important to discuss with you and it needs to be done in person. But I can't stay long, you know how Walter is without me, but I have to talk to you."

Walter was his stepfather, and although they weren't close when he was a child, Malcolm had come to respect the man as an adult. "A visit is completely out of the question."

"Why?" Dinah pouted. "I miss you," Dinah said, trying a softer approach. It almost worked on Malcolm until she followed it up with, "Do you even realize the potential salary you could be earning right now?"

"Medicine has never been about the money to me, Dinah, and you know that," Malcolm replied, his blood slowly starting to boil. Goes to show that the woman knew absolutely nothing about him or what was important to him. You'd think he hadn't come out of her loins.

"Oh?" Dinah laughed sarcastically. "What was that about healing? Because Lord knows, you're not doing much of that in Savannah."

Trust Dinah to hit below the belt. "Is that why you called me, Mother? To remind me of my shortcomings? Because quite frankly, I'm not in the mood."

"Now listen up, Malcolm. Drowning your sorrows in booze will not bring Michael back. So stop this nonsense right now and come back to Boston before you ruin your career and your reputation," Dinah replied, her voice smooth and insistent.

"Is that all you care about, Mother? The recognition that comes from being the mother of an award-winning surgeon?" Malcolm commented, avoiding the subject of his late twin.

"Of course not," she said firmly. "But you have to admit that this…this is a bit over the top even for you. I mean, for Christ's sake. Michael was the spontaneous, fly-by-the-seat-of-your-pants kind. *You* were always the logical and practical one with a good head on your shoulders. This is completely out of character for you."

As she remembered her twins in their youth, a smile crossed Dinah's face. Every time she'd tried to dress the two of them alike, they'd always resisted her urges and found a way to change clothes. "We're fraternal, not identical," Malcolm had always said. And boy, were they different. Michael was the sunshine boy, naturally exuberant and social. He got along with everyone. And women? Her youngest had been God's gift and the ladies fell easily for him. He was never without a girl by his side.

Whereas her oldest, Malcolm, was a loner and given to sullenness except where Michael was concerned. And as far as she knew, Malcolm rarely dated except during those early years with Halle, but that hadn't lasted because the only thing Malcolm was passionate about was medicine.

But he had adored his three-minutes-younger sibling. He always cared for and nurtured Michael as if he were his own father. It had come as quite a shock to his system when Michael had died. How could he survive without his better half?

Malcolm, on the other end of the line, wanted no part of his mother's walk down memory lane. "I'm not coming back," he stated firmly. He'd made a decision to move to Savannah, and Dinah was going to have to live with it.

"Stop this, Malcolm." Dinah began to get frustrated. "You're my only son and I want you here." She was sick and tired of him torturing himself with memories of Michael. It wasn't healthy.

"It's not going to happen, Dinah," Malcolm said, calling his mother by her first name, trying to make his point clear. "Boston holds too many bad memories for me. I need to make a fresh start." Didn't she understand he was a broken man? If he hadn't been so cocky, so sure of himself…

"Why the South? And Savannah of all places? Couldn't you have picked a city close by to get over this funk you're in?" Dinah broke into his self-torture.

"It's not a funk. I'm grieving the loss of my brother. I'd think you'd still be doing the same. Or maybe Michael wasn't that important to you. But he was my twin after all."

"Don't you dare," Dinah replied, standing up from her pedestal stool for effect, even though Malcolm couldn't see her. Tears welled in her eyes. "I may not have been his twin, like you. But I loved my son, just as much as you, Malcolm. You've no right to doubt my love for him."

The hurt in his mother's voice was evident, so Malcolm apologized immediately. "I'm sorry, Mother. But you have to respect my decision and let this go." She had to. He wasn't going to change his mind.

"Fine, if that's the way you want it," Dinah muttered. "Then, I hope you're happy in that hobunk town, because you've just ruined your life."

Seconds later, Malcolm heard the dial tone and hung up the phone. He hoped that he'd finally freed her of any notion that he'd be returning up north. Boston was his past and Savannah was his future.

After supper, when she and Jasmine were on their way upstairs, her father stopped her in the foyer. "I spoke with Felicia and it seems that Mary, one of our maids has to take a leave to take care of her sick mother, which leaves an opening at Parker House."

"And I suppose you expect me to fill it," Sabrina replied.

"If you can spare the time," her father replied.

Sabrina thought about it for the moment. Financially speaking, she was under no strain. She had plenty of money left from the sale of the house, but she also felt irresponsible for not being here to help her parents.

"Okay, Daddy," Sabrina replied. "I suppose I can pinch-hit until Mary returns."

"Splendid," her father replied, grinning from ear to ear. He was quite happy to have procured employment for his baby girl, so Sabrina let him have his moment.

Once they were in her room, Jasmine wasted no time asking for her father. "Can I please call Daddy?"

Sabrina sighed heavily. She didn't relish the idea

of hearing Tre's voice, but she'd promised Jasmine that she would call him. Picking up her phone book and the cordless from the nightstand, Sabrina flipped through the pages to find Tre's new number. Reluctantly her fingers dialed the numbers. While the phone rang, Sabrina's stomach knotted. Please, please, please let Tre pick up.

Luck was not her side. "Hello," Melanie replied breathlessly on the opposite end of the line.

"Hello, Melanie. This is Sabrina. May I speak with Tre?"

"Oh," Melanie drawled. "If it isn't the little mouse." Melanie watched Tre walk into the bedroom and mouth *Who is it?* Shrugging him off, Melanie turned around and continued with her conversation. She so rarely got the opportunity to torture the poor naive twit.

"Eighty-six the name-calling, Melanie, and just put Tre on the phone," Sabrina said, annoyed with Melanie's tactics. It was why she so rarely allowed Jasmine to call. The less dealings she had with that witch, the better.

"I'm sorry, he's busy," Melanie responded cattily.

"Busy doing what?" Sabrina inquired as her blood began to boil. "You mean to tell me he's too busy to talk to his own daughter?"

"You're her mother," Melanie returned. "You're the one that's supposed to take care of her. Tre is too busy with other things. Namely *me*."

"You, you…" Sabrina wanted to call her every

name under the sun, but with Jasmine sitting next to her on the bed, anxiously pulling the phone cord, Sabrina thought better of a verbal combat with Melanie. What purpose would it serve anyway?

"What?" Melanie egged her on.

Sabrina refused to give her the satisfaction. Instead, she handed the phone to Jasmine. "Ask for your father."

Happily, Jasmine accepted the phone. "Hi, Melanie, can I speak to my dad?"

At the sound of Jasmine's voice on the other end, Melanie switched her tone. "Sure, sugarplum," Melanie replied, "I'll go get your dad." Melanie rose from the bed and handed Tre the phone. "It's your little brat," she whispered.

Tre snatched the phone from her before spanking her bottom as she switched away.

Sabrina left the room so he and Jasmine could speak privately. She knew Jasmine was desperate for some sort of father-daughter bond, which was why she was determined that Tre keep his promise and come down and visit her in Savannah later in the summer.

After a half hour, Jasmine came outside on the porch. "It's Dad, he wants to talk to you," she said, handing Sabrina the phone before going back inside.

"What is it, Tre?" Sabrina queried, after accepting the cordless phone.

"Do you really think it's a good idea for Jasmine to be calling so much? She's called me three times in the last week."

"And you have a problem with that?" Sabrina asked. "Jasmine's in a rough place right now and she needs you. In case you forgot, that's what being a father is all about!"

"I don't need you reminding me what my fatherly duties are," Tre returned, reaching for a magazine and turning the pages. "You should be happy you have custody of Jazzy."

"Don't even try it, Tre," Sabrina said. "You wouldn't know what to do with Jasmine full-time. I highly doubt Melanie signed on to play stepmommy. She strikes me as the type who might hit the deck running if she had to deal with a sickly child or go to a PTA meeting."

Fuming, Tre slammed down the magazine he'd been flipping through on the nightstand. "Go to hell, Sabrina," he said and hung up on her.

"You first," Sabrina replied to the thin air. The minute he hung up, Sabrina could have kicked herself. She'd forgotten to ask him if he was still coming for his visit. Why did she continue to let him get to her?

Chapter 6

The following morning, Sabrina dragged herself out of bed for her first day on the job at Parker House. Turning on the taps, she let the steaming hot water wash over her weary flesh. Five minutes later, she emerged, somewhat alive and ready for work.

She was determined to show Felicia and her family she was not above hard work. Sure, she hadn't had to work during her marriage to Tre. Tre's being a labor attorney had provided them with a luxurious lifestyle which she had grown quite accustomed to, but everyone also knew she wasn't born with a silver spoon in her mouth.

To prove it, Sabrina threw on a T-shirt and a pair of paint-splattered jeans and put her curly hair into an unfashionable ponytail. Bounding down the stairs, she searched the foyer for her keys and purse before hurrying out the door.

Thankfully, her mother had generously agreed to keep an eye on Jasmine, allowing Sabrina the opportunity to make some extra cash.

It was dark and still when Sabrina left her parents' home at six-thirty in the morning. She'd phoned Felicia yesterday evening and informed her that she would be reporting to Parker House the following morning. Kicking her convertible into gear, Sabrina backed out of the driveway.

Early morning traffic was very light and she made it to the B and B within fifteen minutes, but when she opened the front door, the B and B was already bustling.

Pausing a moment, Sabrina reacquainted herself with her second home throughout most of her teens. The fresh smell of lemon oil immediately flooded her nose. Glancing down, she noted the hardwood floors had already been buffed and shined.

Sabrina couldn't remember a time when she and Felicia hadn't been polishing floors or helping their mother prepare the guest's buffet breakfast or watching Alton mow the lawn.

The three-floor Victorian was just as luxurious as she remembered. The first floor housed two parlors, a grand dining room for high tea at four o'clock, complete with cucumber sandwiches and Earl Grey, a gourmet kitchen and a wine cellar in the basement.

The parlors were furnished with several pieces of antique furniture. Sabrina didn't relish the thought of dusting each and every one of them.

Glancing up the winding staircase, she thought of the eight master bedrooms with adjoining baths she would have to clean. Each of which had hardwood floors and crown moldings. Most had a spectacular view of the secluded garden in the rear courtyard with the family magnolias. Everything about Parker House stated quality and elegance. It had been a staple in their community for generations. At least eighty years or so, she'd been told.

When she'd been nothing more than a wide-eyed child in love with Dorian, Sabrina had often envisioned them in one of those rooms making love. Sabrina smiled at the teenage memory.

She was just about to head to the kitchen when the back of a regal head caught her eye. Surely it couldn't be Dr. Winters. What was he doing here? It seemed that everywhere she turned up, the doctor was not far behind.

Storming over, Sabrina approached the figure. She was right on the money, when the sound of her hard, quick footsteps on the hardwood floor caused Malcolm to suddenly turn around and focus those coal-dark eyes of his on her.

He was wearing pin-striped trousers accompanied by a pale-blue shirt and an African vest. Somehow he didn't strike her as the Afrocentric type. Then again, what did she know?

"Ah, if it isn't the lovely Ms. Parker," Malcolm said, folding his *Savannah Tribune* and placing it on the small end table next to his coffee cup and half-eaten whole wheat bagel.

Sabrina watched him take the cup in his large masculine hands and bring it to his full sensuous lips. A chill went up her spine as she imagined those very same lips on hers. Shaking herself, Sabrina inquired. "What are you doing here?" Smoothing her hair, she looked an absolute fright.

"As you can see, I'm having my breakfast." Malcolm leaned back and sized her up. He could tell she was excited by the shine in her eyes and the color in her cheeks.

"Not here, here," Sabrina replied, annoyed at the smirk on his face. He was mocking her! "I mean, at my family's bed-and-breakfast?"

"This is your family's place?" Malcolm queried. "I had no idea. When I booked it, I was looking for a place near the clinic."

"C'mon?" Sabrina doubted that very seriously. Had he picked this place because of her? She hadn't seen him in days, since he'd asked her out at the diner and she'd purposely avoided going there for fear she'd run into him.

"No, I did not," Malcolm stated firmly, perhaps a little too firmly when he saw Sabrina's brow narrow in response.

"I find that hard to believe, considering my name is Sabrina Parker."

"And I assume I'm supposed to put two and two together?" Malcolm's left eyebrow rose a fraction. "Parker is a common name."

Once she thought back to the several other occasions she'd been in his presence, she realized his logic was dead-on. Once again, she had egg on her face. "I guess you're right," she admitted.

"Hmmm, seems to me someone is leaping to judgment again. You really must do something about that, Ms. Parker."

"So, we're back to calling each other by our surnames, are we? I guess you were more offended by my turning you down than I'd thought," Sabrina replied through stiff lips.

"Not at all." Malcolm's mouth curved into a smile, revealing very straight pearl-white teeth. "Because you'll change your mind."

"Of all the arrogant things I've heard…" Sabrina replied, putting her hands on her hips.

"Once my charms wear on you, you'll be dying to date me," Malcolm teased.

"You wish," Sabrina retorted.

"I know," Malcolm stated, changing the subject. "So when did you start working here? I don't recall seeing you before." He hoped he'd have the pleasure of her feistiness to start each and every morning. Sabrina Parker was definitely getting under his skin.

"I'm helping my sister out for a time. What's it to you?" Sabrina asked, folding her arms across her chest. Although he wasn't ogling her, she suspected that Dr. Winters did indeed find her attractive. Even with her hair in a ponytail and wearing her ratty jeans.

"Just wanted to know how long I had to work my magic on you," Malcolm replied, picking up his paper and strolling toward the exit. Pretty soon, Sabrina Parker would begging to go out with him.

"You'll never get your way, Dr. Winters," Sabrina replied, standing tall.

"Never say never, Sabrina," Malcolm said. "Because I always get what I want."

Once she was out in the hallway, Sabrina realized that she'd enjoyed the back-and-forth flirtation between them. She hadn't felt that tingle in her belly since the early days with Tre. A night alone with Malcolm could erase all the bad memories of Tre, but she couldn't do that. She couldn't use him that way, he deserved better and so did she. So for now, she would keep her distance.

"Having fun?" Felicia asked when she stopped in the kitchen later that morning to refresh her French-vanilla coffee. She watched Sabrina scour a particularly stubborn pot.

"What do you think?" Sabrina asked, brushing her damp hair back with her hand.

"I *think*," Felicia said, stalking over to the sink and glaring at her younger sister, "that you need to learn the value of working for one's living."

Sabrina recognized contempt when she saw it. "Like you, I suppose?" Sabrina tossed the sponge into the soapy dishwater and spun around to face her. "Oh please. Up until Lucas was born, you were just like me. Content being at home and letting your man support you."

"But I didn't have that chance, did I, little sis?" Felicia slammed down her coffee mug on the Formica counter, spilling some of the drink.

Sabrina stuck her hand in the dishwater and pulled out a sponge to wipe it up, but Felicia snatched it from her and began furiously cleaning the counter. "Dad decided he wanted to retire. And *someone* had to take over Parker House. Sean couldn't do it. He'd been managing the Tybee Island Resort for years. And Alton? Oh please." Felicia tossed her hair across her shoulders. "He'd long since decided he wasn't in the hospitality business. So who do you think the responsibility fell to, Sabrina, while you were off in Baltimore and nowhere to be found?" Felicia pushed Sabrina's shoulder with her forefinger.

"You," Sabrina answered, accepting Felicia's wrath by boldly meeting her gaze. Felicia had waited a long time to have her say, so Sabrina would let her vent. "All you." Sabrina turned away and stared outside. She was beginning to understand some of Felicia's animosity toward her. "You took the load off of Daddy, so he could rest and for that I'll always be eternally grateful." Sabrina swallowed hard, it was a feeble answer but she meant every word. She tried reaching out to her sister, but Felicia jerked away.

A muscle flinched angrily at Felicia's jaw. "I don't

need your sympathy or gratitude," she replied harshly. "I needed some help. But you were too busy enjoying your amazing life in Baltimore. The ironic part is that it turned out to be not all that amazing."

"Does it make you happy, Felicia," Sabrina asked, "to see me in pain, to know that Tre hurt me? Did you get warm fuzzies when you found out my marriage had broken up?" Sabrina fought hard against the tears that threatened. She bit her lip, refusing to let Felicia see her cry.

"Of course not, Sabrina," Felicia stalked across the room to face her sister. "I wouldn't wish that kind of pain on anyone, let alone my sister."

"Well, that's good to hear," Sabrina smiled. "So does this mean that we can finally act like sisters again?"

Felicia opened her arms. "Welcome home."

Malcolm left work early that afternoon for two reasons. One, he needed to renovate the decrepit old house he'd bought from Old Man Sims and two, because despite his busy schedule, thoughts of a certain curly haired single mother kept intruding all morning causing him to lose focus. He was hoping some good old-fashioned brawn and muscle was what was needed to get the place back into mint condition. The two-story home that needed repair just might get his mind off the lovely lady.

Everywhere he went, Sabrina was right there. Either on the side of the road, at lunch and now at his bed-and-breakfast. He couldn't seem to escape her. She even crept into his dreams, causing him to awake with one hell of an erection. So today, he planned on working hard to forget her.

His first project was flooring. It was concrete now, but he planned on adding hardwood floors throughout the foyer, parlor, dining room and his study while the kitchen would have some kind of decorative marble tile. He planned to install plush cut pile carpeting in the upstairs bedrooms. Sure, he could have hired a professional to do the work, but he didn't need to.

He'd hired some day labors to completely gut the place, from the first floor to the attic. A lot of work was ahead of him, but he welcomed the opportunity to work some underused muscles and focus his energies elsewhere. Plus, good old-fashioned exhaustion might cure his insomnia.

His mind was already in overdrive at his plans for the master bath. The interior would be completely remodeled starting with a free-standing tub. Unlike most men, he loved a steaming, hot bath after a long day at work.

He wished he had a little female intuition to help with the decorating. The hardest part would be choosing the right cabinetry, fixtures and accessories that went into making a house a home.

Opening up his cooler, Malcolm reached inside for a Gatorade. He was going to be living off the stuff for months as he whipped the house into shape. Malcolm cracked open the seal and began chugging, when the doorbell ran. It should be his shipment of oak planks that he'd ordered from the Home Depot up the street.

Malcolm opened up the large oak glass door and found Corey Johnson, from the Ace Hardware store.

"Were do you want these?" Corey asked.

"Put them in the parlor," Malcolm ordered.

"Sure thing, sure thing." Corey strode toward the door.

When Corey was finished unloading his truck, he took a handkerchief out his jeans pocket and wiped his sweaty brow.

"Now correct me if I'm wrong," Malcolm began, "but don't you work for Ace Hardware?"

"And your point?"

"I ordered these from Home Depot."

"Well, a man's gotta eat," Corey replied, picking up his baseball cap that had fallen unceremoniously from his head while he unloaded. "And a second job takes care of that."

"Enough said," Malcolm stated and walked towards the door. But for some reason, Corey wasn't taking the hint because he was still standing in the parlor. "Can I do something for you?"

"Well, uh," Corey stuttered. The doctor made him a little bit nervous with his commanding presence. At six-foot-three to his five-foot-nine, Corey felt a bit dwarfed. But he'd been asked to extend the invitation and so he would.

"You see, me and the fellas meet at Mimi's on

Saturday nights and throw back a few beers and shoot pool. You know the usual manly stuff. You should come on down and hang with us."

"Doesn't this look like fun?" Malcolm's arm swung out to the parlor in complete disarray.

"To tell you the truth, no. You're out here all alone and missing out on a good time at Mimi's. Trust me. These truly are a great group of people. When I first moved to this town, they embraced me and now I know just about everyone in the community. Matter of fact, our annual picnic is this weekend."

Malcolm had heard about the picnic and he was thinking of attending if nothing else than to get his name out. "Well, thanks for the info, Corey. But I like my solitude."

Corey shrugged. "It's your loss. But if you ever want to stop by, we're there after work."

"Thanks, I'll keep that in mind," Malcolm retorted, before shutting the door. "Whew, what a relief," he sighed. He had more important things on his mind, like installing a hardwood floor and getting Sabrina Parker out of his head.

"Sabrina, are you ready?" Beverly Parker called upstairs to her daughter as they all prepared to go to the First Baptist Church's annual picnic later that week. Beverly was supplying her famous potato salad and several cakes and pies. Everyone in the church and in the Parker family enjoyed the annual event. There was always plenty of down-home cooking, music, games, prizes and dancing. And it sure had been a while since she and James had done the two-step.

Sabrina poked her head across the banister. "Mom, I'm not ready yet. Give me a few more minutes to finish my makeup." She was excited about a family outing in the beautiful eighty-degree weather.

"Hurry up, child. My group is waiting on me with the rest of the fixins."

"Okay, okay, I'll hustle." Sabrina rushed toward the bathroom and found Jasmine playing in her makeup bag.

"Move aside, darling. You mama's got work to do." With one hip, Sabrina pushed Jasmine aside. Jasmine rebounded by pulling down the toilet seat and sitting atop to watch her mother get ready.

Sabrina applied a small dab of texturizing lotion to her new curls. She just loved this new do and was glad Jasmine had come around. With a little moisturizer, her hair lay in soft waves around her face, giving her a sexy new look.

"You look nice, Mom," Jasmine said, regarding Sabrina's ensemble of an orange halter, cream capris and a pair of mules. It was the perfect outfit considering the high temperature expected for the day.

"Hand me my makeup bag, please."

Jasmine did so, but not before pulling out Sabrina's red lip gloss. "Can I have just a little?" She held the tube up in the air.

"Okay, but just a little," Sabrina took the gloss

from her and applied a small dab to Jasmine's lips. "Mmmwahh," Sabrina kissed her on the cheek.

"What was that for?" Jasmine wiped the kiss away with the back of her hand.

"Because I'm your mother and I love you, that's why. Now let's go," she ordered as they exited the guest bathroom. Sabrina noticed Jasmine's pink T-shirt with the big daisy on the front hanging out of the cute blue denim skirt she'd bought last season while in Boston. "Wait a sec," Sabrina said as they passed her room. Quickly, she fixed Jasmine's shirt and patted her bottom. Together they went bounding down the stairs.

When they arrived at the First Baptist Church annual picnic, the gathering was already in full swing. The church grounds had been transformed with long, buffet tables filled with food, picnic tables, games and prizes and a large temporary dance floor. The men had already abandoned the women's group, who were preparing the food, in favor of playing football in the small grassy knoll behind the church or shooting hoops on the basketball court.

Disembarking from her father's sport-utility vehicle, Sabrina noticed just how many people were actually assembled. Was the whole community part of the congregation?

Her sister Felicia, husband, Sean, and children Destiny, Chynna and Lucas were already there and seated at a large picnic table, while Alton and Danielle sat with his deputies and their wives.

"Well, well, well, if it isn't the dark sheep of the Parker family," Althea Prichard, her parents' neighbor, said upon Sabrina and Jasmine's approach. Sabrina rolled her eyes, but kept her cool as she placed a cake on the buffet table. "Wherever have you been hiding yourself?"

"I'm doing well, Althea. How are you?"

"Oh just fine, just fine." Althea looked Sabrina up and down. "But it looks like we're going to have to fatten you up. What have they been feeding you up north?"

"Nothing but fruits and vegetables," laughed Sabrina. "Though none are as delectable as those in your garden."

Althea smiled at the compliment. Her garden was one of her most prized possessions. "Thank you. I'll be sure to give some to ya mama so we can put some meat on your bones."

"And I'd love to have them," Sabrina replied as she continued down the row. Sabrina continued making introductions until she ran smack dab into her brother Alton and his wife Danielle.

"There you are," Alton said, stopping her. "You're a hard woman to track down these days."

"Really?" Sabrina wondered, feigning ignorance. The truth was she had been avoiding interrogation by her older brother on her failed marriage.

"Yes, you are," Alton replied. "You've been back for well over a month and I've barely seen you."

"I'm sorry, Alton," Sabrina apologized. "Now that

I'm working at the bed-and-breakfast, it's really taking up quite a bit of my time. I'm sorry if I've been neglecting you."

"Well, I was beginning to wonder," Alton murmured. "I was beginning to think it had something to do with the good-looking doctor in town."

"What are you talking about?" Sabrina asked. "What have you heard?"

"Oh, a little of this. A little of that," Alton teased. "Look at him over there—all the ladies are swooning over him. Each just salivating at the idea of landing a rich doctor."

Sabrina glanced around and found Malcolm at a table surrounded by women. With a stethoscope around his neck, Malcolm was checking several women's heart rates, which Sabrina was sure were quite high.

"Oh, he's being quite the hero," Alton replied, "giving everyone free blood pressure and glucose screenings."

Sabrina wasn't surprised. Dr. Winters struck her as the dedicated doctor, one who cared deeply for his patients.

"And? Don't play with me, Alton," Sabrina warned, smacking his shoulder, playfully. "If people are gossiping about me then I want to know it."

"I've heard nothing," said Alton, spinning around and avoiding the sisterly abuse.

"Good," Sabrina said, walking away. Parched, she stopped by the refreshment stand for a cool glass of lemonade, but found a line. When she finally reached the front of a line a football came flying through the air knocking the cup clear out of her hand, spilling onto the man's trousers in front of her.

"Oh, I'm so sorry," Sabrina apologized profusely. Without hazarding a glance, Sabrina accepted the napkin from a volunteer and patted at the man's linen pants, which now held a noticeable wet spot. "I'm so sorry, sir. The boys weren't looking where they were throwing." Sabrina eyed the dreaded football that now stood at her feet. When she bent down to pick it up, and finally looked up at her victim she found a pair of dark irises glowering down at her.

Chapter 7

"**D**r. Winters..." Sabrina began, flustered at his sudden appearance. "I'm sorry I didn't see you." When he didn't respond, she continued fumbling. "I mean...it wasn't intentional." Sabrina attempted a halfhearted smile. "Can I have your pants dry-cleaned?"

She was embarrassed to find herself in yet another compromising situation with the illustrious Boston doctor that she'd heard nothing else about for the last half hour. She'd barely made the social rounds of re-introducing herself and Jasmine to the congregation when women began asking if she'd met Dr. Winters. Like vultures, they smelled fresh meat.

"It's okay." Malcolm's eyes instantly softened

once he realized Sabrina was the culprit who'd soiled his freshly pressed linen trousers. "I'll take care of it." He took the napkin Sabrina procured and patted his pants dry as best he could. Luckily the damage was minimal. He handed Sabrina the soiled napkin. "We really have to stop meeting like this."

"I know." Sabrina gave a halfhearted smile.

"If you don't mind my saying, I like the new look. It suits you." Malcolm noticed Sabrina's hair had changed from long and straight to luscious and sassy curls. It was the very same hair that once or twice his dreams had wandered to when he imagined the two of them making love.

"Oh, this?" Sabrina smoothed her long ringlets. "I needed a change."

"Sometimes change is good," he commented.

Sabrina broke out into a breathtaking smile that threw Malcolm a little off-kilter. "Now if you don't mind, Sabrina, I'm going to grab some food before those teenage boys get hold of everything."

"I think I'll join you," Sabrina said, following behind him to the buffet table. "Because it looks like I've lost my daughter to her new best friend." Sabrina glanced over at Jasmine playing with Monique's children.

Their appearance together at the table did not go by unnoticed. Regina, her mother's good friend and a member of the First Baptist women's church group, stood up upon their arrival.

"What can I get for you, Dr. Winters?" she asked,

holding up a paper plate. Malcolm eyed all the goodies and for once threw practicality out the window. "I'll take a slab of those baby back ribs, some of that potato salad and an ear of corn. Oh yes, and a spoon of those barbecue beans, please."

Regina prepared his request and handed him a plate that said heart disease all over it. But Malcolm supposed one meal wouldn't hurt him. Especially since the women's group had gone through such trouble. "Thank you, Mrs. Douglas."

"And you, Sabrina?" she asked.

"Hmmm, I'll have the same, but replace the ribs with barbecue chicken, please." Sabrina turned and smiled up at Malcolm.

"Dr. Winters, I see you've already met our little Sabrina here," Regina gushed. "We're just so happy to have her back in Savannah."

"Yes, we've met," Malcolm replied after a hearty bite of the baby back ribs. "On several occasions."

And Sabrina could recall every single one of them.

"Good, I'm glad you've made the acquaintance. Sabrina, perhaps you can show Dr. Winters the sights around town. There's plenty to see and do." Regina smiled knowingly.

"There's an empty table over there." Regina pointed to a picnic table that had suddenly become available. Sabrina turned and smiled at Malcolm. He, too, recognized Regina's obvious matchmaking attempt.

"Thank you, Mrs. Douglas, it's so nice of you to

look out for us," Malcolm replied. "Sabrina." He waited for Sabrina to precede him and followed behind her. The table might have been empty, but it was dead center in the middle of the picnic where all eyes could focus on their every move. Had Regina set it up just so?

"It looks like we're the entertainment," Malcolm said as he joined Sabrina at the picnic table.

"It does appear that way." She glanced around and found several curious sets of eyes on them. "Those ladies have nothing better to do but to poke around in other people's business. Don't they know that I don't need a man right now? Matter of fact, that's the last thing I need or want."

"Because of your failed marriage?" Malcolm asked, plowing into his lunch plate.

"Of course," Sabrina replied, biting a piece of chicken. Afterward, she relished the sweet, tangy sauce before taking another bite. "My husband cheated on me, you see and I guess I blame myself."

Malcolm watched Sabrina tear into the barbecue and lick her fingers, and he couldn't help but smile. She was unpretentious and completely herself. If he didn't stop spending time with her quick, he could come to like her even more. "But you shouldn't take all the blame, either. Your husband was a jerk for ever cheating on you. He didn't realize what a gem he had."

Sabrina blinked several times, thinking she'd misheard. Had Malcolm actually called her a gem?

"Mom, Mom." Jasmine came running toward her, proudly holding up a big stuffed horse. "Look at what I won playing horseshoes."

"Why, it's the most beautiful horse I've ever seen. And so are you." Sabrina reached for Jasmine and tried to plant a kiss.

"Mom, stop it. We have company." Jasmine pulled away, and motioned her head toward Malcolm. Seconds passed, before recognition set in. "Wait a second, I remember you. You're the man from the park."

"Guilty as charged," Malcolm replied, putting down his fork and pushing away his empty plate. "I'm Dr. Malcolm Winters." He extended his hand, which Jasmine accepted. Her little hands barely made a dent over his. "And you, young lady, look as pretty as a princess."

"Thank you." Jasmine blushed and turned to face her mother.

"Can I go back and play with Brianna and Brandon? The egg toss is next and I can't wait to throw an egg all over Chynna's shoes." Jasmine laughed as she ran away towards the children's activities.

"Jasmine Matthews!" Sabrina stood up. That child was going to be the death of her!

"Let her go." Malcolm touched Sabrina's arm to halt her. The flesh underneath his fingers burned while his touch rendered Sabrina speechless.

"Hello." Malcolm snapped his fingers in front of her face.

"Hmmm, yes." Sabrina came out of her fog. "Did I miss something?"

"No." Malcolm eyed her curiously before continuing. "I just said to let her go. You know the old adage. Kids will be kids."

"True, but that one is more like a mini-me."

Malcolm laughed heartily. Laughter had been something in short supply these days. It was good to feel happy for a change and not sullen and withdrawn. He was finally remembering what it felt like to enjoy life and not regret that he was still living it.

"Now, whose turn is it to wander off?" Sabrina asked, when she caught Malcolm staring far off in space.

"I'm sorry," Malcolm apologized.

"Forgiven. Now what do you say we go join in on the fun?" Sabrina stood up and pointed to the potato sack race getting ready to begin.

"Isn't that where two people get in a sack and try to hop to the finish line?"

"Yeah," Sabrina grinned mischievously. "You game?"

"Not only am I game, Sabrina, but we're going to win this thing," he said, grabbing her by the hand and running with her across the field.

An hour later, Sabrina returned to their table with a giant overstuffed hippo that she and Malcolm had won for their efforts. The man sure was competitive. He'd nearly carried her across the finish line. But that wasn't all there was. An attraction that had been simmering between them all afternoon had surfaced during the game. Had she felt someone's temperature rising behind her?

Malcolm, on the other hand, had been overjoyed at the turn of events, especially when her delicious curvy bottom had settled between his thighs while racing. When that happened, he'd held Sabrina extra tight, causing his groin to tighten in response and letting him know he was indeed among the living.

"That was a lot of fun," Sabrina said when they made their way back to the refreshment stand for bottled water. The sun was finally starting to set in the west, so the volunteers were setting up a small stage for some live entertainment and a little dancing. "Did you see my brother trying to hop across the field in that potato sack? It was hilarious."

"It was." Malcolm smiled in return as he walked beside her. "I can't remember the last time I let loose like that. I had a lot of fun, Sabrina."

Sabrina stopped and her eyes grew alight with devilry. "Well, you should do so more often. Was that actually a smile I saw?" Sabrina's index finger reached out and touched the slight dimple in Malcolm's cheek. Malcolm quickly grasped her hand, and when he did, the very air around her electrified.

Startled, she pulled away and Malcolm released her. He hadn't realized he'd actually acted out on his desire to touch her. He surveyed Sabrina. He wondered what lay beneath the murky depths of those arresting light brown eyes of hers. From what he'd gathered in their brief conversation, Sabrina was still hurting tremendously over her divorce, but yet he gleamed a spark of interest in her eyes. He wasn't imagining it.

"Would you like to dance?" Malcolm inclined his head towards the dance floor. Several couples had already begun swaying to the smooth rhythmic sounds coming from a local jazz band, and it would finally give him an excuse to do exactly what he'd wanted to do all afternoon and that was to take the beautiful Ms. Parker in his arms.

"Okay," Sabrina said hesitantly.

Malcolm took her arm with gentle authority and they walked to the dance floor. When Sabrina stood nervously looking up at him with those luminous eyes, Malcolm pulled her close and wrapped one hand around her narrow waist until they were separated by a fraction of air while the other clasped one of her delicate hands in his.

Sabrina's body was stiff at first. It had been a while since a man held her tightly and looked at her with such warmth and passion. When she finally hazarded a glance up at him, his gaze was as soft as a caress. It caused a ripple of excitement to shoot through her. It took several minutes for her to finally loosen up and enjoy the music, but when she did, a new and unexpected warmth surged through her veins. Was it the music or the man? Sabrina wondered. It had to be the man, because each time she saw him, the pull was stronger. More and more, she found herself extremely conscious of his virile appeal and this time was no different.

Disconcerted, she forced herself to look away and keep her head low. She was afraid of the feelings that Malcolm evoked in her. Their bodies were meshed so closely together it sent Sabrina's pulse spinning. When some up-tempo music came and she came in close contact with his hips, it was impossible not to notice him. She tried to maintain her composure at the sexual magnetism emanating from his every pore, but she failed. Her body was completely aware of his every move.

And she wasn't alone. Malcolm was experiencing a gamut of emotions being near Sabrina. He knew she had to notice that he was more than a little bit attracted to her by the growing bulge in his pants. His groin was calling out for a release that only she could provide.

Relief flooded through her when the band finally took a break. When they separated, Sabrina and Malcolm turned and found they had indeed caused a commotion because all eyes were on them.

Embarrassed, Sabrina's cheeks became warm. She was glad that the semi-darkness hid the flush in her cheeks. "Thanks for the dance," Sabrina whispered and rushed off the dance floor. She was suddenly anxious to escape his disturbing presence.

"Wait." Malcolm ignored the audience and followed her down the steps. He had to hurry to catch

Sabrina because she was quickly walking back to the picnic area. He caught up with her at a big old oak tree and halted her escape with a firm hand on her arm.

"Malcolm, please," Sabrina said, "Don't come any closer." She held her hand up to stop him. "I can't deal with this right now."

"Why are you running away?" he asked.

"You know why," Sabrina replied. A wave of apprehension had hit her the moment she stepped away from him. "I just ended a ten-year marriage. I'm not capable of anything else right now, Malcolm. All I have room for in my life right now is me and my daughter."

"And all I'm asking is that we spend a little time together. Who knows, you just might enjoy yourself. Kind of like you did tonight."

Malcolm brushed his lips across one delicate hand. "You can't deny the attraction between us, Sabrina. It's been simmering since day one. I know you can feel it."

His strong hands circled around her waist and pulled her snugly against him. With his index finger, Malcolm tenderly traced the line of her cheekbone and then cupped her chin, forcing her to look at him. The smoldering flame Sabrina saw in his eyes caused a delightful shiver to run through her and though every fiber in her body warned her against this, Sabrina wanted him.

But he didn't kiss her right away. Instead he bent down and nibbled at her earlobe before searing a path from her neck and to her shoulders. Sabrina felt her knees weaken, and when his lips finally descended on hers, his kiss was slow and thoughtful, sending spirals of ecstasy through her.

She returned his kiss, savoring every delicious moment as he explored her lips and the soft inner recesses of her mouth. She deliberately shut out any awareness of her surroundings and instead focused all of her attention on Malcolm, drinking him in, starting from his soft and caressing touch on her arm to the sweet intoxicating musk of his cologne tickling her nose.

She drew his face to hers and crushed his lips against hers. He responded by cupping her jaw and tilting her head back for a deeper kiss. He left no part of her mouth untouched, so much so that she didn't remember where she was until the stunt gun sounded signaling the end of the picnic games.

Dragging her mouth from his, Sabrina's senses reeled and she clung to Malcolm's arm for support. Emotions were equally high for him, too, because Malcolm's broad shoulders were heaving and his breathing was labored.

Malcolm stepped back and took a minute to catch his breath. When he finally spoke, he said, "Sabrina, we're so good together," Malcolm whispered. "Please tell me you've changed your mind."

"All right, all right." Sabrina finally gave in. She could no longer fight the inevitable. "I'll go out with you, but just as friends," she threw in.

Malcolm paused. If after that kiss she could still

say they were friends, then she was deluding herself, but he would do it her way for now.

"Okay," Malcolm replied. "How about Saturday night?"

Sabrina was stifling a yawn when a familiar face stopped in front of her. Covering her mouth, she paused to make recognition and realized it was Craig Garrett, her former competitor while in high school.

Short and stocky, she'd always thought of him as sort of a dork. He'd worn wire-framed glasses that were a little too big for his face. Of course, now he'd matured. The short stockiness had turned to lean muscle and the glasses had been replaced with contacts.

"Wow, I heard you were back in town." Craig leaned down to kiss her on the cheek. "It's good to see you."

It amazed Sabrina how easily people forgot. "Craig, it's good to see you, too," she replied in turn. "Have a seat and tell me what you've been up to the last decade."

They were catching up on old times when Craig revealed he was now editor of the local African-American newspaper, the *Savannah Tribune.* A pang of jealousy shot through Sabrina. Craig was living the life she'd always dreamt of. But that was okay, if life hadn't sent her on a detour she would never have had Jazzy. She was home now and on the road to turning her life around and pretty soon, she'd leave Craig Garrett in her dust.

* * *

From the sidelines and several lamps away, Malcolm noted the exchange at the table while he played chess with his patient, Mr. Gibson and was livid. Who was that guy with Sabrina and why was he fawning all over her? And why was he touching her? Malcolm didn't like it one single bit. He wanted to go over there and knock his block off.

It bothered him that some guy was hugging up on Sabrina as if he had the right to. Since when did he become so jealous and possessive? Maybe because Sabrina had finally agreed to go out with him and he was feeling more alive than he'd felt in years.

"Hey, are you with me?" Mr. Gibson asked, waving a hand in front of Malcolm's face. He'd already set up the chess pieces on the board and made his first move.

"Yes, I am," Malcolm replied, turning away from his view of Sabrina and the man she was with. It wasn't long before his attention was diverted from the beautiful divorcée and onto the chess game. Mr. Gibson was quite good and gave Malcolm a run for his money. He'd already captured one of his pawns and they'd only been playing ten minutes.

"How have you been feeling, Mr. Gibson?" Malcolm inquired, staring at the board intently while trying to figure out his next move.

"Still under the weather, Dr. Winters," Mrs. Gibson answered for her husband as she came back to the table with a plate of food. Because of his heart, she'd kept it simple, a few thin slices of barbecue rib roast, potato salad and roasted corn on the cob. "He can't seem to shake the light-headedness and shortness of breath."

"Yeah, doc. What's up with that? I thought this medication was going to fix me right up." Mr. Gibson moved another pawn.

"Still?" Malcolm asked, rubbing his jaw. Then the clot-dissolving medication he'd given Mr. Gibson wasn't working.

"I'd like to see you back in my office on Monday," Malcolm said, moving his pawn one square and capturing Mr. Gibson's pawn.

"Hey, how'd you do that?" Mr. Gibson asked.

Malcolm laughed. "You weren't paying attention." But he would have to be if he intended to fix Mr. Gibson's heart problems. It disturbed him tremendously that the medication wasn't opening up the arteries.

"Wow, it's what, eight o'clock?" Monique said, glancing at her watch as she joined Sabrina's table, "And I finally get to speak to you."

Sabrina blushed.

"Seems someone else took up all your attention this afternoon," Monique commented.

"Yes." Sabrina nodded her head. "And all due to Mrs. Douglas's matchmaking."

Monique laughed. "Don't kid a kidder," she said. "Mrs. Douglas may have been the catalyst, but the two of you did the rest, and boy did ya." Monique chuckled again. "You and the hot new doctor had the gossips buzzing today."

"Oh Lord, did we?" Sabrina asked, touching her chest. Upon reflection, Sabrina thought about the way he'd gazed at her, or the way his compelling eyes gave a lazy appraisal of every inch of her body, or the feel of Malcolm's hand on the small of her back and how she'd tingled with excitement. "Okay, I suppose we did."

"So, what happens next?"

"Dinner and a movie," Sabrina replied evenly.

"And that's all?" Monique asked. "If a sexy doctor had been chasing me for weeks, there would be no question as to where you might find me."

"And where might that be?" Sabrina inquired.

"His bed," Monique stated. "Oh, don't be surprised," Monique responded to Sabrina's shocked expression. "Why shouldn't you spend some time with the good doctor?"

"I don't want to use him as a substitute for Tre. He'd be the rebound guy and that wouldn't be fair."

Monique stood up and looked around for her kids. It was time to leave the picnic. "Girlfriend, I love ya, but I am tired of hearing about Tre. You need to move on from that cheater and what better way than the handsome doc. And if he's ready and willing, then why not? I suggest you grab him up quick because with the amount of single women in this congregation he won't be available for long."

Chapter 8

Life flew by very fast for Sabrina. Her hands were full working at the bed-and-breakfast and rearing Jasmine. She was finally beginning to settle into her new life in Savannah.

After seeing how successful Craig was, she'd immediately gone to Savannah University's registrar's office and registered for the fall semester. She'd discovered that most of her credits from her two years at Georgetown would transfer and that she only had two years remaining to obtain a diploma. And Jasmine was due to start school in a few weeks right along with her. It was all coming together. Had she finally made peace with the cards she'd been dealt?

It certainly appeared so. She was truly happy to

be home and enjoyed the time she spent with her family. She'd renewed her friendship with Monique and formed a new one with Dr. Winters. Although she'd offered friendship, it wasn't the first thought that crossed into her mind when she thought of Malcolm.

Whenever she was around him, she flustered easily or ran at the mouth. Whether it was the warm, melodic tone of his tenor voice, his infectious grin or those dark, unfathomable eyes that penetrated hers whenever she laid eyes on him, Sabrina admitted to herself that she was falling hard for Malcolm. The thought of being with another man, however, terrified her.

Having met in college, Tre was the only man she'd ever been intimate with, unlike Tre, who'd been dipping out on their marriage for quite some time. Sabrina had discovered that interesting tidbit during a heated argument when he was moving out. She'd learned that Melanie was not his first mistress. Apparently, he was tired of having to train her, he'd said. The women he was with knew how to please a man in the bedroom.

Sabrina had no idea what he was referring to. She'd always done as he'd asked or been willing to experiment with different positions. Once, she'd bought an entire stock of Victoria's Secret lingerie and even a few naughty costumes from Frederick's of Hollywood. Tre was wrong about her. If there had been a problem with their sex life, he should have looked in the mirror. And if he thought she was asexual, he was dead wrong. She'd had no problem satisfying herself when the need arose. Now Malcolm, he seemed like the right man to bring out the passion in her!

While washing some dishes at the B and B, Sabrina's mind wandered to a hot daydream with Malcolm as her leading man, but the shrill of the phone interrupted her. And it was none other than the subject of her dream.

"Malcolm." Sabrina blushed at where her daydreams had led. "I'm surprised to hear from you."

"Why? Did you forget about our date?" Malcolm asked, from the other end of the phone. "We're on for the movies and dinner tonight, right?"

"Yes, of course." Sabrina fanned her face with an envelope nearby.

"What time shall I pick you up, then?"

"Umm, pick me up…? Malcolm, you do remember that this is a platonic date?" Sabrina asked. She hoped he didn't think otherwise, despite where her lascivious thoughts had led a moment ago or her mixed signals at the picnic.

"Of course I do," Malcolm answered, exasperated. "But it's the gentlemanly thing for a man to pick a woman up for dinner, but if that's being too forward—" he paused for effect "—then by all means, we can meet at the theater."

"No, no, that's fine," Sabrina was embarrassed. "You can pick me up at six at my parents'."

Malcolm placed the phone in the cradle and leaned back in his leather chair, grinning from ear to ear. He'd been looking forward to his date with Sabrina since he'd left her parents' a couple of weeks ago and now he would have his chance. The thought of gathering Sabrina in his arms and planting another kiss on those sensual lips of hers caused Malcolm's groin to tighten.

Returning to his work, Malcolm signed some scripts and paperwork before locking his office and heading to reception. He had just enough time to run to Parker House and change clothes.

Nurse Turner was turning off the exam-room lights when he exited his office. "I believe these are for you," Malcolm said with a smile, handing the manila folders to his nurse.

Grace smiled back at her boss. Since she'd begun working at the clinic, Dr. Winter's expression had either veered from angry to sad, but never happiness. This new look was a pleasant surprise. From what she'd heard from the local gossips, Grace could only assume it had something to do with a certain single mother.

"Hot date tonight?" Grace queried.

"Something like that," Malcolm answered, not offering any further information. "Don't forget to lock up."

"Going out with Dr. Winters, tonight, huh?" her mother asked from the doorway as Sabrina scrunched her naturally curly hair with a gel to keep the look in place.

"Mom, don't start," Sabrina smiled as she spritzed her earlobes and wrists with her favorite perfume, Casmir. Sure, they had spent some time together, but they were friends, nothing more. "Malcolm and I are just two friends going out to share a meal and a movie."

"You're sure going through an awful lot of trouble for just a *friend,*" her mom commented, indicating Sabrina's new sandals and silk sunflower halter dress.

"Oh, this old thing?" Sabrina smiled knowingly as she added a touch of blush to the honey-brown foundation she'd applied earlier. She'd bought the ensemble for tonight's occasion, eager to look her best. The woman in her wanted Malcolm to find her attractive. When Sabrina was finished with her makeup, she whirled around and posed for her mother. "Well, how do I look?"

Beverly smiled. "You know I think you're beautiful even without all that makeup."

"I know, Mom. But *you* are not who I'm trying to impress," Sabrina said, scooting past her in the doorway and walking to her room for her wrap and purse. Malcolm would be arriving shortly.

"So, you admit you like Dr. Winters?" Beverly pressed for more information.

"I admit only to enjoying the man's company and yes, I admit I like the way he looks at me."

"Don't you think it's entirely too soon to be getting involved with someone so soon after Tre? You're getting over a painful divorce. You were married for nearly a decade, after all," her mother insisted.

"I know all of this, Mom. And truly, I know you mean well, but I'm going to have to ask you to butt out," Sabrina replied. She didn't mean to be cruel or disrespectful, but she was sick and tired of hearing everyone's opinion on how she should live her life.

Jasmine caught Sabrina in the hallway. "Is he here yet?" Jasmine asked, excitedly. Her face broke into a wide open smile, revealing a missing tooth. When it had fallen out last night, Jasmine had been beside herself because she hadn't wanted Dr. Malcolm to see her without her tooth.

"No, not yet, Jazzy," Sabrina replied. "He should be here any minute. Let's go downstairs and wait."

They marched downstairs to await Malcolm's arrival as if Sabrina were a princess going off to a ball. Could Dr. Malcolm Winters be her Prince Charming? A little part of Sabrina hoped it were true. Only time would tell.

The doorbell rang and Sabrina inhaled deeply.

"He's here, Mom!" Jasmine jumped up and down as she looked through the window. Jasmine was excited to see Dr. Winters again. He was really cool and always used big words.

"Calm yourself," Sabrina replied, even though she, too, was excited at the prospect of seeing

Malcolm again. And when she opened the door, he didn't disappoint. She stood frozen in the doorway, letting her eyes travel the length of him. He looked arresting in a tapered black suit, navy silk shirt and Ferragamo shoes. Everything about the man oozed sex appeal.

She caught his appreciative glance and watched those onyx eyes fix on her. She hoped he was pleased because she had gone through a great deal of trouble to look her best.

Malcolm liked everything he saw, especially that touch of cleavage peeking out of the yellow silk dress, which suited her coloring perfectly.

Malcolm caught the eagerness in Sabrina's eyes and the glow to her cheeks as he stepped into the hallway. A tumble of naturally curly dark hair shone even in the low lighting while the silk dress clung to her nubile curves.

"Sabrina." Malcolm brushed his lips lightly against her cheeks. "Good to see you," he said trying to appear nonchalant. "And you, Ms. Jazzy." Malcolm bent down and lifted Jasmine in his arms like she weighed nothing more than a feather. "How's my little munchkin?"

"I'm good now that you're here, Dr. Malcolm," Jasmine replied, squeezing her tiny arms around his neck. Malcolm retuned the hug, before setting her back on solid ground. "Have fun at the movies," she said, joining her grandparents in the living room.

"Ready to go?"

"Yes," Sabrina replied nervously.

The moment they were in the comfort of Malcolm's Jaguar, Sabrina felt more at ease.

"Are you ready for our friendly date?"

"Absolutely." Sabrina raised her eyes to meet his and found him looking in her direction. His eyes were filled with something Sabrina couldn't quite name, but the moment passed and he quickly shifted his gaze back to the road.

They arrived at the theater with enough time for Malcolm to grant Sabrina's wish for popcorn and soda. While they waited for the clerk, Malcolm spoke about how fond he was of Jasmine. "She's really special," Malcolm stated. His heart skipped a beat when she'd looked up at him adoringly at the Parker's home. He didn't know why he felt such a special bond with the eight-year-old, but he did. "You're really lucky."

Sabrina wondered if Malcolm regretted that he didn't have a family of his own. She determined to find out later over dinner at Lady and Son's restaurant.

"Thank you." Sabrina glanced up at Malcolm as she accepted the large bag of popcorn and soda from the clerk. His six-foot-three stature nearly dwarfed her.

Malcolm pulled out a twenty and handed it to the clerk. "Keep the change," Malcolm said, assisting Sabrina by pulling the soda container out of her hand.

"I wish her mother was as equally fond of me," Malcolm said, leading her by the elbow to the theater.

"Fishing for a compliment?" Sabrina queried.

"Absolutely," Malcolm said grinning.

"And when I have one, you'll be the first to know," Sabrina teased, walking in front of him into the movie.

Malcolm chuckled. It was going to be a long night.

When the movie let out two hours later, they were both starved. Luckily, her parents knew the owners of Lady and Son's who'd graciously agreed to hold a table for them even though they didn't usually accept reservations. Known for its good food, the restaurant was always crowded every evening.

The waitress sat them almost immediately upon their arrival in a corner table by the window and handed them their menus.

"We'd like to start off first with a bottle of your best red wine," Malcolm stated to the waitress.

"Mmm, it all looks good," Sabrina commented as they reviewed their menus. "What are you going to order?" Sabrina focused her copper eyes on Malcolm's dark ones.

"Are you on the menu?" Malcolm whispered silkily in her ear as he scooted his chair next to hers and stretched his arm across the back of hers.

The underlying sensuality of his words captivated Sabrina, catching her off guard. "Hmmm, I don't believe that I am," Sabrina replied, her voice a little shakier than she would have liked. "I guess chicken

KIMANI
ROMANCE

An Important Message from the Publisher

Dear Reader,

Because you've chosen to read one of our fine novels, I'd like to say "thank you"! And, as a special way to say thank you, I'm offering to send you two more Kimani Romance novels and two surprise gifts – absolutely FREE! These books will keep it real with true-to-life African American characters that turn up the heat and sizzle with passion.

Please enjoy the free books and gifts with our compliments...

Linda Gill

Publisher, Kimani Press

Peel off Seal and Place Inside...

PUBLISHERS FREE GIFT SEAL THANK YOU

BUSINESS REPLY MAIL
FIRST-CLASS MAIL   PERMIT NO. 717-003   BUFFALO, NY

POSTAGE WILL BE PAID BY ADDRESSEE

THE READER SERVICE
3010 WALDEN AVE
PO BOX 1867
BUFFALO NY 14240-9952

NO POSTAGE
NECESSARY
IF MAILED
IN THE
UNITED STATES

If offer card is missing write to: The Reader Service, 3010 Walden Ave, PO Box 1867, Buffalo, NY 14240-1867 and grits will have to do for you," she said, noting an item on Lady and Son's menu.

"I suppose so," he replied, sending an irresistibly devastating grin her way. "Though I did have something else in mind," he said seductively.

Sabrina wondered at the implication of his words when the waitress returned with a bottle of wine. Malcolm uncorked the bottle and poured Sabrina and himself a generous glass.

"Are you ready to order?" the waitress asked, pulling out a small notepad and pen.

"Definitely," Sabrina stated.

After the waitress left to place their orders—steak and pie for Malcolm and pan-seared tilapia over jasmine rice for Sabrina—the conversation returned to all things conciliatory, giving Sabrina the opportunity to question Malcolm about his past in Boston, from his family life, to his schooling to his career as a renowned cardiologist.

He surprised her by answering all of her probing questions. She discovered that his mother Dinah lived back in Boston with his stepfather Walter and that he'd gone to Johns Hopkins for medical school. However, something about his explanations bothered Sabrina. When he spoke of his family, his voice was kind of cold and impersonal. Sabrina wondered if there was more to his story than he was letting on, and although Malcolm's tone remained dispassionate, his eyes betrayed him and told a different story entirely.

Sabrina learned more in the one dinner than she had from any of their previous encounters. And it all fascinated her. She was more intrigued with Malcolm than ever. Was it his aloofness that piqued her curiosity or was it something more?

Their food had arrived after she'd discovered Malcolm had a passion for sports.

"I enjoy the usual sports: basketball, baseball," Malcolm replied. "Playing, as well as watching."

"Me, too. I'll have to get us some tickets to a Braves or Hawks game sometime."

"That would be great," Malcolm replied.

The waitress returned and sat the steaming hot plates on the table while Malcolm discussed the renovations on his house on Tybee Island. Sabrina wondered why a bachelor his age would buy a five-bedroom house. He had to be looking for a wife to fill it, whether he knew it or not.

"That's an awfully big house you've got there, Malcolm," Sabrina commented. "You must want a really big family."

Malcolm was silent for several long moments and Sabrina wondered if he'd heard her.

He had. It was just that he'd never really thought about starting a family before. In Boston, he'd never had time for a relationship, let alone a wife and kids. "I guess I never seriously thought about it," he replied, honestly.

"Really? Well, you have plenty of room out there. And you're certainly wonderful with Jasmine."

"I adore Jasmine and maybe one day I'll have children of my own," he said. "I'd like to anyway, when I meet the right lady," he said, his eyes burning into hers. His fierce gaze caused Sabrina to look away and stare into her wineglass.

Sabrina surmised from the way he was looking at her that he was thinking she might be that choice, which completely frightened her. Malcolm's intensity scared her at times. So much so that she wasn't sure how to respond.

So instead, she focused on their delectable dinner, after which they shared a decadent dessert of chocolate mousse cake, which Sabrina had to brow beat the extremely health conscious Malcolm to share with her.

All in all, Sabrina enjoyed her evening tremendously and afterward when Malcolm parked in front of her parents' house, she was somewhat reluctant for the evening to end.

"I had a wonderful time," Sabrina said after Malcolm turned off the ignition.

"So did I, Sabrina. You have no idea what tonight meant to me," he began. "To socialize with another person after all this time…" His voice trailed off.

She knew it. She was right. He was hurting over some kind of loss. "What is it, Malcolm?" Sabrina asked. "You can talk to me. Whatever it is that's bothering you, you can tell me."

"I want to, Sabrina," Malcolm replied, "but now is not the right time. We've had such a lovely evening; can't we just leave it at that?"

Sabrina wanted to comfort him, but she was afraid of reaching out to him. She didn't have to because he made the first move by twisting her massive curls in his large hands. He brought Sabrina's face within inches of his and she watched his emotions change from anguish to desire.

His steady gaze traveled a slow, leisurely path to her lips and there it stayed, sending a dizzying current racing through Sabrina as she waited for his lips to brush across hers. His breath was warm and moist against her face and the touch of his fingertips against her lips sent all the blood from her toes surging to her head. She was desperate for him to kiss her again because if he didn't soon she was going to go mad with desire.

A light came on in the distance. "Sabrina," her mother called out to her from across the lawn. "Are you coming in?"

Sabrina pulled away from Malcolm. She knew what her mother was doing. Interfering. And she didn't like it one bit. Rolling down her window, Sabrina replied. "Soon, Ma. I'll be in soon."

"Okay," her mother said, closing the door reluctantly.

"Maybe I should let you go inside," Malcolm said, quickly unbuckling his seat belt and jumping out of the car.

"Darn!" Sabrina swore and folded her arms across her chest. Why couldn't her mother stay out of her life?

In the warm night air, Malcolm took a deep

calming breath and rested his back against the car door. Maybe her mother interrupting was a good thing because if she hadn't, that car would have gotten steamy in minutes.

When he finally caught his breath, Malcolm opened the Jaguar and helped Sabrina out. As he escorted her to the door, the sexual tension between them sizzled.

"Thank you again, Malcolm, for a wonderful evening," Sabrina said, drawn to his profile against the moonlight.

Malcolm studied her intently, trying to read her expression and find out if she, too, was reluctant for the night to end. He found what he was he looking for when she stared back at him with the same intense longing.

Swiftly, Malcolm swept her up in his arms and pressed Sabrina snugly against him. A lurch of excitement leaped through her and the air around them electrified. When her soft curves molded into his lean body, Malcolm knew it was time for another taste of Sabrina. Bending his head, Malcolm claimed Sabrina's lips with an urgency that demanded a response. And Sabrina answered it by returning the velvety warmth of his kiss with some passion of her own—passion she'd been holding inside for months, passion that begged for release.

She began by planting feather-light kisses on his chin as she slowly made her way back to those soft, succulent lips of his. She coaxed open his pliant lips with her tongue, dipping inside to explore the soft recesses of his mouth while his hands lightly caressed the shapely contours of her body. When they came to her full, pert B-cup-sized breasts, Malcolm eagerly caressed them with his fingertips, causing the nipples underneath to blossom into turgid buds. Sabrina quivered at his tantalizing kisses and the touch of his hands as they stroked her arms, the small of her back and her buttocks.

When they finally parted, Malcolm was as shaken as she. His breathing labored. The long-awaited second kiss was even better than the first and had the blood in Malcolm's brain pounding and hot flaming desire running through his loins.

Sabrina's arms stretched and caressed his cheek. "Wow, that was some kiss."

"And well worth the wait," Malcolm replied, gazing at her intently. "I'll call you later."

They'd tried their best for friendship, Sabrina thought as she watched him drive away, but after tonight, all bets were off.

Chapter 9

It was sunny and hot, nearly ninety degrees the Saturday morning Sabrina and Monique volunteered at the refreshment stand for the summer camp's softball team. Their children were playing in the game today, so they'd offered to pitch in. Of course, they had no idea the temperature would spike ninety by noon, causing them to seriously regret their generous offer.

"It's hotter than hell out here," Monique said, wiping her brow with her bandanna. "Why on God's green earth did we ever agree to this?" she asked. She'd much rather be inside sipping on some ice-cold lemonade. The hot baseball uniforms that she and Sabrina were wearing sure weren't helping, either.

"I know, I know," Sabrina said, trying to stay hydrated. She'd already drunk two bottles of water and was well through her third. "Remind me never to suggest this again. It's just that this is one of the few things that has made Jasmine happy this summer and I just wanted to show my support."

"So what's it like doing grunt work for Felicia? I've been dying to hear how it's going," Monique asked, as she prepared a hot dog for yet another parent and his child. "Need anything else?" she asked brusquely. The parent shook his head, handed Monique a five-dollar bill and wandered back to the bleachers.

"Fine, I guess," Sabrina answered, as she selected a hot pretzel and cheese for a pint-sized little girl who couldn't be more than six or seven. "If you can call scrubbing floors and cleaning toilets fun. The problem is I let Felicia back me into a corner about my absence all these years, so I've reluctantly agreed to continue helping out. But don't you worry, when Jasmine and I start school in mid-August, I'll decrease my hours."

"Aren't you going to be burning both sides of the candlestick?" Monique asked, turning to face Sabrina. "I can barely work one job at the diner and manage two kids, let alone school and homework, too."

"I know," Sabrina heard the admonishment in Monique's tone. "It's just when I saw Craig and how well he was doing, it just clicked. School is the missing piece I've been looking for. A good education will help me make a better life for me and Jazzy and get out of Parker House."

Monique stepped back, her hands on her hips. "Are you sure, Sabrina? Because juggling a job, school and Jasmine would be hard work. You are not Superwoman, ya know."

"True…" Sabrina leaned back against the fence. "But I want this, too, so bad, Monique. You just don't know."

"Hmmm, and don't you have something else you want to tell me?" Monique commented.

"Like?" Sabrina smiled.

"You know what," Monique replied. "How did your date with dreamy Dr. Winters go?"

"It was marvelous." Sabrina sighed and looked heavenward.

"Wow, it was that good, huh?" Monique asked at Sabrina's starry eyes.

"Better," Sabrina answered. "He's not only good-looking, he's charming and funny."

"Sounds like someone's hooked," Monique teased, poking her in the arm.

"Oh no, it's not like that." Sabrina squared her shoulders and shook her head in denial. "Malcolm and I just enjoy each other's company. He's a good listener."

"I just bet." Monique chuckled to herself. Sabrina could believe they were just friends if she wanted, but Monique was not convinced.

They continued watching the game and Sabrina cheered when Jasmine hit the ball clear across the field and slid into home base until she saw that her daughter wasn't moving from the ground and the coach was running from the dugout.

Jumping over the counter, Sabrina ran across the field with Monique close behind her.

"Jasmine! Jasmine!" Sabrina yelled as she ran to home base. Coach Carter, an ex-marine, was helping Jasmine off the ground. He was touching her arm and checking for broken bones when Sabrina arrived.

Thank God, she was conscious, thought Sabrina.

"How does that feel?" the coach asked, wiggling Jasmine's arm to the left and to the right, but when he did, Jasmine screamed out in agony. The coach looked over at Sabrina. "Could be broken. We'd better to take her to Doc Winters," he said, lifting Jasmine into his arms as if she weighed no more than a feather.

At the mention of Malcolm's name, Sabrina got butterflies in her stomach. She could still almost feel the touch of his lips on hers as they kissed passionately on the front porch of her parents' house.

"I'm coming with you," Sabrina stated emphatically as she rushed toward his Jeep Cherokee.

"I'm right behind you," Monique yelled.

Gingerly, the coach helped Jasmine into the back seat as she held her left arm. Jasmine's face squinted in pain and her face bunched up in a frown when he set her down on the back seat.

It hurt Sabrina to her very heart to see her child

in so much pain. Sabrina climbed in beside her. "It's going to be okay, baby," Sabrina said, lightly hugging Jasmine.

Malcolm glanced down at his watch. Where were the Gibsons? They had missed a follow-up visit at his clinic and now they were late.

He hadn't spoken with Sabrina since Friday night. It killed him to not pick up the phone and simply call her, so he could hear the sweet melodic sound of her voice. But, he had to. He was trying to give her some space and not overwhelm her.

It surprised him how important she'd become to him. When he'd moved here, he'd planned on keeping a low profile, but since meeting her, everything had changed.

"Dr. Winters, the Gibsons are here," Grace said, poking her head inside his office.

"Thank you, Grace. I'll be there in a moment."

Malcolm hated what was about to come next, but it had to be done. Knocking on the door, he entered the room and saw the inquisitive looks on the Gibsons' faces. He wasted no time in informing them that with continued symptoms of a heart attack, Malcolm wanted to perform an immediate coronary angiography at Memorial Health's Heart Institute as soon as it could be scheduled.

Sabrina arrived at Malcolm's clinic in record time. The coach lifted Jasmine out and headed to the front door. Sabrina met him there, opening it wide for him to enter.

Malcolm was at the reception desk talking to Nurse Turner when the coach brought Jasmine inside. He'd just made arrangements to ensure Mr. Gibson's angiography would be on the schedule for tomorrow morning, when Sabrina and the coach came bursting in carrying Jasmine. Malcolm immediately focused in on Jasmine, who was holding her arm and wincing in pain.

"What happened?" said Malcolm as the coach approached.

"She was running and she lost her footing as she slid into home base. I think the arm could be broken or at the very least sprained," the coach replied. "Where should I put her?"

"In here," Malcolm said, rushing toward Exam One. The coach lay Jasmine on the exam table and left the room.

"I'll be right outside, kiddo." The coach smiled at Jasmine and gave her a thumbs-up. Sabrina, however, was directly on Malcolm's heel following him into the room.

Fifteen minutes later, his initial exam revealed that Jasmine's arm was not broken, but sprained. Just to be on the safe side, he insisted on taking Jasmine to the hospital for X-rays.

Malcolm slid Jasmine's arm into a sling. "This should alleviate some of the pain until we see what the X-rays reveal."

"See, that wasn't so bad, was it?" Sabrina asked, wiping her daughter's tear-stained cheeks.

"No," Jasmine sniffed, holding on to her mother's arm.

Even though her baseball uniform was muddy and her face was smeared with dirt, Jasmine looked like a crestfallen little angel to Malcolm and it tugged at his heartstrings. Somehow this eight-year-old and her mother had slipped under the radar and gotten under his skin.

"Since you've been so brave, I have something for you," Malcolm said, reaching inside his white coat pocket. But instead of handing it to her, Malcolm held it behind his back and teased her. "You have to guess first."

"What is it? What is it?" Jasmine perked up. She pushed her mother aside and reached for Malcolm's coat. Sabrina stepped aside to watch their encounter. She could see that Malcolm really cared for her daughter and it made her feel really good to know Jasmine had a father figure like him in her life. It was also why she thought so very highly of Malcolm. What woman could resist a man who adored her daughter?

"It's a lollipop," Malcolm said, bending down and extending it to Jasmine.

"Thank you, Dr. Malcolm," Jasmine gave him a big hug.

Sabrina watched as surprise registered on Malcolm's face at the tiny act of thankfulness on her daughter's part. He didn't seem to know what to do at first, but after several moments, he returned Jasmine's hug.

Disconcerted, Malcolm rose from the exam table and pulled off his white coat. "Let me give you a ride to the hospital."

"That's very kind of you, Malcolm, but Monique is outside." Sabrina wasn't sure she could sit alone with Malcolm in his car for the twenty-minute ride to the hospital and not rip his clothes off.

"It's no problem at all," Malcolm replied. "I'm finished with my patient load for the day."

"Are you sure?" Sabrina was at a loss for words because there was really no logical reason why she couldn't go with Malcolm, other than the fact that she was extremely attracted to him and therefore he made her nervous.

"I believe Ms. Jackson has two children to attend to, doesn't she?" Malcolm said, grabbing his coat on the back hook of the door. He wanted to drive them because any time spent with Sabrina was better than none at all. "Trust me, with a doctor present, you get treated immediately. But if you'd like to go to the ER and sit for hours waiting to be seen, then by all means, don't let me stop you."

"Well, in that case, how can I resist?" Sabrina helped Jasmine off the exam table and sat her on the floor. "Can you walk, sweetheart?"

"Yes, Mom. I'm better now. It doesn't hurt as bad. Dr. Malcolm made me feel much better. I like him a lot," Jasmine replied as they headed for the doorway.

Sabrina smiled. Apparently, she wasn't the only one Malcolm had made an impression on.

At reception, Malcolm gave Nurse Turner some final orders while Sabrina spoke with the coach. She shook his hand and thanked him for his assistance. Monique, Brianna and Brandon were also in the waiting area, anxious to hear about Jasmine's condition. They rushed over to Jasmine to make sure she was okay.

"She's fine. It's just a sprain," Sabrina said, giving Monique an update. "But Malcolm and I are going to take Jasmine over to the hospital just to be on the safe side."

"Malcolm, huh?" Monique's eyebrow rose and she gave Sabrina secret wink. "Well, then I guess I'm not needed here. Give me a call later and let me know how Jasmine is doing."

"Sure thing."

"C'mon kids," Monique yelled at her crew from the front door. "Let's get home, so I can start dinner." Brianna and Brandon gave Jasmine a quick hug before leaving.

"Aren't they the coolest?" Jasmine stated when they had gone.

"Who's the coolest?" Malcolm asked as he approached the duo.

"I was just telling Mom about my best friends," Jasmine said, taking Malcolm's hand and heading toward the door.

"See you in the morning," Malcolm called out to Grace over his shoulder.

He didn't see it, but from where Grace was, it sure looked as if they were a family.

Once they were alone at the hospital and the technician had taken Jasmine for an X-ray, Malcolm and Sabrina sat in awkward silence in uncomfortable waiting room chairs while they waited. They were both trying to maintain the appearance they were unaffected by the other's presence.

Malcolm was the first to break the ice by walking up to her with an devastatingly irresistible grin. "I really enjoyed our date," he said casually, taking a seat beside her.

"So did I," Sabrina returned politely.

"Then we should do it again," he said, picking up her delicate hand in his large one. "I want to learn more about what makes Sabrina Parker tick."

"Hmmm, you're a mystery to me, too, Malcolm," Sabrina said, pulling her hand out of his. "I don't know if you realize it, but you keep a lot inside. I'd like to know more."

"Do I?" Malcolm laughed. He supposed he kept his feelings close to the vest. But that was him. He'd been more open and honest with her than he had with any other woman.

"Yes, you do."

"Then I guess there's room for improvement on my part, huh?"

Sabrina eagerly shook her head. "And I have just the idea."

"And what might that be?"

Sabrina didn't have time to expound on it any further, because the X-ray tech came back with Jasmine and the test results.

Malcolm rose to speak with the technician while Jasmine came and sat next to Sabrina. Sabrina watched them speak in hushed tones before Malcolm strolled back over.

"Good news," he said, directing his attention Sabrina's way. "The arm isn't broken. Jasmine only needs to take it easy on that arm for a couple of weeks before returning to her normal lifestyle."

"That's great," Sabrina said, smiling up at Malcolm. "After she's better—why don't you come out with Jazzy and me? I promised her we'd go rollerblading in the park sometime soon."

At Malcolm's dumbfounded expression, Sabrina continued. "Kind of like ice skating, but not on ice."

Malcolm shook his head. "Sorry, never done it." And he wasn't all that sure he wanted to learn.

"You'll love it, Dr. Malcolm," Jasmine chimed in. "It's loads of fun even if you do fall on your butt."

If it meant time he could spend with two of his favorite ladies, he supposed he could give it a try. "Sounds dangerous. Sign me up."

"Great." Sabrina assisted Jasmine out of her chair. "I'll set up. You just remember to wear long sleeves."

Chapter 10

"So she's okay?" Tre asked from the other end of the line later that evening when Sabrina called to let him know about Jasmine's fall. She'd felt it was her duty to keep him informed even though he rarely called Jasmine himself. Did he all of a sudden forget he had a daughter now that he had his mistress full-time to service his needs? Since they'd arrived in Savannah, Tre hadn't picked up the phone once to check on Jasmine and see how she was adjusting. And that infuriated Sabrina.

How dare the bastard treat her daughter this way? Didn't he know how much it hurt Jazzy when he didn't return her calls? It killed Sabrina a bit each day.

"Yes, she's fine," Sabrina replied, not offering any further explanation.

"Thank God." Tre breathed a sigh of relief on the other end. "So, how did it happen?"

"Jasmine was playing softball and—"

"Softball—since when did my little girl who plays with Barbies turn into a tomboy?" Tre queried harshly.

"Somewhere between seven and eight," Sabrina offered sarcastically from her perch atop the bed. "Of course, I'm not surprised you didn't notice. You were never very good at paying attention to anyone else's needs but your own."

"Don't start, Sabrina," Tre warned as he paced the floor of Melanie's apartment. "Do you really want to start another fight?"

"No, I don't, Tre," Sabrina began, "but you really should make more time for Jasmine. I realize you have a busy lifestyle, but our daughter still needs a father."

"Well, well. I'm surprised to hear you say that," Tre said. "From the way you've been behaving, you'd think you'd made Jasmine all by yourself. And in case you don't remember," Tre whispered into the phone, "you and I burned up that bedroom in Jamaica and gave passion a new name."

Sabrina remembered all too well the night they'd conceived Jasmine. It was one of those rare occasions early on in their marriage when Tre had actually taken the time to be romantic. He'd gotten a bonus from his job and had splurged on a weekend getaway to Jamaica. They'd frolicked in the sun, basking in the crystal-blue water and made love until the sun rose the following morning, but Sabrina didn't want to go down that road with Tre. He was the one who'd been unfaithful and destroyed their marriage. And every happy memory they'd ever shared was now sullied by that one act.

"Tre, honey. Aren't you coming back to bed?" Sabrina heard a female voice coo through the phone. She deduced it could only be one person, Melanie, the evil, deceptive witch who had ruined her marriage. Just thinking of that woman caused Sabrina to see red and served to remind her of what a jerk Tre really was. Here he was in another's woman bed and still trying to flirt with Sabrina, his ex-wife!

"Well, I've got to go, Sabrina," Tre replied as he watched Melanie parade in front of him in a sexy Frederick's of Hollywood number.

"Don't you want to talk to Jasmine?" Sabrina asked, annoyed.

"No, not right now," Tre said. "But tell her I love her and I'll call her." Seconds later, Sabrina heard a dial tone. Furious, she slammed the telephone back on the charger and plopped back down on the bed.

Why did she let Melanie get to her? Because Melanie knew they were on the phone discussing their daughter, she'd deliberately brought Tre's focus and attention back on her. The woman was evil incarnate. And Tre was led by the wrong head, following right behind her. It infuriated Sabrina to know that Jasmine did not come first with him. Yet, lately she seemed to love Tre the most while she treated Sabrina like a second-class citizen.

Turning off the lights and pulling the comforter over her head, Sabrina could only hope that one day Tre would not break their daughter's heart.

The next morning, Malcolm nervously drove to Memorial Health. Why hadn't the clog-dissolving medication worked? Why did he have to have a cardiac patient so soon into his family practice? He'd thought he wouldn't see a heart case for quite some time at the clinic. Nervous tension ran through his entire body at the prospect of having to perform an angiography. He hadn't been in a catheterization lab in well over a year and he wasn't all that sure he was ready, but what other choice did he have? Dr. Baker was retired, therefore, he was the only one qualified enough to perform the procedure. It wasn't like he wasn't well-skilled, so why did he have a nagging feeling in the pit of his stomach. Had he lost his nerve?

Once he arrived at the hospital, he stopped by the catheterization lab. He found everything in order and had enough time to change clothes before checking in on Mr. Gibson.

The familiar scent of antiseptic greeted him as he walked through the halls of Memorial Health on his way to Mr. Gibson's room. Several candy stripers smiled adoringly up at him as he passed them along the way. Now, *that* he remembered.

He found Mr. Gibson prepped and ready for surgery.

"How are you feeling?" Malcolm inquired, stepping into the room.

"Oh, I'm fine," Mr. Gibson said, "but this one is kind of scared." He pointed to his wife.

His wife's eyes brimmed with tears. "Please take care of him, doc."

Malcolm smiled inwardly. Never let them see you sweat.

"I'll do my best," Malcolm replied. He wished he could reassure her more, but he no longer believed that miracles were possible every time.

Once his patient was settled comfortably and had been given a local anesthetic and intravenous sedation, Malcolm went into the viewing area to wash his hands again. In the mirror, he stared at the reflection of the scared man in front of him. What had happened to the invincible Dr. Malcolm Winters, superman of Cardiology, who was able to perform miracles in a single bound?

Malcolm didn't see that superhero standing in front of him now. Instead, he saw a scared rookie afraid of performing his first solo procedure. Images of Michael, as he fell to the floor in slow motion at Dinah and Walter's anniversary party haunted him.

Malcolm shook his head, blinked several times to erase the negative image from his head while furiously scrubbing his hands. *Get it together, Malcolm!* He told himself before entering the catheterization lab. The X-ray technician was standing by, waiting for word from Malcolm on when to begin.

When the cath lab nurse handed Malcolm the catheter attached to a fluoroscope, he stared at it and her for several long moments before finally accepting. The instrument shook in his hands. It was all up to him now.

"Are you ready, Dr. Winters?" the X-ray technician asked. "I can insert the radiographic contrast if you are."

Taking a deep breath, Malcolm replied. "Yes, let's begin."

The procedure was over fairly quickly, taking Malcolm only two hours to perform. Once it was complete, he sutured up Mr. Gibson's leg. There was a small risk of complication from the angiography, but although he'd been nervous, the procedure was a success.

"He's all yours, Dr. Jeffries," Malcolm commented to the anesthesiologist as he pulled off his mask and left the lab.

Once he was back in the locker room, Malcolm forced air back into his lungs. He hadn't realized it, he'd hardly taken a breath during the procedure for fear he'd make a wrong move. Thank God it was over. But it had shown him one thing and that was he hadn't lost his touch.

"Great job, Dr. Winters," the anesthesiologist

replied a short while later as Malcolm packed up his bag in the locker room.

"Thanks. Thanks a lot." Malcolm replied, leaving the locker room.

He found Mrs. Gibson sitting in the waiting room. When she saw Malcolm, she rose from her chair and rushed towards him. "How is he, Dr. Malcolm?"

"He's doing just fine, Mrs. Gibson. You can take him home in a few hours once he's regained consciousness." Malcolm sought to reassure the frazzled woman's nerves. "Now it's just a wait-and-see game."

Malcolm woke up with a start, bathed in sweat. He'd been having that dream again. The same one he'd been having since Michael's death. The one where he was in surgery trying to repair Michael's aortic dissection except this time, he was the surgeon and try as he might he couldn't repair the damage and his twin died on the operating table.

Jumping up from the king-size bed, Malcolm padded to the adjoining bathroom. He flicked on the light switch, flooding the room with light. The cold water he splashed on his face did little to ease the nightmare that had plagued him for the last year. Instead he relived the last year.

His twin had come to him several months before his death complaining of chest pains. Malcolm had run all kinds of tests and had found nothing. He'd missed something and because of it Michael was dead. The guilt crippled him.

After Michael's death, he'd felt inept as a cardiologist. Why hadn't he seen the clues? He'd been so paralyzed with fear that he hadn't been able to treat his patients. Sure, he'd taken some customary time off as the chief of staff had suggested, but it had done little to alleviate his guilt.

He'd just replayed his actions over and over again. The chest X-ray and MRI had revealed nothing, causing Malcolm to allow Michael to resume his normal lifestyle. And normal to Michael had meant skiing, rock climbing or white-water rafting with his buddies. Malcolm hated that Michael had an affinity for risking his life, but his stubborn twin had refused to listen and reason. "I like taking risks," he'd told Malcolm. "That's what makes me who I am."

And so Malcolm had let him continue as if nothing was wrong. No precautions. He just threw his brother to the wind. And he'd been wrong. Dead wrong.

He should have insisted on another opinion, allowed a fellow heart man to take a look. Top of his field at the time, he'd been cocky and assumed that he was infallible. How could he have known that his thirty-five-year-old brother would have a tear in the inner wall of his abdominal aortic artery? It was a condition normally found in men much older.

How could he have seen a heart attack in Michael's future when all signs indicated that he was the picture of health? Was there anything he could have done to prevent it? That's what lived with him each and every day, and killed him bit by bit.

Could they have performed surgery and repaired the aortic rupture if he'd diagnosed it earlier? If the tear was caught prior to a rupture, at least half of the patients survived. Of course, now he would never know. And he would forever be haunted by the last image of Michael at Dinah and Walter's anniversary party when Michael crumpled to the floor. Malcolm would never forget Michael's pallor and clammy skin, the profuse sweating and shortness of breath he'd experienced. And the feeling of powerlessness Malcolm had felt as he'd desperately tried to save him.

He'd done his best before the ambulance had arrived. He'd given Michael mouth-to-mouth to resuscitate him, but it hadn't worked. The rapid blood loss had caused a shock to Michael's system that was irreversible. Once they'd admitted him and gotten Michael to surgery, he'd died on the table.

Malcolm glanced up at the ravaged image in the mirror. He looked haggard with bloodshot eyes. Quickly, he turned on his heel into the bedroom. He found his sweatpants on a nearby chair and pulled them over his hips. Throwing on the matching sweater over his head, Malcolm rushed out the door.

Malcolm frantically walked down the corridor of Memorial to the nurses' station. "Excuse me, nurse, I'm Dr. Winters and I'm here to check on my patient, Mr. Gibson?"

The redhead reviewed the charts and responded. "I'm sorry, Dr. Winters. Mr. Gibson suffered a massive heart attack earlier this evening and was taken up to the coronary-care unit. I think the surgeon on duty is working on him now."

Horror crossed Malcolm's face. "He's in surgery? Why in the hell wasn't I paged? I'm his primary-care physician, after all." Malcolm snatched his pager off his hip and checked the memory. There were no earlier messages on it. He was furious with the Memorial Health University Medical Center staff. How dare they not call him in such a vital matter of life or death!

At the thunderous expression on Malcolm's face, the nurse attempted to explain. "I'm sorry, Doctor. There wasn't time. The surgeon wanted to get him to surgery."

"So what," Malcolm yelled, running his fingers across his forehead. "After the surgeon took him to the OR, someone could have paged me. How inept is this hospital?" Malcolm said, rushing down the hall to the elevators.

Frantically, he pressed the button and paced the floor. When the elevator finally arrived, Malcolm was going out of his mind with worry and rushed inside. What had gone wrong? Had he missed a diagnosis? Had he done something wrong in the angiography? All these thoughts echoed in his mind.

When the doors finally opened, Malcolm shot through them and ran down the hall, nearly colliding with a stack of supplies. He pushed through the Intensive Care doors and was on his way to the OR, when he saw Mrs. Gibson sitting in the waiting room.

She was clutching a handkerchief in her hand. He could see that she had been crying because her eyes were all puffy and swollen.

"Mrs. Gibson?" Malcolm said, striding toward her with his hands extended. "Have you heard anything?" he asked, taking a seat beside her.

"No, Dr. Winters. They haven't told me anything." She took both his hands and squeezed them tightly. "I've been out here for an hour and no one's told me what's happened to my husband."

Malcolm released her hand and jumped up. "Stay right here, Mrs. Gibson. I'll find out your husband's condition." He stormed over to the nurses' desk. "I want an update on Mr. Gibson's condition." He pulled out his ID and flashed it to the nurse. "I'm his primary doctor, Dr. Winters."

"I understand, sir," the nurse acknowledged, "but the surgery is still ongoing."

"What OR?" Malcolm asked, glancing toward the swinging doors.

"You can't go in, Dr. Winters. You're not scrubbed in," she replied.

"I didn't ask you that," Malcolm said, annoyed with the young nurse. He understood she was trying to follow protocol, but he needed to find out Mr. Gibson's condition. "I asked you what OR he was in."

Afraid of offending him, the nurse supplied the room number. "OR Five," she said nervously and watched Malcolm rush through the doors.

Running down the hall, Malcolm glanced at each operating room until he found number five. When he pushed open the front door and looked through the window, he didn't like what he saw. The crash cart was out and the cardiac monitor was flatlined. He heard the surgeon say, "Time of death 10:30 p.m."

"No!" Malcolm rushed inside the room.

The surgeon walked toward him. "Dr. Winters, I presume," the surgeon said, glancing at the ID badge hanging from Malcolm's neck and extending his hand. "I'm Dr. Moore. I'm sorry, but Mr. Gibson did not make it. I did my best, but the damage from the massive heart attack was too severe."

Malcolm was silent as he looked down at the surgeon's extended hand. He completely ignored him and walked toward Mr. Gibson's lifeless body on the operating table. After everything he'd done, Mr. Gibson had still died.

The surgeon patted him on the shoulder as he walked away. "It's rough to lose a patient. Would you like me to tell the wife?"

Malcolm shook his head. "No, I'll do it." Somehow he would walk out those doors and inform Mrs. Gibson that the love of her life had passed away. Somewhere he had to find the inner strength.

As he stared down at Mr. Gibson's lifeless body with his chest cracked open, Malcolm inwardly screamed to himself, the gods or whoever else was listening at how unfair life was. How could this have happened again? He was supposed to get it right this time. A lonely teardrop fell down his cheek at the injustice of the world. Disgusted, he stormed out of the OR.

Mrs. Gibson was waiting for him on the other side, hopeful that all was well with her husband. He hated to deliver the heartbreaking news, but better it come from him than someone else. The moment she saw him, however, she knew the truth. His head was hanging low and defeat was etched across his whole face.

"No!" she screamed, "No!" Mrs. Gibson cried out and collapsed to the floor. Malcolm and the nurse from the station reached her at the same time.

"Let's get her into a chair," Malcolm said, lifting her into his arms and gently placing her into a chair. She came around slightly once she was seated, muttering under her breath. "Nurse—" he turned to the young nurse whom he'd treated terribly before "—get me a cold cloth and a sedative.

"It's okay, Mrs. Gibson." Malcolm soothed the older woman in his arms. "We'll get you through this."

And that's how Malcolm ended his evening, sitting by Mrs. Gibson's side until her sister arrived to take her home. He'd given her a mild sedative in the hopes that it would alleviate some of the pain and get her through the night. But the real test would begin in the morning, when she would have to face the world alone.

Chapter 11

Sabrina didn't have to wait long to see Malcolm again because she ran into him when she and Monique stopped by Mimi's for happy hour.

After a hard day's work, she and Monique were commiserating their fates over a smart cocktail when Sabrina noticed Malcolm sitting alone at the bar. There was an air of isolation surrounding him and it seemed as if he wanted it that way, if the way he ranted at the barkeep was any indication. His mood was a far cry from the Malcolm she and Jasmine encountered when Jasmine sprained her arm. His profile was rugged and somber.

"Excuse me for a moment," Sabrina said to Monique.

"Go get him, tiger," Monique teased.

Sabrina slid off the bar stool and sashayed toward Malcolm. She glanced over her shoulder and saw Monique giving her a thumbs-up.

"Malcolm, long time no see," Sabrina attempted casualness.

Malcolm glanced up from his eighth shot of tequila and through his slightly blurred vision, saw Sabrina. He didn't respond though, instead he pulled the tequila bottle over toward him and poured himself another drink.

"So I take it you intend to tie one on?" Sabrina asked glancing at Malcolm, except he didn't bother to look her way.

It was the first time she'd seen him completely disheveled. His hair was uncombed and his white shirt was hanging out of his jeans. But it was his eyes that Sabrina noticed the most. Though they were bloodshot, there was something more. The hurt and pain lying in those murky dark depths was evident. Something had happened. Something devastating that had rocked him to his very core.

"Are you okay?" she asked, touching him on the shoulder. Malcolm flinched when she did and moved away. Sabrina felt horrible. She wished she knew what was eating him up inside. She knew about that kind of pain because she'd lived through it and was still standing. When she'd discovered Tre's infidelity, it had taken her days to get out of bed, but eventually she did.

"Malcolm, whatever it is, you can talk to me about it." Sabrina sat beside him on the adjacent stool. "I'm your friend. You can tell me anything."

He didn't respond at first, instead he just stared remotely into his glass. After several minutes had passed, he finally turned to her and said, "I know you mean well, Sabrina, but you can't help me, okay? Just go back to Monique."

Sabrina's eyes welled up seeing him this way. "Malcolm, please," she whispered, scooting closer to him. She grabbed his arm when he tried to move away and hung on tighter this time around. "Please tell me what happened. Sometimes talking it out helps."

Malcolm shook his head. She couldn't help him. No one could. No matter how hard he tried to fight it, to beat the odds, death was a part of life and he was just going to have to accept it. Maybe he should tell her about it. It might help.

Sabrina watched Malcolm look up and roll his eyes heavenward. Was he praying for something? If so, she hoped he prayed for inner peace.

"I lost a patient yesterday," Malcolm whispered, his voice barely audible.

He spoke so low, his words were barely discernible. "What did you say?" she asked.

"I said, I lost a patient," he repeated, taking a generous gulp of tequila and turning to face her. "He came to me with symptoms of a heart attack. And I did everything I could, everything I knew of to save him, but he still died of a massive heart attack."

"Oh, I'm so sorry, Malcolm." She shuddered inwardly at the thought of what he must be going through. Sabrina leaned over, squeezed his shoulders and covered his hand with hers. "How's his family?"

"His wife is completely devastated. And I feel so bad, Sabrina." Malcolm's voice cracked. "I told her I could save him and she believed me."

"Malcolm, this is not your fault," Sabrina said, but he shook his head.

"You don't understand."

"Yes, I do," Sabrina replied. "You're blaming yourself right now for his death, but didn't you say you did everything you could? Everything you knew how? Listen to me." She grabbed him by the jaw. "This is not your fault, Malcolm. You did your best."

"My *best* wasn't good enough," Malcolm said.

"So now what?" Sabrina asked, fast becoming annoyed. "You're going to wallow in self-pity and drink yourself into a drunken stupor."

"Sounds good to me."

"Well, that's not going to happen," Sabrina said.

"And what do you have to say about it?"

Sabrina jumped off the stool. "I'm your friend, that's what. And as your friend, I'm taking you home to Parker House. Barkeep," she called, "close out his tab, please." The bartender nodded.

"Excuse me for a moment." Sabrina went back to Monique at the end of the bar. "Listen, girl. Malcolm lost a patient yesterday and is pretty upset about it. I'm going to take him back to Parker House."

"And is that all you're going to do?" Monique asked, teasing.

Sabrina blushed. "Yes, that's all. I'm going to put him to bed and leave. So, grab your things and let's go. We'll drop him off on the way home."

"All right, girl," Monique said, opening her purse and throwing several bills on the table, "But if I were you I'd be hitting *that* with the quickness."

"Is sex all you think about? Let's go," Sabrina said. When they returned to the bar, Sabrina found Malcolm nearly passed out. The bartender slid his tab her way. "Do you have a credit card?" Sabrina asked Malcolm.

"Breast pocket," he mumbled. His head rose from the table for a brief second. Sabrina slid the card in the bartender's direction. He returned with a receipt, which Malcolm scribbled his name across. Sabrina and Monique assisted him out of the bar. Malcolm rather enjoyed having two women with him, one on either side.

"Hmmm, I think I like being the man in the middle," he said jokingly.

"Hush your mouth," Sabrina replied, fumbling to get her keys out of her jeans pocket while holding him upright. Once the car door was open, she and Monique slid him onto the back seat, where he promptly passed out and stayed that way until they reached the Parker House.

"Girl, you ought to be sainted," Monique said as she helped Sabrina pull the big man out of the car.

Sabrina grabbed Malcolm under one arm, while Monique took the other.

Malcolm mumbled underneath his breath about how beautiful Sabrina was and how much he loved being her friend while they carried him through the foyer.

"Is that so?" Monique said, glancing in Sabrina's direction as they rushed toward the elevator.

Sabrina blushed and pressed the Up button several times. She was grateful her parents had had the foresight to install an elevator for the handicapped. It arrived thankfully seconds later and they hauled Malcolm's one-hundred-and-eighty-pound self onto the elevator.

"He's heavy," Monique said.

"No kidding," Sabrina said. "Imagine how I feel in these heels." Monique glanced down at Sabrina's three-inch sandals.

Once the doors opened on the third floor, Monique and Sabrina dragged Malcolm down the hall to his room.

"Sabrina, did I tell you about my twin, Michael?" Malcolm sputtered. "He was the best."

Sabrina peered at him strangely. "Did he just say twin?"

"Sounds like it to me," Monique replied.

"Hmmm, he never mentioned one before," Sabrina commented. When they arrived at his door, Sabrina reached inside Malcolm's breast pocket and produced his key. Inserting it in the cylinder, she twisted the lock and opened the door.

"C'mon, boy," Sabrina said, flicked on the light switch, bathing the room in soft lighting. Sabrina was shocked to find the room a sight. What had happened? Clothes were everywhere, as were several empty pizza boxes and take-out containers. It didn't go with her image of Malcolm as the pristine doctor. No wonder a permanent "Do Not Disturb" sign had been on his door. She would be sure to come in here and clean up tomorrow. "Let's get him to the bed."

Together, she and Monique carried him over to the bed and plopped him down. The second his head hit the pillow, Malcolm conked out.

"Thank the Lord," Monique said, sitting on the bed and holding her heaving chest. She was completely out of breath. "That man weighs a ton."

Sabrina glanced down at Malcolm. From the tall, athletic physique she'd seen and just felt, he was all muscle. "Indeed he is. Well, I'd better get you home."

"Do we have to go home, just yet?" Monique said, reluctantly rising from the bed. "Can't we go out and party some more?"

"No, sister," Sabrina said, pulling her toward the door. "Your kids are waiting for you. I'm sure they'd like to see Mommy before bedtime."

Monique rolled her eyes. "You're right. I guess I'd better get home."

Sabrina hazarded one more glance at Malcolm sleeping soundly on the king-size bed. He would have a major hangover in the morning. She just hoped talking about losing his patient had helped. "Good night, sweet prince," she said, turning off the lights and closing the door.

Chapter 12

"Mom, can I have this?" Jasmine held up some Cocoa Pebbles in her hand while she and Sabrina shopped for groceries at the local Winn-Dixie one Friday evening after work. Several weeks had passed and Malcolm was still MIA. Jasmine and Sabrina had both begun school and still no Malcolm. She wondered where the reclusive doctor had disappeared to.

"No," Sabrina replied, going down the next aisle. "Too much sugar."

"How about this?" Jasmine asked, holding up some Oreo cookies.

"Jasmine," Sabrina said, annoyed. "Why don't you go look for some fruit because that's the only thing you're going to get." She and Jasmine were on their own tonight because her parents had been invited back over to her mother's friend Regina's for dinner after Bible study.

When several minutes passed and Jasmine still hadn't returned, Sabrina began to worry and started searching every aisle of the store. When she made it to the meat department, she finally came across Jasmine, but she was not alone.

"Look who I found," Jasmine smiled adoringly at Malcolm.

The man had impeccable timing in catching Sabrina off guard and looking like a ragamuffin. When she'd thrown on a pair of old Capris to go to the store she hadn't expected to run into anyone.

"Malcolm." Sabrina's face broke into a smile. Why did he have to look like he'd just stepped out the pages of *GQ* magazine? At least he looked much better since the last time she saw him. He was smiling of course, revealing a beautiful set of perfect white teeth. Tailored maroon slacks, a crisp white shirt, casually opened at the top had Sabrina licking her lips. "It's good to see you. How are you doing?" she asked. Clearly, he had recovered from his previous bout of depression.

A foggy image came to Malcolm reminding him that Sabrina and Monique had put him to bed when he'd bottomed out over Mr. Gibson's death. He'd have to thank her later for her generosity. "Well. And you?" Malcolm asked civilly as he peered down at Sabrina. A quick glance affirmed what he already knew—that Sabrina had a shapely figure. The chill in the air was causing her nipples to peak out underneath her tank top while her low-rise capris revealed a shapely bottom that he'd love to roam his hands over.

"What are you doing here, Dr. Malcolm?" Jasmine was the first to ask what was on Sabrina's mind. "Aren't you staying at the Parker House? Don't they have a restaurant?"

"Yes, Jasmine, I—" Malcolm bent down to Jasmine's level.

"Call me Jazzy," Jasmine said, interrupting him. "Mom does." Sabrina smiled at her forward daughter. Jasmine was as smitten with the good doctor as was she. Feeling such an emotion so soon after Tre, both overwhelmed and terrified her.

"All right, Jazzy. I'm here picking up some fruit, snacks and protein drinks. I like to keep myself healthy," Malcolm responded.

"Well, that's no fun," Jasmine remarked. "You should come eat with us. Mom's making meat loaf and mashed potatoes. I'm sure there's enough."

"Jasmine." Sabrina couldn't believe Jasmine's audacity. "I'm sure Malcolm has other plans." She sure hoped not. The thought of sharing a meal with Malcolm pleased her immensely. The attraction between them was hard to ignore. Her stomach would probably be tied up in knots sitting across from that good-looking face all evening. She wondered how long it would be before they acted on it.

"As a matter of fact, I don't," Malcolm replied, rising to his full six-foot-three height. "And I would sure love to have a home-cooked meal." He'd been down in Savannah for months since he'd come from Boston and yes, he ate at the B and B, but most times he grabbed a salad on the go, which was fast becoming a bore.

"Well, uh…" Sabrina was at a loss for words.

"It's set then," Jasmine said, grabbing Malcolm's large hand in her tiny one and pushing him toward the checkout. "You'll come over to Grandma's and have dinner with me and Mom."

Malcolm halted the pushy little midget and turned to face Sabrina. "That is if you don't mind." he said. He hoped she didn't; they hadn't spent much time together since their first date, a fact Malcolm intended to rectify.

Sabrina shrugged her shoulders. "Of course not." She was eager to spend more time with Malcolm. Since his patient's death, he'd been distant. Sabrina understood and had given him his space, but she missed his company and his amazing gift of listening. "Jazzy's right. There's plenty to go round." Sabrina halted Malcolm. "Give me a minute to grab the ground beef and we'll be on our way."

After Sabrina bought two pounds of Angus ground beef from the butcher, they were out the door. Malcolm was ever the gentleman and helped her carry the bags to the car.

"Thank you." Sabrina smiled back at him as she accepted her keys. "Did anyone ever tell you that you're quite the gentleman?"

"I think I've heard it once or twice," Malcolm replied. Was he flirting with her? If so, the evening was sure to be interesting.

Malcolm followed behind Sabrina as she drove the short distance to her parents' home. He was looking forward to spending time with Sabrina. She'd shown such kindness taking care of him. It made him adore her all the more.

Pulling up behind her, he turned off his engine and jumped out to assist her with groceries.

Sabrina flicked on the kitchen light and held the door open for him to pass.

"Where do you want these?" he asked, holding up the bags.

"On the table is fine," Sabrina replied.

Malcolm placed the bags on the kitchen table and turned to her. He owed her a huge thank you. They stood facing each other for several awkward moments until Jasmine chirped up. "Would you like a tour of the house?"

Malcolm smiled at his pint-sized hostess. "I would love one. If you don't mind?" he replied, hazarding a glance at Sabrina, who was busy putting away groceries. Although he didn't mind a tour, he would have preferred to sit in the kitchen and watch Sabrina. He thought *he* was guarded, but Sabrina gave new meaning to the word. He wished he knew what she was thinking…feeling, but he couldn't read her closed expression.

"Why would she mind?" Jasmine asked, holding out her hand for Malcolm to take. "This isn't even her house."

Malcolm laughed at the wisecrack. Jasmine certainly was a little firecracker, just like her mother.

"C'mon." Jasmine pulled him along toward the front of the house.

Sabrina grabbed her mother's apron off the hook and wrapped it around her middle.

"Wait a sec," Malcolm replied, coming to Sabrina's aid and tying it for her.

He lingered a moment longer than necessary, breathing in Sabrina's sweet scent before stepping away. He was infatuated with this woman and her spitfire of a daughter.

Jasmine was anxious to begin her tour and spurred him along. She didn't notice the appreciative glance Malcolm sent her mother's way, but Sabrina sure did.

She turned red and immediately began gathering all the ingredients and spices to prepare her delicious Italian meat loaf. When she was finished Malcolm would be salivating.

It didn't take long for Sabrina to mix all the ingredients and form a loaf to put in the oven. When Malcolm returned to the kitchen without his companion Jasmine, who'd gone upstairs in search of board games, he found Sabrina cutting up potatoes.

"So?" Sabrina asked, looking up from her task at the kitchen sink. "What do you think?" she asked.

"Your parents have a lovely place," Malcolm replied, "Very lived-in and homey."

"I couldn't agree with you more," Sabrina said, placing the potatoes on the stove to boil. "It's why I came back."

"For the sense of security that only your parents could provide?" Malcolm asked.

"Yes," Sabrina agreed, grabbing the ingredients for a salad out of the fridge. How did he always seem to know what she was thinking?

"And has being home done that?" he asked, leaning against the counter to watch her.

"It has," Sabrina answered nervously. She could feel Malcolm's eyes on her as she cut up the vegetables, so she kept her eyes focused on the task ahead. "I've never felt so safe."

When she finally turned around and their eyes made contact and locked on each other, Sabrina's emotions went spinning out of control. Malcolm's close proximity was causing her body to go haywire. Her heart thumped loudly in her chest as his nearness both excited and disturbed her, because she wasn't all that sure she was ready for what came next.

Long before she felt his breath on the back of her neck, Sabrina sensed Malcolm's presence behind her.

"Have I told you thank you for your help the other

evening?" Malcolm whispered in her ear. "You really pulled me out of a rough place."

"Umm, no, I don't believe you did."

"Then by all means, let me say thank you." Slowly, he began to massage her shoulders with his strong, narrow fingers until he felt her relaxing slightly. He heard her sigh deeply as she turned around to face him. Malcolm decreased the distance between them by wrapping his arms around her midriff, gathering her closer to him. He was ready for their relationship to move to the next level, but was she? He regarded her quizzically for a moment, gauging whether to pursue his impure thoughts, when Sabrina reached out and softly touched his cheek. That tiny action was all the indication Malcolm needed.

He lightly brushed his lips across her forehead, trailing soft kisses down her face until his lips were a hairsbreadth away from hers.

"I want you so much, Sabrina," he said huskily.

She surprised herself when she said, "I want you, too."

He paused for what seemed like an eternity before smothering her lips with demanding mastery. Sabrina's lips parted in response and she drank in the sweetness of his kiss. When she wound her arms around his neck, Malcolm stepped forward and clasped her body tightly to his, pressing her against the counter.

He fused his lips with hers, her breasts, stomach and thighs melded like perfection against his rock-hard body and when she gripped his back and purred like a kitten, Malcolm nearly devoured her. That's until he heard tiny little footsteps on the back stairs leading into the kitchen. They both pulled away quickly, startled by the interruption.

Reality came whirling back to Sabrina when Jasmine, oblivious to the adults' recent interlude, came bounding into the room.

"I found the games, Malcolm," Jasmine announced, setting the boxes for Life and Monopoly on the kitchen table. "Grandma had these upstairs in the guest closet," Jasmine continued. "Do you want to play until dinner's ready?"

Shaken, Sabrina refused to look Malcolm's way even though she could feel his eyes burning a hole in the back of her head. She scooted over to the sink, desperate to get away from Malcolm. Being near the man was dangerous to her sensibilities.

When Sabrina quickly moved out of his embrace, Malcolm felt bereft. He'd been so ready for that kiss and the promise of what it offered: a chance to hold and caress Sabrina in his arms. Sabrina roused a passion in him that he hadn't felt in a long time and he wanted more. Which was why it was probably a good thing that the little midget interrupted them. He looked down at Jasmine who was pulling on his shirt. She was bubbling over with excitement at having a play pal.

"Malcolm?" Jasmine asked, getting annoyed from his lack of response. "Don't you want to play with me?"

"Of course I do, sweetheart," Malcolm said, bending down to reply to Jasmine's height. Maybe a little time to clear his head was a good idea. Malcolm stood up and walked over behind Sabrina at the stove.

He whispered in her ear, "I'll be in the other room if you want me."

Of course she wanted him! That much was obvious. He had to know that from her response. If Jasmine hadn't interrupted, she'd been ready to offer herself up to him on a silver platter. He probably thought she was a tease, seeing as how only a couple of months ago she'd stressed friendship and nothing more. And today, she hadn't stuck to that resolve. With all she had going, she had no business even contemplating getting involved with another man. Let alone someone as commanding and charismatic as Malcolm Winters. Sabrina determined to a put a halt to any further intimacies between them. With someone like him, she could easily have her heart broken and Sabrina didn't want a repeat performance of Tre Matthews. She was just now getting over that mistake. She needn't make another.

She managed to finish dinner by banishing all thoughts of Malcolm out of her head. Forty-five minutes later, an Italian meat loaf, mashed potatoes, green beans and salad were on the table.

"Ready to dig in?" Sabrina asked, stopping by the living the room to check on Malcolm and Jasmine, who'd been surprisingly quiet throughout her dinner preparation.

"Yes," Malcolm replied, looking up from the Monopoly board. He'd been trying to get out of jail after little Ms. Jasmine had trounced on him for the majority of the game. Surprisingly, she'd been quite good for a eight-year-old. "I'm starved," he said, rising to his feet.

"So am I," Jasmine said as Malcolm lent a hand to help her up. Together, they walked toward the dining room where Sabrina had already set the table and laid out supper.

Before they began, Sabrina stopped Malcolm. "Let's say grace."

"I'm not really into that," Malcolm retorted.

"What?"

"Religion."

"Then maybe you should be," Sabrina returned, grabbing Jasmine with one hand. "Have you ever thought that some prayer might help you get over the traumatic events in your life?" she asked.

"No, I hadn't. Although my mother attended services, it was more for show than anything else." And Malcolm wasn't all that sure that he believed in God anymore. There was something wrong with a world that would take his brother.

"I understand you've lost your faith, Malcolm, but a little religion might be good for your soul." Her other slender hand reached out and grasped Malcolm's strong, massive hand in hers. He resisted, but Sabrina held on firmly.

At first, Malcolm didn't know how to react to

Sabrina's spirituality, but he soon followed suit when she and Jasmine bent their heads in prayer. "Lord, we thank you for this food we are about to receive," Sabrina began. "and we pray that you will see your way to guiding those who may be lost back home to your safe haven. Amen."

Sabrina glanced up and looked over at Malcolm. His expression was unreadable, but he did say, "Amen," before digging into his meal.

Dinner was uneventful. Malcolm and Sabrina tried to ignore the sexual pull between them by catering to Jasmine's every whim. Sabrina could see how happy Jasmine was in Malcolm's company. It was so obvious to Sabrina that her daughter missed that male companionship, that father-daughter bond between her and Tre.

Somehow, Malcolm was providing exactly what Jasmine needed at the moment and Sabrina was grateful. He didn't seem to mind at all that Jasmine had taken a liking to him. He listened to all her school stories and answered her questions when asked. Sabrina glanced up from her dinner plate and when she did, her eyes made contact with Malcolm's dark irises. When he smiled at her and she was hit with the sure power of his magnetism, a delicious shudder heated her body. God, help me, thought Sabrina, he's sexy as hell. Back in the kitchen, she'd wanted more, more than just a kiss.

It was no mystery what he was thinking when he looked at her with those bedroom eyes. The good doctor wanted to take her to bed and she doubted she'd resist.

"Mom, what do you think?" Jasmine asked.

"What was that, baby?" Sabrina said, shaking her head to clear her thoughts, which was close to impossible since Malcolm hadn't taken his eyes off her. Wherever she moved, his eyes followed her.

"Malcolm said he's remodeling his house, and I thought maybe we could help. He's painting his parlor on Saturday, isn't that right, Dr. Malcolm?"

"Yes, it is, Jazzy," Malcolm answered, turning his gaze from Sabrina for a moment and leaning across the table to squeeze Jasmine's nose.

"Hey, stop that," Jasmine laughed.

"What, this?" Malcolm said, squeezing it again.

"Stop!" Jasmine pushed his massive hand away when he attempted it again. "Mom!" Jasmine pushed her chair away and prepared to run. She glanced at her mother for help.

"Hey, you." Sabrina smiled at Malcolm. "You wanna give it a rest?"

"Why? What are you going to do about it? Are you going to try and stop me?" Malcolm teased. "'Cause if so, I'd sure like to see you try."

"You think I can't?" Sabrina asked, rising to the challenge. "Well, I'll show you." She boldly lunged at him. Malcolm halted her assault by swinging an arm around her middle, landing her directly in his lap. Sabrina used the opportunity to tickle Malcolm's center. When she did, Malcolm let out a hearty masculine laugh. "Jasmine, help!" Sabrina called out to her daughter.

Jasmine assisted and pretty soon they were all tickling each other. Sabrina and Jasmine managed to push Malcolm out of the chair and onto the floor. Their loud laughter drowned out the noise of the front door opening and closing.

"Ahem," Beverly and James Parker said loudly, coughing from the doorway. They were rather surprised to find their daughter and granddaughter sprawled across Dr. Winters.

"Excuse us," James said, grabbing his shocked wife by the arm and lead her to the living room.

"Did you see…?" Beverly began. She couldn't believe her daughter's outrageous behavior.

"Yes," Sabrina heard her father say. "And she's a grown woman."

"With an impressionable daughter," Beverly added for emphasis.

Sabrina heard every word from her location across Malcolm's chest. It was pretty hard not to. Her mother made no secret of her displeasure.

Malcolm rose and stood up, helping Sabrina and Jasmine to their feet. "Listen, I'm sorry about that," he said. "I didn't mean any disrespect to you and your family."

"It's okay," Sabrina said, rearranging her clothes, even though she was completely embarrassed at being found in a compromising position by her parents.

"Jasmine, why don't you go in the living room

with Grandma and Grandpa, while I show Dr. Malcolm out?" Sabrina ordered.

"Do I have to?" Jasmine pouted, folding her arms across her chest. "Can't I stay with you guys?"

"Go on, Jasmine," Malcolm warned. "Do as your mother ordered. We'll see each other real soon."

"Promise?" Jasmine's big eyes fixed on Malcolm and he knew he was a goner.

"I promise." Malcolm crossed his heart.

Sabrina glanced back and forth at Malcolm and her daughter. An alliance between the two had been formed before her very eyes. Sabrina watched Malcolm shake Jasmine's hand before she disappeared into the living room. Clearly, the duo trusted each other.

"You have a wonderful daughter," Malcolm told Sabrina once Jasmine had gone.

"The feeling is reciprocal," Sabrina replied with a smile. "Jasmine adores you."

"As do I," Malcolm said, "but she's not the only one I like."

Sabrina didn't respond to Malcolm's flirty comment. Instead, she said, "Let me fix you a plate to take home."

"That would be great," Malcolm said, following her to the kitchen.

Sabrina fixed Malcolm a styrofoam paper plate filled with leftovers, covered it with aluminum foil and handed it to him by the back door.

"Thank you, Sabrina, for a wonderful dinner,"

Malcolm said. "It was surely better than eating dinner alone. I really enjoyed myself."

"So did I," Sabrina said.

Malcolm was turning away to leave when he swooped down and planted a ravishing kiss on her lips. Before she had time to protest, he broke the barrier of her lips and teeth and plundered her mouth and she had no choice but to surrender completely to his masterful seduction.

When he kissed her, it was divine ecstasy and when he finally pulled away she had a burning desire, an aching need for another kiss.

"I can't take this anymore, Sabrina. You're driving me insane." Malcolm inhaled to force some air into his lungs. They had reached the point where their relationship had to be resolved. "It's time we became lovers."

"I wouldn't have it any other way," Sabrina smiled seductively. The admission was dredged from a place beyond logic and reason. It was basic and instinctive.

Malcolm smiled broadly. Finally, they made progress. "Well, I look forward to that time," he stated and closed the door behind him.

Sabrina stood and stared at the door several long moments, remembering the soft touch of Malcolm's lips before turning and walking away.

Chapter 13

"Hello?" Malcolm answered the phone beside his bed.

"Malcolm, darling. Don't be such a grouch. It's your mother," Dinah replied.

"Mom?" Malcolm wiped the sleep from his eyes and sat upright. "What are you doing calling me this early?" he asked, pushing the pillows back with his fist and leaning against the headboard.

"It's nearly noon," Dinah returned. "Aren't you a morning person? You're usually up with the roosters." Dinah remembered her son's habit of getting up early for his morning exercise.

"Well, I had a long night," he answered harshly. But one he had enjoyed tremendously. And he was looking forward to picking up where they'd left off the next time he saw Sabrina. He was in such a good mood, why ruin it by talking to his mother, especially when he hadn't even had his morning cup of coffee.

"Well, wake up," Dinah voiced loudly, "because I'm here in Savannah. And I want you to come by and pick me up."

"What!" Malcolm yelled. What was Dinah doing down South? She said nothing was good this far south of the Mason-Dixon Line. "What are you doing here?"

"I came to convince you to move back home with your family, among other matters."

"What other matters?" Malcolm queried.

"All in due time, all in due time," she replied. "Why don't you pick me up for lunch first and I'll tell you all about it."

"Mother…" Malcolm began.

"Don't start, Malcolm. Meet me at Foley House within the hour." Perturbed by his behavior, Dinah hung up the phone on him. Malcolm rubbed his chin thoughtfully, wondering what Dinah's agenda was. Once he'd showered, he'd soon find out.

Malcolm showed up within the hour to pick up Dinah for lunch. He came appropriately attired in khakis, a navy polo shirt and cream blazer.

Foley House was as luxurious a bed-and-breakfast as they came, not that he expected anything less. Only the best for Dinah Armstrong!

Inhaling deeply, he opened the front door. "Mrs. Armstrong, please? Can you let her know I'm here?"

"Mrs. Armstrong advised us you'd be coming. She's waiting in the parlor," the female clerk said. She was giving him her best come-hither look, but Malcolm was not interested. He'd tasted heaven last night and he wanted another helping.

The clerk led him to the parlor where he found Dinah sitting on a chaise, sipping tea as she flipped through *Home and Garden*. "Mother," he said, raising his voice slightly.

At the sound of his voice, Dinah whipped around. "Malcolm!" she cried, standing up and rushing toward him. Dinah greeted her older son with an affectionate hug, which Malcolm received stiffly. She didn't seem to notice his less than enthusiastic response.

Elegantly dressed in a cream Dolce & Gabbana pantsuit with matching shoes, Dinah Armstrong oozed sophistication with a capital *S*. Covered in pearls from the choker on her neck to the earrings on her lobes, her look said old money. And boy did she have lots of it.

When he and Michael were seven years old, Dinah had begun working as a secretary for Walter Armstrong. Walter was nearly twenty years her senior, but that hadn't mattered. With an older man like Walter and a good-looking woman like Dinah rearing twins, it hadn't taken long for Walter to bend down on one knee and beg her to let him take care of her and the boys. Now whether Dinah married for love or money, Malcolm didn't know. But from what he'd seen, it did eventually turn into a deep abiding love, which surprised him, considering he'd never felt a true mother-son connection with Dinah. Her affection had always been reserved for Michael.

"It's so good to see you," Dinah gushed. "Let me look at you." She held either side of his face and stared at her often distant son, kissing him on both cheeks. Malcolm blushed at the show of affection and moved away. No lovey-dovey stuff for him, Dinah thought. Sometimes she wished he was more like Michael. But it was too late to teach an old dog new tricks. "You look just as handsome as ever," Dinah said, taking a seat.

"So, Dinah, what brings you to Savannah?" Malcolm asked, folding his arms across his chest.

"Must you call me by my first name?" Dinah asked. "It's so…so disrespectful. Have you forgotten your manners, as well as your brains down here in the land of Dixie?"

"No, I haven't. And if I've offended you, then I'm deeply sorry," Malcolm apologized. Yet he couldn't help but wonder what was truly going on, what had brought her here.

"Why don't we go have some lunch and catch up," Dinah said, rising to her feet. "Allow me to get my wrap and I'll be ready to go." Dinah left Malcolm standing there, waiting for what, he didn't know.

Twenty minutes later, they were seated outside at

a café along Riverwalk, while a waiter filled both their glasses with Evian. Dinah waited until he'd gone before speaking.

Leaning over, she grasped Malcolm's hand in hers. "It's been too long, son," she stated.

Malcolm pulled away his hand. "Yes, it has. I'm sorry I've stayed away this long. It truly wasn't my intention. I guess I got caught up in my new life here."

"And forgot that you have a mother that still cares about you and would like to know what's going on in your life," Dinah stated. "Won't you tell me about it?"

Malcolm heard the beseeching tone in her voice and acquiesced. He wasn't purposely trying to be evasive. He was a private person and Dinah knew that, but she was his mother, so he supposed he should make an effort. "What do you want to know?"

She shrugged. "Whatever you'd like to share with me. I'm just so happy to be here with you." Dinah's eyes misted with tears.

Malcolm patted her hand. "All right," Malcolm said, removing his blazer and setting it on the back of his chair. "I've taken over a family practice and I now have my own clinic."

"Oh, really?" Dinah said quietly.

"And," Malcolm continued, "I recently purchased and renovated an historic house on the Tybee Island. Mother, if you could see it, it's beautiful. It's got five bedrooms, with a parlor and study and lots of wide-open space outdoors."

"Since when do you like the country?" Dinah asked sarcastically.

The waiter came back carrying their salad plates and set them on the table before Malcolm could answer, which was a good thing because he didn't really care for her tone.

"Since I needed to get away from the pressures in Boston," Malcolm answered unapologetically. He hoped Dinah wasn't going to start in about him moving back there, because if so, she'd be wasting her breath. He liked his new life and his new woman here in Savannah and if Dinah didn't like it, that was too darn bad.

"I don't understand you, Malcolm, with a brilliant career like the one you had, you blow it to smithereens. Why? What possible purpose will it serve? You're giving up your dream of being the best cardiac surgeon in the country."

Malcolm couldn't answer that. All he knew was that somewhere along the way his dream had changed. Being the best cardiologist no longer mattered, he was tired of being alone and now he didn't have to be. "I know it's hard for you to understand, but I'm happy here. Can't you take that at face value?"

"I wish I could, Malcolm." Dinah shook her head. "If that's all there was to it, but it's not." He knew it, Dinah was being too coy. She had a secret that she was keeping from him and she'd come to Savannah to reveal it.

"What's so important you couldn't tell me over the phone?"

Dinah paused to take a long gulp of her Evian before proceeding. "There's no easy way to tell you this…"

"Mother, whatever it is, just tell me."

"A woman named Tasha has come forward claiming that she had an intimate relationship with your brother that resulted in a child. Michael's child. His son." The words tumbled out of Dinah's mouth before she had time to prepare Malcolm. Complete shock was etched across Malcolm's face at the news.

Malcolm was floored. "A son!" he muttered, leaning back in his chair. Could there really be the possibly that another Michael existed? If it were true, it would just be too…

"Malcolm, did you hear a word I've said?" Dinah asked. She wanted to offer a shoulder, but he remained distant across the table. She could see his mind was a million miles away. She should have known what this news would do to him.

Could it be true? After several long deadening moments, Malcolm finally found his voice. "So do you think she's telling the truth?" Malcolm asked. Could his twin have left behind a child for them all to love? The news caused Malcolm's heartbeat to speed up rapidly and made him feel lightheaded. Of course, he hadn't eaten a thing on his lunch plate since it arrived.

"Of course not," Dinah said, pulling out a cigarette. "If Michael had a son, we'd know. You and I were both very close to him. If he'd gotten a woman pregnant, he would have told us." Dinah refused to believe otherwise.

"So you think this woman is after his money?"

"Yes," Dinah stated emphatically. "Michael's estate is sizeable and she could be looking for a way to subsidize her lifestyle."

Malcolm punched his fist down on the table for emphasis. "As executor of his will, I'd never allow that to happen."

Dinah smiled. There was the fearless, determined son she remembered! Malcolm's anger was encouraging. She knew her son would wipe slate with this scheming conniver.

"So, what's the next step?" Malcolm asked, because Dinah always had a plan.

"Well, I'd dismissed her claims for the last few months, but she's hired an attorney and now it has come down to a court-ordered paternity test."

"Then, I guess, we'll find out soon enough," Malcolm replied. The results would speak for themselves.

"Hey, girl," Monique gave Sabrina a quick hug. "Come on in. Forgive the mess," she said when Sabrina entered and found Monique's single-story bungalow in complete disarray. Toys were all over the front room while Brandon and Brianna had the television blaring in the background.

And Monique, well, that was another story

entirely. Monique came to the front door wearing skintight denim capris and a tank top two sizes two small for her overly large bosom. Her beautiful face was covered in makeup and bright red lipstick, which she really didn't need. Monique was a beautiful girl she didn't need all the extras.

"Look who's here." Monique glanced in her children's direction. The twins looked up from their video game and beckoned Jasmine to join them on the couch.

"Come on back to the kitchen with me," Monique ordered.

Sabrina followed, taking in her surroundings. The bungalow was a modest size with only a large living room, three bedrooms, one bath and a large eat-in kitchen.

"I hope you don't mind takeout," Monique said and pulled off several Boston Market bags from the stove while Sabrina took a seat. "I really had every intention of making dinner tonight." She pulled out several paper plates and plastic tumblers. "But the diner was busy because that trifling waitress of mine called off sick again to be with her boyfriend, leaving me holding the bag. I had to complete her shift until help arrived. Lord, I swear that restaurant is going to be the death of me."

"Then let me help," Sabrina rose from her seat, found a sponge in the sink and proceeded to clean the table.

"Thanks, Binks," Monique commented, opening

up the roast chicken, macaroni and cheese and creamed spinach she'd brought. It wasn't her home cooking, but it would do in a pinch. "So how's everything going?"

"Did I tell you that Mary isn't coming back to Parker House? And now that classes have begun, I'm working and going to school."

"So why don't you tell Felicia to find someone else?" Monique asked. "Dinner's ready!" she yelled to the children.

"I can't." Sabrina tossed the sponge in the sink. "I have to show her that I'm capable of hard work."

Minutes later, Jasmine, Brianna and Brandon came stomping into the room causing a ruckus. "None of that in this house, ya hear," Monique warned her two children. After being scolded by their mother, Brianna and Brandon quickly sat down.

Sabrina was starved, but fixed a plate for Jasmine first.

"I don't like spinach." Jasmine frowned, scrunching up her nose at the offending vegetable when Sabrina set the plate in front of her.

"Spinach is good for you," Sabrina explained, trying to be calm because she didn't really care for Jasmine's tone.

"I'm not eating it," Jasmine replied, pushing her plate away from the table and folding her arms across her chest. Brianna and Brandon both looked across the table at their mother. If they ever tried that move in front of company their mother would kill them.

"Yes, you are," Sabrina said, fast becoming annoyed with Jasmine's attitude.

"No, I'm not and you can't make me," Jasmine pouted.

Sabrina counted to ten before she lost her temper.

Monique glanced in her friend's direction and intervened before World War I broke out. "Listen up, Jasmine," Monique's voice rose in an authoritative tone. "In *this* house, children do as they're told. You're going to sit there and eat your vegetables like the rest of the children at this table. And if you don't, you won't be eating at all. So, what's it going to be?" Monique asked.

Jasmine looked back and forth at Brianna and Brandon for help, but they shrugged. Defeated, Jasmine acquiesced and pulled the plate back toward her.

Sabrina breathed a sigh of relief that a disaster was averted. Thank God for Monique! She may be rough around the edges, but she sure knew how to rule her roost.

Later, when she and Monique sat out on the couch drinking coffee and listening to Roberta Flack, they commiserated on the sad, pitiful state of their love lives.

Monique told Sabrina about her failed relationship with Brianna and Brandon's father. "Sabrina—" Monique shook her head as she tucked her legs underneath her "—the man was incredibly gifted in a certain department if you know what I mean and I was too young and naive to realize he was bad news. But when he got involved with the wrong crowd and started bringing those thugs around my babies, that's when I told him he had to go."

"Good for you," Sabrina said. "Though you should consider yourself lucky that you didn't have Tre Matthews."

"Oh, I do." Monique patted her thigh. "But now that you've found Malcolm, that must ease the pain somewhat."

"It has." Could she admit her true feelings to a dear old friend, someone who wouldn't judge her? Sabrina thought so. "He's wonderful, Monique," Sabrina admitted aloud. "He makes me feel special and treasured in a way I've only dreamed of. And you should see him with his patients and with Jasmine. He's so kind and giving."

"Have you acted on this attraction?" Monique asked, sipping her coffee.

"Sort of. I mean, we've made out several times. He's a supremely good kisser. And I must admit it's made me want more."

"What are you waiting for? You're a grown woman. And you've got to be horny. When was the last time you had any?"

Sabrina laughed out loud. Trust Monique to be brutally honest. "It has been a while."

"Don't be afraid to take a chance. The man obviously desires you, Sabrina. Even I've seen it. Find that Sabrina of old. You do remember her, don't you? The fearless girl who left town to pursue her writing career? You haven't lost that person, Sabrina. She's still inside you. So, go after what your want."

"I don't know, Monique."

"Don't act like the idea sounds preposterous to you. The best way to get over an old man is to find yourself a new one. And with a doctor as fine as Malcolm, you'd be a fool not to." Monique laughed aloud at her own joke.

"You do have a point," Sabrina replied. "Perhaps it's time I turned our relationship up a notch."

"So, what do you think?" Malcolm asked after he'd given his mother a complete tour of the property and the house.

"It's really quite amazing," Dinah said after they'd come back inside for a glass of wine. The merlot warmed her after the cool night temperature.

"I did all the work myself," Malcolm replied proudly.

"Without any help?" Dinah queried.

"With my own two hands," Malcolm replied.

"I never thought I'd see the day, when you'd become so domesticated." She couldn't imagine him getting his hands dirty. A chill ran through her and Dinah tossed her wrap around her shoulders.

"Cold?" Malcolm asked. "This house can take care of it. It comes with two working fireplaces."

"Well, you sure are the real estate agent."

Malcolm didn't like Dinah's tone. "I don't need to sell you on my home," he said. "It's already a done deal. But if you're asking if I want you to be proud of my work, then yes, I am. I've worked very hard on this place." Malcolm fingered the doorframe still left to be painted.

"So, it's been cathartic?" Dinah asked.

Malcolm nodded. "Yes, it has."

"Then come home," Dinah started in on him again. "Once you're done renovating, sell it and move back where you belong."

Annoyed, Malcolm became silent and faced the window. After the news he'd heard, he was really in no mood for another round. "You don't get it, do you?" Malcolm spun around to face his mother. "*This* is my home."

"You're wrong." Dinah shook her head. "I refuse to believe it. Listen to me, Malcolm. You're not too old to learn a thing or two from your mother. I've been around the block a time or two. Trust me, an ordinary life is not in the cards for you. Please, come back with me." Dinah held out her arms to him.

"No." The word got his point across.

Dinah stomped her heel. "Why must you be so stubborn?" she said. "After everything I've done for you." Dinah reached in her Louis Vuitton bag and pulled out a lace handkerchief. "After the life I've given you, the clothes, the cars and the education. I've given you the best of everything. Please, look at what you're doing to yourself!"

"I never asked you for any of those things," Malcolm replied.

"No, but you sure didn't mind them, did you?" Dinah asked sarcastically. "I implore you to stop this farce. Enough is enough. This…this life of poverty will not bring Michael back!"

Rage shot through Malcolm and he stormed across the room to confront his mother. "Don't you dare bring Michael's name into this conversation! His name has no place here."

"Like hell it doesn't," Dinah returned and grasped him by the shoulders. "You've been grieving for over a year. Well, enough is enough, Malcolm. Get on with life!"

"Why? So you can feel better?"

"No, so you can," Dinah replied. "I'm doing fine. I'm coping. I'm not the one who feels guilty for my role in Michael's death."

"What did you just say?" Malcolm asked, halting her with one hand. Maybe they were finally down to the heart of the matter.

"Nothing," Dinah backtracked. "I have no idea what you're talking about."

"Oh yes, you do," Malcolm roared, stepping away from her. "Why don't you finish what you started, Dinah." Malcolm returned to the use of her first name. "You started down a path. Why stop yourself? Since we're *talking*—" Malcolm imitated quotation marks "—then why don't you say what's really on your mind. Tell me how you truly feel."

Dinah looked around the room for her purse. Once she found it, she walked to the front door. "I'm not going to do this. I'm not going to feed into your masochism. Kindly take me back to the hotel, please." Dinah rushed toward the glass front door.

"Why are you running, Dinah? Are you too afraid to reveal the real truth!" Malcolm roared.

"And what might that be?" Dinah asked.

"That you blame me," Malcolm snapped. His eyes met Dinah's from across the living room and they were as cold as ice. Dinah's blood ran cold seeing that lethal look in Malcolm's eye. It was the same look she'd seen the night Michael died, when the light had gone out of Malcolm's eyes.

"That's right." He saw her café au lait coloring turn scarlet at the statement. "Yes, Dinah." Malcolm nodded his head. "Can't we be 'honest' here? Admit that you blame me for Michael's death."

"No." Dinah shook her head.

But Malcolm wouldn't stop. He continued to press her. "I'm the one that misdiagnosed Michael's heart condition, right? Admit that you hold me responsible."

"All right!" Dinah yelled, unable to hear any more accusations. "Yes," she screamed back at him. "Yes, I hold you responsible. You...you were the renowned cardiologist. You should have seen the tear in his aorta."

Malcolm's expression turned to stone. "Finally." He clapped his hands. "Finally, you say what's been in your heart this entire time. Thank you, Mother. It's nice to know that you think I murdered my own brother." Malcolm stormed toward the door. "If you have your things, I'll take you back to your hotel."

The instant she'd said the words, Dinah wished she could take them back, but it was too late. "Malcolm, I didn't…" Dinah began, but he was already out the door.

The second he was outside in the fresh, clean air, Malcolm wondered why he'd done it. Why had he called her out on her feelings regarding Michael's death? Why couldn't he have let sleeping dogs lie? Could it be because he thought she was right?

Chapter 14

A week later, Sabrina questioned her own sanity when she stopped by Malcolm's on her way home from work, purely on impulse. She hadn't heard from Malcolm since that night on her doorstep, when he'd said they would become lovers. She was sure he would phone her to make another date, but he hadn't. Had she done something to push him away? Was her fear of getting involved causing him to run in the opposite direction? Because one moment he was as cold as ice and the next he was this romantic fellow dancing with her under the stars at the picnic. Why was he keeping her at arm's length? Weren't they getting closer?

Sabrina discovered from Nurse Turner that

Malcolm had moved out of Parker House and was now living in his remodeled house. Was the house even finished yet? Driving on 95, she pulled off the road and into a beautiful residential district on the Tybee Island. When she pulled up in front of the house, she was surprised at how traditional his home was. The exterior had been given a complete update as had the carport, which now housed Malcolm's Jag. Sabrina pulled alongside it.

She knew she had her work cut out for her because from what she'd heard from Nurse Turner, Malcolm hadn't been to the clinic in a week. She'd rescheduled all his appointments, which meant he'd had a lot of free time on his hands to brood.

Today, though, she was determined to find out his deep dark secret and let him know that she wanted him with the same intensity that he wanted her.

Turning off the ignition, Sabrina stepped out of her convertible wearing a bias-cut skirt, camisole and matching sweater. Closing the door behind her, she prepared to face Malcolm.

Opening the white picket-fence gate, Sabrina climbed the wooden porch steps of the two-story pale green house. Glancing around her, Sabrina saw a father and son outside playing with their dog and an elderly man outside watering his lawn. It was so surreal for Sabrina to picture Malcolm in this family setting. There was so much more to the man than even she'd realized.

Nervous tension ran through her veins as she

pressed the doorbell. Several minutes passed and
when no one answered, Sabrina knocked on the glass
door. When he still didn't answer, Sabrina banged
even harder and harder with her fists until Malcolm
would have no choice but to answer if he wanted the
racket to end.

Sabrina began to wonder if he was there when the
door suddenly swung open and Malcolm appeared,
shirtless, bathed in sweat and holding a hammer. He
looked haggard and exhausted. Seven-day-old
stubble surrounded his regal jaw while he wore a
paint-splattered pair of jeans.

His body was so incredible to look at that Sabrina stuttered. "M…Malcolm?" Sabrina nearly lost
her voice.

"Sabrina," Malcolm greeted her in a husky
whisper. "What are you doing here?"

"I came to surprise you."

"Trust me, I've had enough surprises."

"Indeed." Sabrina smiled. "Can I come in?" She
tried stepping inside, but Malcolm blocked the
doorway.

"Now isn't it a good time," he muttered.

So, she was in for a battle. Well, Malcolm would
soon discover that she was just as stubborn as he was
and that she didn't cower easily, at least not anymore.

Sabrina found her voice. "Yes, well, uh…I was in
the neighborhood and thought I'd finally stop by and
see this masterpiece you've been working on for
months," she said, squeezing underneath his arm and

rushing inside before he could stop her. Malcolm couldn't resist smiling at her ingenuity. At five foot two, Sabrina could manage tiny spots.

Once inside, however, he wondered why she'd come. His home was completely out of her way. "Where's Jazzy?" he asked, looking for his ray of sunshine. He could use that right now.

"I'm sorry. I came alone," Sabrina responded. "I hope that's okay?"

"Yeah, it's fine. Now that you're here, would you like a tour of the house?" he asked, wiping the sweat from his brow with his hand.

"Yes, I'd love one." Sabrina smiled. When she entered the hallway, the smell of oak greeted her and tickled her nose. "The floors are beautiful, Malcolm," she commented as she walked into the empty living room. "And this fireplace…" Sabrina walked over to the mantel and ran her fingers across the cold marble. "It's magnificent. Does it work?"

"Of course," Malcolm replied. "What would be the purpose in having a fireplace and not utilizing it? Let me show you the rest of the house." His arms swung open.

When he was several meters away, Sabrina turned and found his gaze riveted on her as he gave her a lazy appraisal. She was entranced by the sexual magnetism emanating from him and his bare, rock-hard chest. It made her want to touch him. Feel the strength and warmth of his masculine flesh against hers in a purely sensual experience, but she didn't dare be that bold. So she moved away instead and continued touring the house.

The parlor, study and dining room had been beautifully restored like the rest of the house. Most of the rooms were empty except for his study which he'd decorated with the furniture from Boston that had been in storage. But he still needed help with the living room and parlor. His current modern living room set had no place in a house like this. "This home requires warmth and style, not a leather interior," he informed her.

"Everything looks good," she commented, glancing around the kitchen. It was completely masculine with hardwood floors, maple cabinets and stainless-steel appliances. The two large windows by the sink overlooked a small retention pond with a lapping fountain. "But it could use a woman's touch. Like some curtains," Sabrina suggested.

Malcolm watched her from the doorway wondering why she'd come. "Are you volunteering?" he asked.

"Maybe, but then again, that would mean you would have to return my calls."

"There's a lot going on that you don't know," Malcolm replied.

"So why don't you tell me?" Sabrina returned.

"You wouldn't understand my crazy family dynamics."

Sabrina fumed over his refusal to open up and share his feelings, so instead she glared out the side window at a happy older couple taking in their groceries.

When she remained silent, Malcolm tried again. "Listen, Sabrina," he said, jumping up and plopping on his island counter. "I'm going through something right now and I just need time alone."

"Oh please, Malcolm." Sabrina spun around. "What could have happened within the last week that would change you this drastically?"

"I don't want to discuss it," he said, avoiding her eyes and looking at a spot on the wall. He couldn't bear looking into those beautiful light brown eyes for fear he'd lose himself in them. *Would that be so bad?* an inner voice asked.

"Well, you're going to," Sabrina walked towards him and stood in between Malcolm's legs.

"Sabrina." Malcolm tried pushing her away by the shoulders, but she ignored him and lightly caressed his chin.

"Don't even think of acting like you're unaffected by me," Sabrina said, touching his messy hair. For once it wasn't slickly laid down in waves across his head. "Because I know otherwise." She inhaled deeply and plunged ahead. "Why don't you tell me what's going on, Malcolm. Get it out in the open. I'm here to listen."

"I can't," he said, lowering his head.

"That's a load of hogwash. Yes, you can. You just have to try." She cupped his chin and lifted his head to meet hers. "Wouldn't it be nice to tell someone? You know, unload."

"I can't do that to you," Malcolm jumped off the island.

Sabrina refused to be dismissed and came behind him, wrapping her arms around his middle. "And why not?" she said, turning her head and glancing up at him. "I've got strong shoulders, I can handle it." Sabrina posed for him, revealing her buff forearms.

"You know, I don't deserve you," Malcolm said, turning around and gathering her in his arms.

"Why on earth would you say something like that?" she said.

"Come with me and I'll tell you," Malcolm replied, taking her hand and leading her to his study. It was the only comfortable place to sit and talk considering his limited accommodations.

Once they were seated on the leather reading sofa, Malcolm recounted the details of Michael's diagnosis and subsequent death.

"How could I have missed the tear?" Malcolm's voice broke as he relived the last few weeks of his brother's life.

"Didn't you say it's nearly impossible to diagnose?" Sabrina queried.

"Yes. But I should have let another physician check him out. I was too close to assess the situation and provide an unbiased opinion." Malcolm ran his fingers through his wildly unkempt hair. "I should have known better."

"Oh, Malcolm." Sadness filled Sabrina's eyes as she thought about the depth of grief that Malcolm must be experiencing. The guilt he must be feeling over the loss of his brother, it had to be tremendous, which would explain his life-altering decision to give up practicing cardiology full-time. Clearly, Malcolm loved medicine too much to give it up completely, but in his role as family practitioner, heart patients would be few and far between.

"I'm so sorry for your loss," Sabrina cried for him. "What can I do? Is there anything I can do for you?"

Malcolm shook his head. There was nothing anyone could do. He'd have to live with the guilt for the rest of his life. "No, Sabrina. I wish there were, but there's more. I'm not done with the story."

"There's more?" How much more could he possibly handle?

"Yes," Malcolm continued on. Sabrina was right, telling someone made him feel less alone. Less isolated. "My mother was here for a visit."

"When?"

"Last week," Malcolm replied.

Understanding dawned on Sabrina's face. That was why she hadn't heard from him. What could his mother have done or said to make him revert to his loner lifestyle? "And what happened?" Sabrina asked.

Malcolm let out a long reluctant sigh. "She said that she held me accountable for Michael's death."

"No…" Horror crossed Sabrina's face and her eyebrows furrowed together. How could his own mother say something so cruel?

"Oh yes, she did. Though I don't know why it

upsets me so much. It's not like it's not anything I haven't already said to myself a thousand times."

"But, Malcolm, it's not your fault," Sabrina said.

"Wasn't it? Maybe subconsciously I wanted him to die for some reason. I mean, he was the twin everyone adored. He was the center of Dinah's life. I was always left out in the cold, wishing for just a little bit of that attention." Malcolm stood up and he bit back the tears that stung at his eyes. He didn't want Sabrina to see him like this. So weak. So unglued.

"No, no, no." Sabrina rose and grabbed Malcolm's hand. "That's not true. Not the gentleman I know, that has cared for my daughter like she were his own," Sabrina replied defiantly. "I refuse to believe it. And you can't convince me otherwise."

Malcolm looked down at his little spitfire and attempted a halfhearted smile. "Wow, such an impassioned speech! Has anyone ever told you that you're amazing?"

"Not recently, he's been a little preoccupied," Sabrina answered.

"I'm sorry, Sabrina."

"It's okay. I just hope next time you'll know that you can tell me anything because I always fight for the people I care about."

"And you care about me?" Malcolm inquired.

"Of course I do," Sabrina replied nervously. "Why else would I be here?"

"Why else indeed?" Malcolm wondered aloud.

Even though she'd said the words, Malcolm could feel Sabrina's anxiety even though they'd yet to make love. Was she afraid of the emotions going on in her head and her body? Didn't she know that he understood how she felt? It had been a long time since he'd shared a woman's company. Hell, even wanted a woman's company, but his desire for Sabrina was rapidly rising and he could no longer deny it. He wanted her in his bed and if she admitted it to herself, so did she.

Malcolm didn't want to wait any longer for what he knew they both wanted. Why else would she come by unannounced without Jasmine? She wanted him, too, and he intended to show her just how much.

With two quick steps he was at the study's fireplace, sweeping Sabrina into his arms and kissing her all over.

Desire flooded her as Malcolm's hands crept up to cup her breasts underneath the lacy exterior of her camisole, so he quickly dispensed with her shirt. At his touch, her full breasts rose and Malcolm bent down to have his first taste through her bra. Sabrina smelled of lavender and tasted as sweet as a Georgia peach.

The feel of Malcolm's bare chest against hers sent Sabrina into overdrive. Burying her face in his neck, she responded by planting a hot moist kiss on Malcolm's neck, burning a path of fire all the way to his earlobe before laving it generously with her tongue. Malcolm moaned sensuously when Sabrina continued kissing the pulsing hollow at the base of his throat. When she suckled on the spot, Malcolm stopped her before he lost control.

"So you're not afraid that your feelings for me have deepened to something more than friendship?" he asked her in a passion-filled haze.

"No, I'm not afraid anymore. It's time."

"Oh yes, it is. And I promise you we'll both enjoy it," he said.

With two long strides backward he had her pinned against the wall, reclaiming her lips. His mouth covered hers hungrily as he devoured every inch of her honeyed softness.

"Do you know how much I want you?" he whispered against her earlobe.

Just about as much as she wanted him, Sabrina imagined, responding to his demanding kisses with equal fervor.

He embraced not only her face but her body. His hands explored every inch of her fevered flesh and when he eased the lacy cup of her bra aside to fasten his lips on one small turgid peak, Sabrina didn't stop him. She couldn't think, let alone speak. She felt transported on a soft and wispy cloud. And when Malcolm finally turned to the other breast and with equal attention bathed it with his hot wet tongue, Sabrina finally succumbed and gave in to the desire rising within her.

"How does that feel?" Malcolm whispered huskily as his teeth teased one swollen nipple.

"So good, so good," Sabrina moaned aloud.

At that moment, Malcolm knew that Sabrina Parker was finally his for the taking. He wanted to undress her slowly, savoring each moment as he worshipped her luxurious body. Lifting her off the floor, he quickly marched out of the study and up the stairs.

He took the steps two at a time and when he made it to the bedroom, he kicked the door open and stalked over to his king-sized poster bed. That's when Sabrina took over. Her arms reached out and encircled his waist while her hands and fingers traveled the length of his back. When she squeezed his buttocks, Malcolm let out a tormented groan. He'd fantasized about this moment and now his fantasy was fast becoming a reality.

"Are you sure you're ready for this?" Malcolm asked, because he wasn't sure he could stop once they started.

"I'm not a china doll, Malcolm," Sabrina replied. "You don't have to treat me with kid gloves. Trust me, if I didn't want to be with you, I wouldn't be here."

Unzipping her skirt, Malcolm let it fall in a puddle on the floor, allowing him better access to the soft lines of her waist and her hips before falling to his knees and exploring the soft lusciousness of her thighs. He slowly laid her down on the bed before reaching down to caress her intimately. When he did, he found her bikini underwear slick and wet.

Oh yes, Sabrina was ready for him. Malcolm hooked on to the tiny fabric and skimmed it down her shapely thighs and legs before tossing it over his shoulder. Before long Sabrina would be screaming out his name.

Nudging her legs apart, Malcolm bent his head between her thighs and laved the tiny nub at the center of her womanhood and when that wasn't enough he inserted his narrow, lean finger inside her moist cavern, sending Sabrina soaring higher than she'd ever known possible. Her body tightened around his finger as he eased in and out.

She surrendered quickly to him as her breath came in quick, uneven tones. When he looked up and found her eyes open and bright with desire for him, he nearly lost control. Without taking her eyes off him, she unzipped his jeans, pushing them down his hips. Quickly and succinctly he moved them down his legs giving Sabrina her first view of his magnificent piece of manhood. She had felt his body against hers before, but the sight of his erection made Sabrina's heart pound loudly in her chest. Knowing he wanted her as much as she wanted him, gave her self-confidence.

"Come here," she murmured, opening her arms wide. When he was an arm's length away, she reached out and pushed him down onto the bed and straddled his waist.

"You've had your fun," she said, smiling. "Now, it's my turn." Pretty soon, he would be quivering underneath her skilled touch. Tre was very wrong indeed. She had a high sex drive.

Caressing him with her palm, Sabrina's mouth closed around his thick, hard member. Flicking her agile tongue back and forth across the shaft caused Malcolm's groans to become louder. All the while her hands trailed upward to squeeze and caress the nipples on his chest. Malcolm wasn't a bystander for long, though. In the midst of his ecstasy, his hands found her gorgeous mass of ringlets and slowly he allowed his hands to sink in its luscious depth. He wasn't surprised when her hair was soft and light to his touch.

Once Sabrina had worked her magic and had him close to the precipice, he stopped her and leaned over to grab a pack of condoms in his nightstand drawer.

"And you just happen to have those lying around?"

"I've been waiting for you," Malcolm said honestly, reaching across to gather her in his arms and shower her face with kisses. But Sabrina was as eager as he and when he fumbled with the condom wrapper, Sabrina snatched it from him and opened it herself. Easing the condom onto his enlarged member, Sabrina slid herself back on top of Malcolm. She didn't know what had come over her, but she wanted to ride him like there was no tomorrow.

Malcolm marveled at Sabrina's aggressiveness and allowed her to take the lead. He loved the gentle sway of her hips and the tight feel of her around his engorged shaft.

"Yes, baby, yes," Malcolm moaned, grabbing her firm buttocks.

"You like that, huh," Sabrina said, seductively. "Then you're going to love this," she said, bending down to brush her lips across his. His lips parted, allowing easy access for Sabrina's tongue to dart out and delve into his interior. Their tongues met as hers challenged his to a duel that she didn't win because Malcolm was ready to take back the lead.

Flipping her over, he caught both her hands and put them above her head and threw one leg over his shoulder. Then he slowly began thrusting in and out. Cocooned in her warmth, Malcolm felt like they were two pieces of the same whole. Their bodies meshed together perfectly as he penetrated her deeper and deeper.

They found a rhythm and it wasn't long after that Sabrina's back arched, lifting her off the bed as she reached an earth-shattering climax. Malcolm came right after her, giving a loud shout as his body released itself and he collapsed on top of her.

Rolling onto his side, Malcolm quickly relieved her of his weight, but Sabrina hadn't cared. Exhausted, she lay on her back with her beautifully dark hair spread across his pillow like a fan, just like he'd envisioned in his dreams.

"My, my." Malcolm sat up on one arm and looked down at her, while the other gently caressed the side of her face.

"Where did all that unbridled passion come from?"

Sabrina blushed. "I don't know. Probably from years of sexual repression."

"You mean to tell me that you and Tre didn't set the world on fire like we did just now?" Malcolm teased, fingering one tendril in between his thumb and index finger.

Sabrina shook her head. "No, I'm afraid Tre didn't always find *the* spot." Sabrina smiled. "Often I faked it just to end it."

Malcolm's onyx eyes fixed on hers. "Well, there will be no faking between us, got it? If you don't like anything I'm doing, tell me. And I'll find another way to please you."

"Hmmm, I like the sound of that," Sabrina said, reaching out and pulling his head down toward her. "Why don't you begin right now?"

"I would love to," Malcolm replied, his arms encircling her waist and gathering her firmly to him. It wasn't long before they were making love again until the wee hours of the morning.

Malcolm awoke first and peered down to watch Sabrina sleeping peacefully. Last night had been everything he'd dreamed it might be. Their coupling had been hot and passionate and extremely pleasurable. Sabrina had given herself to him completely without any qualms. He'd been amazed at her tenacity and aggressive behavior, but he'd loved every minute of it. He only hoped that she felt the same way in the morning light.

He glanced down at Sabrina, who was slowly beginning to awaken and become aware of her surroundings. He watched her do a double take, however, when she glanced at her watch. A look of horror crossed her face when she realized the time. When she tried to get up, Malcolm halted her with his arm. He wanted them to stay in bed all day.

Sabrina, on the other hand, was beside herself. She hadn't meant to stay out all night. What must her parents think? It was most certainly not that she'd just had the best sex of her life!

Sabrina spoke. "Malcolm, I've gotta go," she said, pushing his arm away. She threw back the covers and began gathering her clothes and underwear scattered across the floor. She couldn't believe she'd slept in Malcolm's bed all night long. She'd intended to get up and leave, but their activities had exhausted her.

"Can't you stay for just a little while longer?" Malcolm asked, following her lead and jumping off the bed. Naked, he was unashamed to walk over to where she stood and gather her in his arms. "There's a lot more I have in store for you," he said, lightly nipping at her neck. His lips traveled upwards and found their way to her lips, crushing them beneath his.

"Hmmm," Sabrina moaned, but pulled away and slipped on her underwear. "As much as I would love to stay…"

"I know. You have to get home."

"Yes. Jasmine's probably wondering where I am, while I'm sure my parents are worried sick."

"I guess I was kind of selfish keeping you all to myself all night," he replied, watching her slide on her camisole and zip up her skirt.

When she was fully clothed, she rushed over and planted a searing kiss on Malcolm's inviting lips. "You were. But make no mistake, I wanted to be here," Sabrina responded, before rushing out the door. "Call me later," she tossed over her shoulder.

Chapter 15

Sabrina made it home in twenty minutes, but found the house thankfully empty. She hadn't wanted to face the disapproving looks at her scandalous behavior. She knew a lecture would be forthcoming from her mother about the example she was setting for Jasmine.

And truly, Sabrina knew all that, but she'd done something completely for herself and it had felt good. Being with Malcolm last night had been incredible and oh so pleasurable and no one was going to make her feel ashamed of that, not even her mother. Creeping up the stairs, Sabrina entered her bedroom and stripped down to her skivvies. She was almost to the bathroom when she heard the front door closing. Rushing into the bathroom, she turned on the taps and got under the pulsating water. She would hear the lecture after a long, hot shower.

Fifteen minutes later, she emerged in her robe feeling energized and ready for her day. It was surprising what a night of good sex could do for you. Feeling more alive and full of energy than she had in years, she headed to her room and was looking for an outfit in the closet when she heard a knock on the door.

"Mom, you're home," Jasmine cried, coming in and throwing herself into Sabrina's arms. Her behavior was a surprise considering she'd been Jasmine's least favorite person of late. "Where were you?" she asked. "We thought something terrible had happened to you."

"I'm sorry, sweetheart. Mommy stayed over at a friend's," Sabrina replied, returning her hug with a firm squeeze. "I didn't mean to make you worry, pumpkin."

"I'm just happy you're home," Jasmine replied.

"So am I, Jazzy. So am I." Sabrina returned to the closet and found what she was looking for in some pale peach trousers and short-sleeve beaded top. When she turned around, her mother was staring at her reproachfully from the doorway.

"Hey, Mom." Sabrina came forward and kissed her mother's cheek. "I'm sorry I made you worry," she whispered in her ear.

Beverly didn't answer, instead she motioned to her granddaughter. "Jazzy, if you still want to help me bake the cookies for Sunday school, I'm getting started now."

"I sure do, Grandma," Jasmine said, running toward her.

"And you—" her mother pointed "—I'll have a word with downstairs once you're dressed." Beverly closed Sabrina's door behind her.

Sabrina sucked in a deep breath. She was in for it now.

When she finally made it downstairs, her mother was waiting for her in the living room and wasted no time scolding her. She thought Sabrina's behavior was highly inappropriate.

"I'm a grown woman, Momma," Sabrina replied. "I don't need your permission to spend the night over at a man's house."

"No, you don't," her mother said. "But you do need to inform me if you're going to stay out all night. You and your daughter are living here, after all. How did you know your father and I didn't have plans for Friday night?" her mother queried.

Sabrina hadn't thought about that. She'd just assumed her mother would always be there. "And for that I apologize. I truly didn't think about that." All she'd been focusing on last night was Malcolm.

"As you said, you're grown, so I'm not going to lecture you, but a phone call letting me know when you'll be home and wishing your daughter a good night is not too much to ask."

"I agree," Sabrina said. "And if I promise to call

next time, can we end this discussion? It's really uncomfortable talking to one's mother about your sex life."

"I couldn't agree more," her mother replied.

"So you and the hot doctor finally did the do," Monique smiled knowingly as she wiped and shined the counters at the diner the day after Malcolm and Sabrina had slept together. Of course, she'd seen their attraction coming from a mile away, but the two of them had been a little slow on the pickup. "You go, girl." Monique extended a hand for Sabrina to slap. Leaning across the counter, Sabrina gladly obliged.

"It all happened so fast." Sabrina shook her head as she sat back down.

Monique smiled. "Do you need me to tell you about the birds and bees? 'Cause I think you already know."

"You don't understand, Monique. One minute I'm there discussing his past and our burgeoning feelings and the next I'm up against a wall in a passionate embrace."

"Sounds good to me," Monique laughed. "Where can I sign up?"

Sabrina giggled. "I'm sorry to tell ya, but he's taken."

"Good for you because whatever he did sure got you glowing," Monique said.

Sabrina grabbed a nearby steel napkin holder and peered at her image. Monique was right. She was glowing like a neon light.

"I'll be right back." Monique stepped away to the pantry and returned several minutes later carrying large packages of napkins and two tubs of ketchup and mustard.

"Let me help you with that," Sabrina said, jumping off her stool and rushing to her aid.

"Thanks," Monique replied, out of breath. "So what's next?"

"What do you mean?" Sabrina asked, wide-eyed.

"Now that you've been intimate, does this mean that you're a couple?" Monique inquired as she went around the diner and collected empty napkin holders.

Sabrina assisted by picking up the condiment bottles. "Hmmm, I don't know," she replied, taking the bottles to the counter and pulling a container toward her. "I guess we haven't had the chance to discuss it yet." She also hadn't had the chance to tell Malcolm that Tre would be here any day now for a visit with Jasmine. Sabrina still hadn't decided how she was going to deal with that.

"Then don't rush it. Sounds to me like you and Dr. Strangelove are off to a good start." Monique laughed aloud. She took a large handful of napkins and placed them in an empty holder. "If I were you, I'd enjoy him."

Sabrina smiled knowingly. "Oh, I intend to do just that."

But first, Sabrina and Malcolm had to go rollerblading wih Jasmine. She hadn't forgotten and had kept bugging her until Sabrina finally set a date with Malcolm.

Sabrina was equally excited as she and Jasmine waited for Malcolm in Forsyth Park to go rollerblading. Her mind kept wandering to her and Malcolm in bed; she hadn't been able to think of anything else. She'd been so resistant at first to a relationship and now everything had changed. The dichotomy unnerved her.

"This is going to be so much fun," Jasmine said, excitedly tying on her rollerblades.

Sabrina smiled. Malcolm was exactly what they both needed. He'd shown them such kindness. It had been a long time since a man had shown Sabrina that emotion. "Here, put these on." Sabrina handed Jasmine a bicycle helmet, knee and elbow pads and wrist guards. The Rollerblade instructor had advised her that injuries were caused by people not wearing the proper protection.

Sabrina and Jasmine were suiting up when Malcolm arrived five minutes later. Devastatingly handsome in blue jeans and a polo shirt that fit his perfectly toned body like a glove, Sabrina warmed almost immediately.

"Are you ready for some fun in the summertime?" Sabrina asked, smiling up at him as she put on her knee pads over her jeans.

Malcolm laughed. "Sure," he replied, bending down and capturing her lips with his before sitting beside her. "Though I must admit I'm a little nervous at the prospect."

"I understand," Sabrina said, quivering at his tender kiss. "When I promised Jasmine we'd do this, I forgot how involved it was. There's even an instructor here hired by the park district who'll run through the basics."

"Good," Malcolm replied. "Because I'm sure I'm going to need it." He watched Jasmine zoom around up the sidewalk toward him.

"Are you two a couple now?" Jasmine queried aloud. "Because you're doing an awful lot of kissing and hugging. Just like my mom and dad used to."

"Jasmine!" Sabrina replied, embarrassed for herself, as well as Malcolm. Jasmine was so precocious. Sometimes she wanted to wring the living daylights out of her.

"We are indeed," Malcolm answered. "Do you have a problem with that, Ms. Jazzy?"

"Nope, I like you," she said matter-of-factly, and she held out her hand. "C'mon Dr. Malcolm, I'll take you to get your gear." Jasmine inclined her head in the direction of the Rollerblade hut.

Sabrina and Malcolm were relieved that Jasmine did not have a problem with their relationship because they both had been somewhat concerned.

"Lead the way." Malcolm walked behind Jasmine as she skated ahead of him. He turned around and gave Sabrina a seductive wink. When they reached the hut, the instructor advised Malcolm of the necessary equipment and helped him select the proper size skates. Malcolm handed him a twenty.

"Don't worry," the young man said, walking beside him. "I'll walk you and Ms. Parker through the whole thing. It's a breeze. You'll catch on in no time."

"From your lips to God's ears," Sabrina said as Malcolm sat down next to her to put on his gear.

"If you're ready, we can begin your lesson," the young blond man replied after Malcolm laced up his skates.

"Yes, we're all set," Malcolm replied, attempting to rise from the park bench. Instead of balancing himself Malcolm stumbled. He hated being so inept.

"Yes, we are," Jasmine said, excitedly gliding over to them.

"Here, let me help you," the instructor said, assisting Malcolm up from the bench. "Rollerblading is all about balance, but I'll show you some safety measures like braking to help you out. Let's get started."

An hour later, Malcolm was happy to safely make it back to the bench. He'd nearly broken his arm half a dozen times. Sabrina had skated circles around him. His mishaps had taken up the entire hour and boy did his bottom feel it. Even though he'd worn jeans, he was sure to be black and blue in the morning.

Sabrina and Jasmine pulled up the rear behind him and sat down next to Malcolm to remove their gear.

"So, how'd you like it?" Jasmine inquired, grinning mischievously as she removed her skates.

Malcolm frowned. Jasmine and Sabrina had to have seen him fall unceremoniously on his behind. It was embarrassing that he hadn't been able to master rollerblading. It disarmed him. Usually he was good at everything. "It was great, Ms. Jazzy," Malcolm replied, attempting a half smile. Jasmine chuckled as she walked away to return her skates.

Sabrina glanced over at him and found no malice in his smile or tone. "Don't worry." She patted his knee. "You made a gallant effort."

"C'mon, I was terrible." He wasn't too proud to admit the truth. He stunk!

"Aw, you weren't that bad," Sabrina lied. She knew how fragile the male ego was. "You just need a little bit of practice."

"You didn't need any," Malcolm stated derisively.

"That's because I went a couple of times with Tre and Jasmine, so naturally it came back to me. I was just like you the first time I tried rollerblading, but it got better and eventually I wasn't half bad. Eventually, I left the activity to the two of them. You know, father-daughter time. But now that Tre's not here, I'm all Jasmine has so…"

"So what are we going to do now?" Jasmine asked once she returned from dropping off her equipment.

"How about some ice cream?" Sabrina suggested. "I'd love something cool and Carvel makes the best. What do you think, Malcolm?"

"Ice cream would be great. Let me return these skates, first."

Once he'd returned the equipment, the three of them walked the short distance to Malcolm's car for a quick five-minute drive to Carvel.

Several folks from the community were seated outside the ice cream shop as they approached holding hands. Malcolm wanted no part of the local gossip, so he went inside first with Jasmine, while Sabrina stopped and said hello.

"So," Adriana Hunter smiled. "Are you and the handsome doctor an item now?"

"Pardon me?"

"C'mon, don't play coy, Sabrina. That man has been the cause of every woman's wet dream at the church. Don't act like you haven't noticed."

Sabrina's lips twisted in a cynical smile. Of course she had, but she'd never let these gossips know it.

"No, I hadn't realized that." Sabrina glanced inside the glass windows.

"And available," Adriana responded. "If I were you, I'd snap him up quick because if you don't someone else will." Adriana tossed her head and returned to her conversation.

As she walked inside, Sabrina was sure those biddies would be spreading gossip about her and Malcolm all over church. But why didn't that bother her? Had Malcolm become more important than she realized?

"Mom, I'm going to have Rocky Road," Jasmine said. Her eyes were wide as she stared at all the different flavors through the glass case.

"What are you going to get?" Sabrina pinched Malcolm's side.

"Yogurt," Malcolm replied unequivocally.

Sabrina smiled at Mr. Health Conscious. "That's too bad, 'cause I'm having that," she said to the clerk, pointing at the Jamoca Almond Fudge.

The clerk slid open the freezer and generously scooped their selections. Jasmine opted for an ice cream cone while Sabrina and Malcolm each asked for cups. Malcolm quickly paid for their snacks before joining them at the table.

"What do you say when you're treated, Jasmine?" Sabrina asked.

"Thank you, Dr. Malcolm." Jasmine smiled up at him.

"You're welcome." Malcolm ruffled Jasmine's ringlets.

It amazed him though that he was this taken with a child. He'd never been this kid-friendly before, but somehow this little munchkin had stolen his heart. And when she smiled back at him with those big brown eyes, Malcolm knew the feeling was mutual.

"Thanks." Sabrina gave him a knowing smile.

They both reached for a napkin at the same time, but Malcolm took it from her. "Here, let me," He dabbed at either side of her mouth.

Their eyes met, but then Sabrina caught the ladies outside openly staring at them through the glass. "I guess we'd better get going," she said, looking at her watch.

Malcolm turned and saw the direction of her gaze. He didn't care two bits about the gossips. "Stay, finish your ice cream," Malcolm replied. "Then *I'll* take you back."

After they enjoyed their ice cream, Malcolm dropped them both off at Forsyth Park.

"Thank you for a lovely afternoon," Sabrina said at her car. She stood on her tiptoes and kissed Malcolm's square jaw.

He was tempted to turn his face slightly and have her kiss land on his lips instead, but with Jasmine around, he refrained. There would be more time for them later.

"I'll see you soon," he said, curving his lips into a smile. "Bye, Jazzy."

Jazzy came from around the passenger side and Malcolm bent down to accept the hug she bestowed. "See ya soon."

Sabrina blew a kiss at him and drove away.

Chapter 16

Sabrina returned to Malcolm's the following evening for some TLC and Malcolm was only too happy to oblige. He started by devouring her lips as soon as she arrived.

"I missed you," Sabrina said, circling her arms around his neck.

"So did I," Malcolm replied. He'd been eagerly awaiting her return. She'd unleashed a passion that had been stored up inside of him for months. He was so hungry for her that he lifted her off her feet without any preamble and carried her straight to his bedroom.

He took two steps at a time, until he made it to the top floor. He barely made it to the bed before his lips crushed Sabrina's.

Her lips felt soft against his and Malcolm's emotions turned to red-hot desire instantly when Sabrina hugged him tighter. He felt her firm breasts through his thin T-shirt and it turned him on instantly.

His fingers slid their way up her shirt and he began massaging the tiny little pebbles underneath.

"Hmmm, that feels good," Sabrina moaned in his ear.

"Want some more?"

"What do you got?" Sabrina queried flirtatiously.

"This," Malcolm replied, lifting her shirt and lowering his head. Pushing her bra aside, he bent his head and tugged on one nipple, until Sabrina cried out his name. And while his mouth worshipped her breast, his hands touched and caressed her fevered flesh. She wanted to reciprocate, but couldn't, instead she closed her eyes and let the erotic rush of sensation wash over her sensitized skin. She enjoyed the path Malcolm's tongue took as it traveled the length of her and when his mouth covered her *there*, Sabrina couldn't resist moaning aloud as the most spectacular climax she'd ever had overtook her. At some point, she opened her eyes and found Malcolm staring at her.

She met his gaze and the desire she saw shook her to her very core and she wasn't alone. Sabrina was so hot and ready for him that Malcolm strained in his shorts, eager for a release. He wanted to be inside her, feeling her warm cocoon clenched around him.

Swiftly, he disposed of their clothes, slipped on a

condom and entered Sabrina. As he pumped inside her, thrusting deeper and deeper, Sabrina welcomed him, twisting her hips and drawing him in farther. She accepted him and every part of her immediately came alive. She didn't hold back any part of herself; instead, she gave herself to Malcolm mind, body and soul. She could even hear the sighs and moans of their lovemaking echo throughout the room. When Malcolm's final plunge came, it pushed them both into oblivion as waves of pleasure washed over them causing them to collapse in each other's arms.

Afterward Sabrina fell sound asleep on his chest.

Sabrina heard her cell phone ringing as she drove home after leaving Malcolm's, but she couldn't reach it, so she kept her eyes firmly planted on the road. Pulling over to the side, she opened her purse, flipping it open on the last ring.

"Hello, hello," she spoke rapidly into the phone.

"Sabrina, is that you?" Tre asked from the other end.

Sabrina exhaled. Great! Tre was the last person she wanted to speak to after such a fine evening. "Yes, Tre. What can I do for you?" she asked glumly, watching other cars pass her by from the side of the road.

"Wow, don't sound so enthusiastic," Tre said as he unpacked his suitcase, throwing items into a hotel drawer. "I just wanted to let you know that I'd arrived."

"Glad to hear it," Sabrina replied. "Jazzy will be very excited." Curiosity got the better of her though and she had to ask the question lingering in the air. "Did you come alone?"

"Of course not," Tre muttered. "Melanie *is* my girlfriend and she decided that it was high time she got to know Jazzy better, since she'll be visiting us during the summer."

"How magnanimous of her," Sabrina replied, pulling her favorite MAC lipstick out of her purse and freshening her face. After spending all afternoon with Malcolm, her lips had been kissed clean.

"Sabrina," Tre warned, "don't tell me you're still sore over Melanie and me."

"No, I'm not still sore," Sabrina imitated Tre's tone, "but I don't think now is the appropriate time to be flaunting your relationship in Jazzy's face. It's been a really difficult six months for her. And I don't want her traumatized any further."

"Traumatized?" Tre queried. "Don't you think that's a rather harsh word? I don't think that Jazzy's spending time with Melanie for a weekend will have any effect on her one way or the other."

"That's how little you know about your own daughter," Sabrina replied testily. Tre had no idea who Jasmine really was.

"You're the one who has a problem with Melanie being here and now you're making a federal case out of it." Tre was getting really annoyed with Sabrina's attitude. Melanie was in his life to stay and Sabrina was going to have to accept it.

Sabrina chuckled heartily and Tre sniffed on the

other end. "That's utterly ridiculous. I've got much better ways to spend my time than think about you and your mistress."

"My girlfriend," Tre uttered. "You and I are no longer married."

"Thank the Lord for that." Sabrina couldn't resist one final comment. "So when are you coming to pick up Jazzy?"

Tre sighed. "Well, I thought that since it was so late and it is our first night here…" His voice trailed off.

"That I wouldn't tell Jasmine you're here until tomorrow," Sabrina finished. "How typical."

Tre laughed. "Ah, you know me so well. Would that work for you?"

"I guess I have no choice. Call me tomorrow." Sabrina closed her cell before she could hear another syllable of that rat's voice. Here he was in town and still wouldn't come see his own daughter. Sabrina shook her head and dismissed all thoughts of Tre from her mind. She had someone else much better to think about.

Jasmine, on the other hand, was tickled pink when she heard Tre was in Savannah and would come by tomorrow and rushed straight to her room to select the perfect ensemble for the occasion.

"Well, it's good to see you home this evening," James Parker commented to his younger daughter. "You have been rather missing in action these days."

"Have I?" Sabrina lowered her head. "I suppose I have been," she said cutting up onions for her father's spicy chili. When she was done, Sabrina peeked her head over his shoulder. "Hmmm, that smells good. Can I have a taste?"

"Sure can." James reached inside a drawer and pulled out a small spoon for Sabrina to taste. "How is it? It's not too spicy, I hope? Your mother hates it when I make it too spicy."

Sabrina licked her lips. "No, Dad. It's perfect. You're right on the money, as always."

"Ah, you say that now," James laughed. "Wish someone had listened to me way back then. The first time I ever met Tre, I thought, he isn't the one for my baby doll."

Sabrina smiled. "Would anyone have been right for me?" she asked.

"Well, no," James chuckled. "But at least they would have been better than him."

"But I might not have had Jazzy. And no matter how much Tre hurt me in the past, I will always be grateful for that little girl upstairs."

"Amen!" James replied. "Now pass me that chili powder. I think this chili is missing something."

The following morning, when Sabrina padded downstairs in her bunny slippers to the kitchen, she found Jasmine wide awake and already dressed for the day. Wearing a yellow camisole and blue denim skirt with a belt, Jasmine looked adorable.

"Morning, Jazzy," Sabrina said, covering her mouth to stifle a yawn and walked straight toward the coffeepot. "So, you excited to see Daddy today?"

"Yes, Mom. I've missed him so much," Jasmine said.

"Is that why you're up so early?" Sabrina inquired, taking down a filter and pulling the coffee canister toward her.

"Yes, Daddy said he'd be here at nine to pick me up for breakfast."

"That early, huh?" Sabrina wiped the sleep from her eyes, pulled her robe closed and sat down at the kitchen table waiting for the coffee to percolate. Once she did, she realized she'd forgotten a cup. "Can you pull Mommy down a mug, please?"

"Sure," Jasmine answered, going to the step stool and pulling down a mug for her mother. "He said he'd take me to breakfast, just the two of us, before Melanie wakes up."

Sabrina glanced at her watch. It read nine-fifteen. "Guess he's running late, sweetie." Sabrina found the energy to move from her seat and kissed Jasmine on the head before pouring herself a strong cup of coffee. "If you want, you can use my cell and give him a call. It's in my purse in the hallway."

Jasmine raced out of the room and Sabrina heard her talking to Tre. "Dad, how could you forget? You promised me you'd be here," Sabrina heard Jasmine say. Damn that Tre! Why couldn't he keep his word? "All right, Daddy. I'll be waiting."

Jasmine returned to the kitchen with a sad face. "Is he on his way?" Sabrina asked cheerily.

Jasmine frowned. "He said to give him thirty minutes."

"Then he'll be here. You know your father. He was never an early riser." Sabrina attempted to ease the situation even though she wanted to strangle Tre with her bare hands.

When Tre arrived forty-five minutes later, Sabrina was livid. She waited until Jasmine was out of earshot, running upstairs to get her overnight bag, before telling him so.

"How dare you have Jazzy waiting here for over an hour," Sabrina snapped, confronting Tre in her robe in the hallway. It wasn't the impression she'd envisioned making the first time Tre saw her again, but hell, he'd seen much more of her than anyone else, except Malcolm.

Tre noticed the move and Sabrina followed the direction of his leering gaze to the V of her robe where the swell of her breasts was evident. Tre was a pig! Sabrina clutched her robe shut.

"It's way too early, Sabrina," Tre began.

"Don't shhh me," Sabrina hissed. "I'm not the one having my daughter waiting an hour for me."

"No, but you sure would like to make me out to be the villain. I'm not the one who moved our daughter to this godforsaken town. I got lost getting here from the riverfront."

Sabrina stared back at Tre. What a liar! He'd been

in bed with Melanie. What had she ever seen in a jerk like him? Was it the hazel eyes or the milky skin? It may have appealed to her when she was nineteen, but when she looked at him now, Tre completely turned her off.

"Is there a problem?" Tre asked.

"The problem is you, Tre," Sabrina responded. "You really have to stop taking Jasmine for granted. She's going through a tough period of adjustment since the divorce and she needs you."

"Wow." Tre stepped back. "Did I actually hear you say she needs me?" he asked.

Sabrina sucked in a deep breath. She would not let him get the better of her and descend to his level. "Listen, Tre. All I'm asking is that you stop being so selfish and think of Jasmine."

"You know, *Sabrina,* I'm sick and tired of all your warnings and your high and mighty attitude. I just got here, for Christ's sake! If you keep this up…"

"What? You'll leave. Go ahead then, Tre. Leave." Sabrina waved her hand. "It's what you do best." She was tired of trying to get through to him, but Jasmine came bounding downstairs with her overnight bag in tow.

Tre handed Jasmine the rent-a-car keys. "Go on, honey, and put your bag in the convertible. I'll be out in a moment." Tre opened the front door and allowed Jasmine to exit before closing it behind him.

When Tre whirled back around to face Sabrina, his facial expression had turned from angry to menacing. "Don't dismiss me ever again, Sabrina," he hissed. "Listen up, darling, like you, I'm quite capable of providing and caring for Jasmine and don't you ever forget it."

Turning on his heel, Tre swung open the front door and slammed it behind him.

Sabrina tightened her robe around her. The thought of Tre rearing their daughter brought chills to her stomach. And if he thought she'd ever let that happen, he was dead wrong.

Chapter 17

"I'd hoped this evening would cheer you up," Malcolm said as he and Sabrina sat down to dinner at the River Grill. He himself was in no mood for being in public, but if he continued to stay at home and brood until the blood results came back from the laboratory, he would go mad. Waiting was agony. It was like pulling a hangnail slowly. And Dinah, well, she'd left several apologetic messages for him, but he wasn't ready to hear them.

"I'm sorry, Malcolm." Sabrina forced a smile as she glanced at him over her wine goblet. Two glasses of merlot had done little to soften Sabrina's mood or the brick at the bottom of her belly at Tre's parting words. She hadn't even told Malcolm about the implication.

Tre was her problem and she would have to deal with it. "Guess I'm not much company this evening."

Malcolm bent down and brought her delicately soft hands to his lips. He brushed them ever so lightly across hers and glanced up. His eyes were riveted on her natural beauty. Whether it was her smooth honey coloring, vibrant light brown eyes or radiant smile, Malcolm was falling head over heels for Sabrina Parker. He shouldn't be surprised. Matter of fact, he probably knew the first time when he laid eyes on her and her beautiful daughter stranded on the side of the road.

"Malcolm, are you okay?" Sabrina asked, breaking into his reverie. He was wearing a rather odd expression.

"Yes, sweetheart, I'm, uh, I'm fine," Malcolm replied. When he tried to reach for his water glass, his cuff link caught a hold of the remaining contents, sending water spilling across the floor.

Sabrina jumped up to help him and was patting his lap when she heard a feline voice say, "Well, how apropos, darling. Sabrina on her hands and knees." Melanie stood behind her.

If Sabrina could have melted into a pool of water herself, she'd have been happy. Instead, she stood tall, brushed off her dress and looked up at her nemesis, who loomed over her at five feet eleven.

The evil witch was exactly the same as Sabrina remembered. Same fake weave. Same overly made-up high yellow skin. Same designer duds that Sabrina was sure Tre was paying for.

She would have said something, but Tre and Jasmine were behind her. Was that her baby all dressed up in a ruffly concoction *again!* Dear heavens, when would everyone learn that Jasmine hated girlie clothes! "Baby, what are you wearing?"

Jasmine's face went into a huge pout. "Melanie made me wear it."

"Well, I had to. The child had absolutely nothing to wear in that entire bag of clothes you sent over." Melanie grinned devilishly.

Sabrina deigned not to answer her with Jasmine in their presence. "Y'all have a pleasant evening," Sabrina said in her best imitation of a Southern drawl. "While Malcolm and I'll sit here and sop up our ham hocks and chitlins."

Melanie turned red and rushed away to their table the waiter was holding open for them, but Malcolm let out a hearty laugh.

"Ham hocks and chitlins?" Malcolm asked. "I don't think I've ever ate such a thing in my life."

"Well, it is a southern delicacy."

"If you say so," Malcolm replied.

He was fascinated as he watched the family scene playing out before him. So, this was the infamous Tre he'd heard so much about when he'd first arrived. Barely six feet, slender build. He wasn't much to speak of except for the Hugo Boss suit he wore and maybe the eyes. Women dug hazel eyes.

And the piece he brought with him, well, she was nothing more than one of those bottom-feeding women he'd encountered during his cardiologist days in Boston. She was just another viper looking for her next victim and she'd found it in gullible Tre Matthews. Did he really think he was any better than the others she'd no doubt used and abused until the next sucker came along?

He was surprised when Tre stopped along the way to finally acknowledge his presence. "Listen, you must be Malcolm, right?" Tre offered a hand that Malcolm declined to take.

At Malcolm's glower, Tre pulled it away quickly. "Jasmine's told me a lot about you, but listen up, my man." Tre put a hand on Malcolm's shoulder and bent down to whisper in his ear. "Jasmine has a father and she has no need for a new one. Got it?" Slapping Malcolm's shoulder, Tre walked away.

"Tre," Sabrina whispered, attempting to avoid a scene, but apparently several patrons were already watching their encounter. And one of them just so happened to be her mother's friend Regina from the women's group sitting with her husband. No doubt this would get back to her parents. Since she'd arrived, she'd been nothing but an embarrassment to them, so she stopped mid-sentence.

Once Tre was finally seated at his table, Malcolm let out a swear word under his breath. "I could...I could..." The thought of that slimy bastard touching his Sabrina... There. There it was again. His Sabrina.

But that was indeed how he felt. She was the only woman he wanted to be with, spend time with. The only woman he wanted to talk to, make love to. His heart welled up with joy at the thought. How did a cold, hard-nosed doctor like him ever fall in love with such a warm, kind, sensitive woman like Sabrina?

It couldn't be luck. It had to be fate. They'd been destined to meet.

"Malcolm." Sabrina waved her hand back and forth in front of his face. "Are you with me?"

"Yes, I am most definitely with you," Malcolm said.

Sabrina heard a flirty giggle, when she turned around she caught Melanie smiling as she leaned over and rubbed her hand suggestively across Tre's arm. And to make matters worse, Sabrina saw Melanie fixing Jasmine's hair and clothes. She gave Melanie a harsh glare before turning back to Malcolm.

"We have to go," Sabrina said, suddenly standing up. "I can't stand watching that witch carry on with my daughter *and* my ex-husband."

"You're not jealous seeing Melanie with Tre, are you?" Malcolm wondered, because Sabrina was acting a little like the jilted lover.

Sabrina glanced over at Tre and the mealy-mouthed Melanie and laughed. "Of course not. That's utterly ridiculous. Melanie can have his sorry behind."

"Then why leave?" Malcolm asked. "We are not going to let that bastard run us off. No, I don't think so. Sit down." Malcolm grabbed Sabrina's forearm and helped her back in her seat. "Listen up, today we're not running. So let's order dessert," he ordered.

Malcolm yelled out to the waiter passing by. "Waiter!"

Sabrina burst into a fit of giggles at Malcolm's caveman routine. "Okay, okay," she said, nearly in tears. "We'll stay."

When the waiter arrived and asked what they wanted, they both said in unison, "Crème brûlée."

"You're right," Tre admitted to Sabrina the following day when he came to pick up a change of clothes for Jasmine.

"About?" Sabrina asked, closing the door behind him.

"I think I'm going to stay another day or so. Jasmine's been very clingy and I'd like to spend some more time with her."

"Excellent idea," Sabrina said. "Now where is she?" Sabrina looked over his shoulder.

"I left her at the hotel with Melanie, so you and I can talk freely." Tre swung his arm open, indicating Sabrina should walk ahead of him into the living room. Sabrina noted the look of disdain on Tre's face at her mother's outdated furniture. Sure, it was no Ethan Allen, but it was well-kept.

Sabrina sat down. "What would you like to talk about, Tre?"

"You're moving back to Baltimore," Tre said with no preamble.

Sabrina chuckled at his wannabe tough routine. "That's not going to happen, Tre."

"It's in Jasmine's best interest to have both her parents in her life, don't you agree?" Tre questioned.

"Which is why you should take full advantage of your summer visit together," Sabrina countered.

"Clearly, you can see that's not enough," Tre stood up, annoyed that the conversation was not going his way. What was with this new, defiant woman sitting across from him? He used to be able to convince Sabrina to do anything he wanted. What had changed?

Sabrina glared back at him. She didn't appreciate Tre trying to change the terms of their custody arrangement. "What I can see is that she's going through a period. First the divorce and now the move. She needs time to heal and then she'll be just fine."

Tre shook his head. "I disagree, what she needs is her father." He handed Sabrina an envelope.

Fear knotted in the pit of her stomach. She prayed this wasn't what she thought it was. "What is this, Tre?" Sabrina queried.

"I think you have some idea." Tre's eyes turned cold as he spoke. Suddenly, they weren't the warm hazel eyes of days past.

"Why don't you just say it?" Sabrina replied.

"Fine," Tre muttered. His expression stilled and grew serious. "I'm suing you for sole custody."

Hearing those words caused all the air in Sabrina's lungs to evaporate and she thought she would nearly faint. She grasped at a water pitcher on the table, poured herself a cup, gulping it down quickly. Several moments passed with the house as quiet as a mouse. It didn't take long for Sabrina to find her voice and her courage. She was not some naive nineteen-year-old that Tre could walk over. She was a grown woman.

"I am willing," Tre began, "to amend the petition to joint custody, if you'll agree to move back to Baltimore." Tre's tone was chilly and edged with steel.

"So now you're resorting to blackmail?" Sabrina's eyes widened in amazement. "How dare you come into *my* parents' home and threaten me? Have you no shame, Tre Matthews?"

"Not when it comes to my daughter," Tre replied, fingering her family photos on the fireplace mantel. "You should know me better than that."

Sabrina shook her head. "You'd do anything to have your way, wouldn't you? Even if means uprooting Jasmine again right when she's beginning to adjust and make new friends, but you'd take her away from all of that, just to spite me. You're despicable. You really are."

"New friends like your Dr. Malcolm?" Tre inquired in a nasty tone.

"What's it to you?"

Tre let out a long, audible laugh. "Nothing at all," he responded, shrugging his less-than-buff shoulders. He was nothing like Malcolm, thought Sabrina. In fact, he was the antithesis of him. "But for you it might be. Are you willing to give up your daughter to keep him? Move back to Baltimore and all will be well. Or stay here and face the consequences."

Sabrina rolled her eyes and prayed for the strength not to put a hurting on Tre. "You'd really put Jasmine through a court battle? Because I'm here to tell you that's what I'll take. I will fight you tooth and nail."

"Whatever it takes, Sabrina. I mean, look at this place." Tre swung his arm around her parents' living room. "Can you honestly tell me that this dump surpasses what I could provide Jasmine?"

"First of all, don't call my home, the home I was raised in, a dump. Second, this stunt proves what I already knew when I left Baltimore."

"And that is?"

"That you're not qualified to raise my child," Sabrina answered unequivocally, stiffening her back and standing up straight. "So, take your strong-arm tactics and get the hell out of my house." Sabrina pointed to the door. "And if you ever make another threat against me, you'll see just how dangerous I can be."

"Like you have any power," Tre replied.

"Don't push me, Tre, my brother is sheriff and he'd like nothing better than to throw your sorry butt in jail."

At the fury etched across her face, Tre moved quickly toward the door, but not before leaving one parting comment. "You'll regret this," he said, closing the door behind him.

How wrong he was. What Sabrina regretted most

was all the time she'd spent grieving over him. Tre simply wasn't worth it.

"The results are in," Dinah said on the other end of the line. There was an awkward silence after she spoke. She hated that this was the first time they'd spoken since she'd accused him of causing Michael's death, but she hadn't known what to do. What could she ever say that would make up for it? Malcolm was stalwart. He understood these matters. In time, he would get over the affront and let her back in his life.

The results of the paternity test gave her hope and reason to pick up the phone. This was a call he would assuredly take.

Malcolm's breath caught in his chest. This was the call he'd been waiting for nearly two weeks, but now that it was here, all he felt was fear. If it were true, it would mean that God had granted them a miracle, but if it wasn't true, it would be a devastating blow. It would mean that Michael was truly gone forever. It would be like losing him all over again.

"Malcolm, are you still there?" Dinah asked.

"Yes, I am," he said, finding his voice. "So, what were the laboratory's findings?"

Dinah didn't mistake the bitterness in his voice, but she continued, "Malcolm, are you really prepared to hear this?"

"I don't have much choice now, do I? If this

woman is who she claims she is, then as executor of Michael's will, some changes will have to be made," Malcolm answered.

"Okay, I'll tell you," Dinah said. "The test came back positive, Malcolm. With an accuracy of ninety-nine percent, Michael fathered a son."

"Dear God." Malcolm dropped the phone. All the air in his lungs rushed out and he fell to the floor.

When Dinah didn't hear him on the other end, she yelled into the phone. Her voice rose several octaves. "Malcolm, Malcolm. Please pick up. Malcolm!"

After a long pause, Dinah's voice finally broke through Malcolm's haze. Reaching across the hardwood floor of his living room, he found the cell phone and put it to his ear. "I'm here, okay. You can stop yelling."

"Thank God. Are you all right? Did you faint?" Dinah fired questions at him.

"I'm fine."

"I know this must come as quite a shock."

"You have no idea," Malcolm scratched his head. "And they're sure?"

"The test was done three times for verification."

"Then it's true." Malcolm's voice faded. "My brother has a son. I have a nephew." The words seemed strange on his tongue. "What is his name, Mom?"

Dinah paused and her heart filled with joy. She couldn't remember the last time he'd called her *Mom*. "His name is Jayden Thomas Winters."

"Winters?"

"Yes, Tasha gave him his father's last name when he was born." Dinah had seen her grandson and he was truly the most beautiful thing she'd ever seen in her whole entire life. Michael might be gone, but a part of him would live on in Jayden. She'd apologized immediately to Tasha for her disbelief, but she'd had to be sure. Tasha had understood and vowed that Dinah would always be a big part of Jayden's life because that's what Michael would have wanted.

"How old is he?"

"Fourteen months," Dinah replied. And what a beauty he was! Tasha had been kind enough to fly up to Boston and bring Jayden for a visit to meet his paternal grandmother. He looked exactly like Michael did at that age. A mop of curly hair and beautiful skin the color of mocha. Dinah was positive she was looking at another heartbreaker.

Malcolm paused. Could Michael have known he'd had a son before he died? If so, why hadn't he told him, his twin, of all people?

"I'm not sure if he knew," Dinah said, reading Malcolm's thoughts, "and I don't want to know. What difference would it make now, but to sully this moment? Do you know how lucky we are, Malcolm? We've been given another chance." Dinah's voice broke and Malcolm could hear her crying in the background.

"You're right," Malcolm acknowledged. "All that matters now is Jayden and what's best for him." His mind started working a mile a minute. He would have to call Michael's attorney and have him set up a trust in Jayden's name immediately. No matter what, Malcolm would always be sure to take care of his brother's son.

"I guess the next question is, where is she?" he asked.

"In South Carolina," Dinah said.

"What?" Malcolm wondered aloud. "You mean she's been here underneath my nose the entire time?"

"Afraid so," Dinah answered.

"C'mon, haven't you wondered why Michael chose Savannah of all places as his favorite? It's why you moved there, to feel closer to him," Dinah said.

"I believe she lives in Hilton Head, which is about thirty-five miles north of Savannah, but close enough to drive."

"You have got to be joking," Malcolm laughed derisively, leaning back against the wall. All this time, his nephew had been right under his nose and he hadn't even known it. "But why did she wait so long to come forward?"

"Fear, plain and simple," Dinah replied. "She thought we might try and take Jayden from her and she doesn't make very much. She thought we'd fight her for custody."

"It doesn't matter how much money she makes. As long as she loves and provides for him, we'd never fight her. And as executor of Michael's will, I'll make sure she never has to worry about it."

"We know that, but she doesn't. Now it's up to you to let her know that she has nothing to fear from us."

"You're right," Malcolm replied. But the thought of looking into Jayden's eyes and seeing his twin scared the living daylights out of him. "It's just…"

"Don't delay, Malcolm. You'll never know how much joy he could bring to your life," Dinah said. "Because he's already brought so much to mine."

"Oh, Mom," Malcolm said. It was the first time his tone changed. Dinah was thrilled to have him call her mom again.

"Let me finish," she interrupted. "You're right there, Malcolm. You can become a huge influence in his life and tell him what a great person his father truly was. Promise you'll go see him. And soon."

"I will, Mom. I promise I will," Malcolm replied. He'd come full circle. His twin had left behind a son and Malcolm was now an uncle. It was funny how life surprised you when you least expected it.

He'd come to Savannah to escape the pain, only to discover that he'd left a precious gift behind. Then, he'd met Sabrina. A beautiful, smart, funny, sexy, vibrant woman who was everything he'd been looking for his entire life. After losing Michael, he'd said he could never love anyone or anything that much ever again.

He'd been wrong. Sabrina had changed all that. She'd changed him and opened up his heart, allowing the love to come pouring in. Glancing upward, Malcolm thanked God for his blessings.

Chapter 18

The smell of fresh coffee and frying bacon wafted through the air when Sabrina emerged the next morning.

Her tummy instantly did flip-flops. A solid breakfast would suit her just fine. She was starved, having not eaten the night before. It was hard to have much of an appetite when the whole world was falling apart.

Shock registered on her face when she found Felicia in the kitchen wearing an apron. She turned around from the stove when she heard Sabrina's footsteps.

"Good, you're finally up," she said, stirring her pot of grits.

Stunned, Sabrina regarded Felicia strangely as

she took a seat at the kitchen table. "Why are you here?" Sabrina asked.

"Mom told me about the threats and I thought you might need a hearty breakfast for the fight ahead," Felicia said, walking to the coffeepot and filling a cup on the counter. She handed it to a stunned Sabrina. "'Cause fight you shall," Felicia said, pulling a chair out and getting directly in Sabrina's face. "The Parkers are not quitters. We do not run. We do not hide. We do not let some outsider come and intimidate us."

Sabrina couldn't believe the fervor with which Felicia spoke. What had gotten into her?

"I have a friend from high school. She's a big-time family lawyer now. I've already spoken with her this morning. I only gave her a few facts, but she's willing to take your case."

Sabrina's eyes welled up with tears. "You did that for me? Why?"

"Of course I did," Felicia said, getting up and walking away to check on her stove. "I'm proud of you, Sabrina. I've seen how hard you've worked the last few months and you've been amazing."

Felicia shook her head at Sabrina's misty eyes. She hated when Sabrina got all teary eyed. Even when she was a kid, it had been the hardest thing for Felicia to bear. It was why she and Alton had always taken the brunt of the punishments even if they'd all done wrong. Sabrina was the baby of the family and they had always looked out for her.

"Unlike the divorce, you're not alone," Felicia said with her back turned. "You're home now and your family supports you."

Sabrina couldn't believe her ears. Pushing her chair back, she rose and walked up behind Felicia. "Thank you, sis." Sabrina hugged Felicia tight for several moments before Felicia pulled away.

"Enough of that," Felicia said, averting her eyes from Sabrina and returning her focus to breakfast. "I don't do mushy, okay?" Felicia finished up the bacon and grits and prepared some eggs and toast to go along with them. When she was done, she brought the platters to the table.

"Now dig in," she said, pushing the food towards Sabrina. "I've got to go."

"Aren't you going to stay and have breakfast with me?" Sabrina asked, giving Felicia a puppy-dog look.

"Sorry, kid, that stopped working when I was nine. Listen, I've got to get back to the B and B, but we'll talk later." Felicia waved and headed out the door. "Call Mom and Dad down, too, I made enough for them." Seconds later, she was out the back door.

Had she become delusional? Had her sister really made breakfast for her? Wonders never ceased.

"Can I get you anything else, Malcolm?" Monique asked the next morning when he sat at the diner counter. He'd been nursing that one cup of coffee for quite some time. Not to mention it looked as if he'd slept in those clothes he was wearing. Monique couldn't recall a time when she'd seen the doctor unkempt and unshaven. Well, except for that one time at Mimi's.

Malcolm looked down at the remaining contents. "A refill would be nice." Unable to reach Sabrina either at home or on her cell, he'd come to the diner to get away from his house, give himself some breathing room and a chance to think. For some reason, he'd felt isolated and needed some company even if they were strangers.

"I think I can handle that," Monique said, going to the warmer and pulling off the pot of decaf. She returned and filled his mug and the mugs of several other patrons sitting at the counter.

Monique took a check from a customer and rung him up at the register. "Here's your change. Come again." She handed the customer a five-dollar bill and some coins. When she was finished she walked back and stood in front of Malcolm, but he didn't seem to see her; his expression was far away.

"Why do I have the feeling though that Sabrina isn't the only thing on your mind?"

Malcolm glanced in Monique's direction. "You would be correct. I received some very shocking news last night and I'm trying to process it."

"Can I help?"

"No, this next step requires action on my part, except I'm kind of afraid to take it," Malcolm replied. Taking risks had always been his twin's department, not his. He'd always been much more cautious. But why was he afraid of meeting a child? His brother's child? He couldn't understand it.

"Well, I for one have always been the kind to jump right in if you know what I'm saying."

Malcolm grinned from ear to ear. "Now why doesn't that surprise me, Monique?"

"So, Sabrina's told you a story or two about me, uh?" Monique said. She glanced over at the door when the bell chimed indicating another patron. Monique smiled Malcolm's way. "Believe every word, because it's probably true."

As Monique walked away, Malcolm wondered where Sabrina was. He was eager to share with her his news about Michael and Jayden and wrap himself in the comfort of her arms. He hoped everything was okay.

"Oh baby, I am so happy to hear from you," Sabrina said once she heard Jasmine's high-pitched voice on the other end. "Have you been having fun with your father?" Sabrina asked. No matter how angry she was with Tre, she must not let Jasmine see it. That was the sign of a good parent.

"Yes, Dad and I went to the zoo and to the aquarium. Then we went shopping for new sneakers," Jasmine replied, less than enthusiastically.

"That's good 'cause those Nikes were on their way out," Sabrina said, but she wondered why Jasmine didn't sound excited. "Is something wrong, Jazzy?"

"Mom, I'm ready to come home."

Sabrina breathed a sigh of relief. Thank God nothing was wrong. On the other hand, she was secretly thrilled that Jasmine wanted to be with her and not Tre. "Do you really?" Sabrina asked.

"Yes, I love spending time with Daddy, but I hate Melanie. Why did she have to come? Why can't she just go away and leave us alone?"

Sabrina paused for a moment before answering. "*Hate* is such a strong word, Jazzy. I know you dislike Melanie, but your time with her is limited. Focus on the positive, like spending time with your father."

"I know, Mom, but she's just so miserable. She complains about everything. She's rude to the hotel staff. She's just plain mean."

Sabrina smiled. From the mouths of babes! That was exactly how she felt about her ex's choice of companion. "Some people are mean to others because they are unhappy themselves, Jasmine. But I've taught you better than that. You just always remember to be kind and courteous."

"I will, Mom," Jasmine promised.

"Where's your father now?"

Jasmine glanced at the master-bedroom door of the suite, which had remained closed all morning. "They haven't made it out of bed yet and the door is locked."

"Well, go ahead and call room service and order yourself up some breakfast. If your father has any problem with that, tell him I told you to do it."

"Okay, Mom. I'll see you soon. And I promise I'll

take care of Melanie," Jasmine replied. Seconds later, Sabrina heard a dial tone. What had Jasmine meant when she'd said she would take care of Melanie? What was her daughter up to?

Chapter 19

"I'm glad we finally have some time to ourselves," Malcolm said, when he finally found Sabrina. She'd finally picked up her voice mail and he stopped by to pick her up on the way to his place. He'd been waiting for the appropriate time to bring up the test results, but he hadn't had the opportunity. Now, they finally had the chance.

"I'm so sorry, Malcolm." Sabrina turned to face him. "Tre's visit riled me up."

"It's okay," Malcolm replied. "I know that Tre has a way of pushing your buttons. So what has he done now?"

Sabrina didn't want to ruin their evening with bad news. "Let's not talk about Tre," she replied, placing

Malcolm's hand in hers. She had a funny feeling that fate would take care of Tre for her or maybe a certain mischievous daughter? "Let's focus on us instead. Or more importantly: you. Please accept my sincere apology for neglecting you."

"No apologies are needed," Malcolm replied, bringing her hand to his lips. "But I would like to talk to you about something important once we get to my place."

She was glad Jasmine had one more night with Tre because it would give them an entire evening together. And this time, she'd told her mother not to expect her until tomorrow.

When they arrived at Malcolm's house, he pulled into the carport and jumped out to open the passenger door.

Once inside, Malcolm flicked on a lamp nearby, flooding the room with light. Sabrina was surprised to find the living room had been fully furnished. When did he have the time?

"Where did you get all this?" she asked.

"Ethan Allen."

"It's lovely," Sabrina said, eyeing the four-piece living room set, area rug and tapestries. It was very masculine.

While Sabrina made herself comfortable, Malcolm started making a fire. The evening had turned chilly and it was the perfect night for one.

"Do you have any wine?"

"A bottle is in the fridge."

"Excellent." Sabrina removed her pumps and suit jacket and went to the kitchen to find the essentials for a romantic evening. A bottle of wine, wineglasses, candles and a lighter.

Once she'd arranged them, she sat down on the couch and watched Malcolm stoke the fire. Once it was in full swing, Malcolm joined her, snuggling between her thighs on the sofa.

"So," Sabrina asked, rubbing his head, "what did you want to talk to me about?"

Suddenly, Malcolm became unusually quiet, which made Sabrina know whatever he had to tell her was pretty serious.

It took several moments, before he finally spoke. "I left something out about Dinah's visit," Malcolm said, turning around to face her.

"What was it? And why didn't you tell me?"

"Because I wasn't sure of the outcome. Now I am."

"That's no excuse, especially when it's important, but I'll forgive you this once." Sabrina couldn't believe he hadn't confided in her. Was she really that self-involved? Thanks to Tre, she had been.

"You'll hardly believe it when I tell you," Malcolm said, shaking his head. "Hell, when Dinah first told me I was flabbergasted."

His mysteriousness had Sabrina's mind wandering all over the place. What could it possibly be?

"A woman came forward claiming that she conceived Michael's son."

Shock registered over Sabrina's face. "What?

How can this be? I don't understand. Why did she wait nearly a year after his death to come forward with this news?"

"Fear, plain and simple. She thought Dinah or I might sue her for custody. And maybe she might have been right. At the time, neither Dinah nor I was in the best shape emotionally." Malcolm went on. "Needless to say, Dinah did not believe her and requested a court-ordered paternity test."

"And?" Sabrina eyes were wide. She was dying from curiosity. "What were the results?" If the woman was honestly telling the truth, it could change Malcolm's life forever.

"I have a nephew," Malcolm blurted out.

"Ohmigod," Sabrina cried, covering her mouth with her hand. "Are they certain?"

"Yes. The test was ninety-nine percent accurate," Malcolm answered.

"That's wonderful. You and Dinah must be thrilled at the news." Sabrina leaned over and gave Malcolm a big bear hug.

"It does come as quite a shock," Malcolm said when they separated.

"Have you seen him yet? What's his name?" Sabrina fired a million questions at him.

"Jayden Thomas Winters. And no, not yet."

"And why haven't you?" Sabrina inquired with her hands on her hips.

Malcolm rose from the sofa and went to the fireplace. He moved the wood strategically around with the poker. "To be quite honest, I don't know. I guess I've been afraid, which is why I was hoping you might join me when I go."

"You want me to be there the first time you meet Michael's son?" Sabrina was overwhelmed. That he was willing to share such a momentous occasion like this with her showed her how deeply he cared for her.

Could there be more? Was Malcolm feeling the way she was? Her heart swelled with a feeling she had thought was long since dead. Could it be love? She'd been feeling that she was falling in love with the brilliant doctor for some time, but she had yet to share her feelings with him or anyone. Was now the right time? They both had so much going on in their lives. He had a new nephew and she had a potential custody battle looming. Her head told her maybe it was better to wait and err on the side of caution, but her heart said go for it and reveal to him just how much she was in love with him.

She hadn't realized it until this very moment, when he'd opened up to her and laid his heart completely bare that she was truly, madly, deeply, head-over-heels in love with Dr. Malcolm Winters. How could this have happened? She'd thought she'd been protecting her heart so well and then bam! Love snuck in.

"Absolutely," Malcolm replied as if there were no doubt in his mind. Was he that sure of her? Obviously, he believed in her more than she believed in herself.

"Then my answer is yes." Sabrina walked toward him and grabbed his large masculine hands in hers. "Of course, I'll go with you."

"It's a date then." Malcolm grinned. "I'll make the arrangements and call Tasha, Jayden's mother, and set up a time."

"Excellent." Sabrina smiled.

Malcolm caressed her cheek. He had truly found the woman for him and he wanted to shout it from the rooftops. He wanted to tell her that his love for her had deepened with each passing day before he lost his nerve. "Sabrina," Malcolm began. "I love you."

Sabrina's eyes filled with tears at hearing Malcolm say those three little words.

"I don't know when or where or how it happened, but I do. And I don't expect you to say it back, at least not right away. I know you've been through a great ordeal, but in time I was hoping that you would come to feel the same way as I do."

Sabrina stopped him from speaking with the tip of her index finger. "Can I say something, too?" she asked.

Malcolm nodded.

"When I left Baltimore, I was a broken, tattered woman who'd vowed to never love anyone ever again. 'Cause I didn't want to feel that way…" Sabrina's voice cracked. "To feel that kind of hurt and pain ever again."

As Malcolm stared down at her, he realized that he saw the same emotion he felt and it filled him with such joy that he thought he would burst at the seams. "And now?" Malcolm asked.

"And no matter how hard I tried to deny it," Sabrina whispered, "to resist you. I couldn't. I had fallen for you." Sabrina caressed his face. "Malcolm, I love you with all my heart. I love you more than I thought possible."

Tears fell from Malcolm's eyes at hearing Sabrina's heartfelt declaration of love. "I feel the same way," he murmured. "I love you so much. I don't know what I would do without you."

"Oh God, Malcolm, stop. Do you know how happy you've made me?"

He kissed her face over and over. "No more than you've done for me. You've changed my life, Sabrina." She wiped away the tears streaming down his face with the back of her hand. "I was a walking dead man before you and Jazzy came into my life. The guilt and grief over the loss of my brother consumed me. But once I met you and opened up my heart, I was a goner. I thank God for you, Sabrina, every day."

Malcolm bent down and swept Sabrina up in his arms. Quickly, he marched out of the room, carrying her. Within minutes he was laying her down on his massive king-size bed and joining her himself.

"I want to show you just how much I love you, Sabrina," Malcolm murmured silkily in her ear as he nipped on one earlobe. "Let me love you."

"Yes, oh yes," Sabrina moaned, savoring the

moment of skin-to-skin contact. "Love me, Malcolm. Please."

Malcolm complied by combing his fingers through her mass of ebony hair and planting playful kisses on her forehead, brow, eyelids and the tip of her nose. When he found the sensitive area at her neck, Sabrina moaned aloud again. "Hmmm, you're very good at that, Dr. Winters," she murmured.

"I'm good at a lot of other things, too," he whispered, tracing the edge of her lips with the tip of his tongue before darting inside. Languidly, he rolled his tongue over her teeth, following the moist contours of her mouth before dancing together with her tongue in an up-tempo swing. Every cell of Sabrina's body came alive at his tender kiss.

She responded by covering his face with a carpet of kisses as they slowly undressed each other, peeling off layer after layer of clothing like the skin of a forbidden fruit. When Malcolm reached her lacy underwear, he edged them down, squeezing her buttocks gently.

And once their clothes were finally removed, they wasted no time in caressing and stroking the length of each other's bodies.

Malcolm began first kneading her breasts, squeezing them between his fingers before bending his head and flicking his tongue across one nipple. He licked and nipped it until it turned into a rock-hard pebble beneath his hot wet tongue. While one hand stimulated one breast, his other softly stroked her belly and navel, traveling downward until he made it to her feminine core.

Sabrina moaned. When he inserted a finger into her and simulated the action he prepared to take with his manhood, she clung to his shoulders, crying out in ecstasy.

Malcolm's erection tightened in response. He wanted to show her just how much he treasured her by worshipping her body. He spread her legs wide and dipped his head lower to her feminine center. Gently he nuzzled her, teasing her with his tongue. He stroked her softly at first and then changed his thrusts as she became more and more aroused. When he sucked gently on the nub at the center of her womanhood and flicked his tongue from side to side, Sabrina nearly bucked off the bed as the pressure built deep within her. Seconds later, she came with quick short breaths.

"Oh, Malcolm. That was incredible."

"I'm glad you enjoyed it," Malcolm said, shifting his weight to one side and tenderly brushing her hair away from her face.

"Well, let me return the favor," Sabrina said, turning toward him.

"Relax a moment," Malcolm laughed, pushing her back onto the pillow and opening the drawer to pull out protection. "We've got all night."

Unable to sleep after a rousing evening of love-making, Sabrina crept downstairs for the wine bottle, hoping to finish the job when she heard her cell phone ringing. She rushed to her purse and found the display reading 10:00 p.m.

"Hello," she said, flipping it open.

"Sabrina, it's Tre," he replied curtly. A little too curtly for her taste.

"What is it, Tre?" Sabrina asked, annoyed. Why had she answered the phone? She was in no mood for Tre's shenanigans. She had a good man like Malcolm Winters waiting for her upstairs who just so happened to love her with his whole heart and was the best lover. Sabrina was blissfully happy. Malcolm's love brought bottomless peace to her soul.

"I need you to come and get Jasmine. I have to leave town unexpectedly."

"Whatever for?" Sabrina queried. "I thought you wanted to spend more time with your daughter? Well, you got it, buddy. Deal."

"Do you mean to tell me you're not going to come get her?"

"Why should I do you any favors?"

"I suppose not. I see that Jasmine's behavior this evening is a reflection of you," Tre commented.

"Pardon me?" Sabrina's tone changed from teasing to angry in two seconds flat. Tre had a way of doing that.

"Don't act like you didn't have anything to do with Jasmine behaving like a spoiled brat the entire day."

Had Jasmine done something wrong? "I have no

idea what you're talking about." Sabrina feigned ignorance. Did this call have something to do with Jasmine's final comment that she would take care of Melanie?

"Jasmine has been completely miserable today. She's practically terrorized Melanie all day, putting a frog on her chair at the pool, refusing every plate brought for lunch, but the final straw was *accidentally* spilling red wine all over Melanie's cream sleeveless gown. So, Melanie came upstairs, packed her bags and fled town. She called me from the airport to say she was returning to Baltimore immediately."

"Did she?" Sabrina acted horrified, but inwardly, she giggled. So, Jasmine had played devil child and scared the woman off. Good for her!

"Don't act like you care in the slightest bit, Sabrina. Hypocrisy doesn't become you."

"Okay, fine. I won't." Sabrina didn't feel bad in the slightest. "So, why do I need to pick up Jasmine? Now you have all the time in the world to spend with her."

"No, I don't. I'm going back to Baltimore to repair the damage your daughter's caused."

"Oh, now she's *my* daughter."

"Yes, she is," Tre replied. "You needn't worry about a custody suit, either." His bags were already packed and he'd called the concierge and requested a limo. But he needed Sabrina to come fetch Jasmine first. He had to get back to Baltimore and smooth Melanie's ruffled feathers.

"What's wrong? Is Melanie not prepared to be Mommy Dearest?" Sabrina chuckled.

"Go ahead, gloat," Tre replied. "You win, Sabrina. Melanie has told me in no uncertain terms that she does not want Jasmine living with us full-time. A week here or a month in the summer there is all she's willing to abide."

Sabrina breathed a sigh of relief. Thank God for small miracles. "I'm glad to hear you both have come to your senses. Jazzy is much better off with me. And of course, I would be more than happy to come and pick up my child. Give me about forty-five minutes."

"No can do," Tre said. "If I want to catch Melanie, I've got to leave now." He looked over at Jasmine playing with her Game Boy on the hotel sofa. He hated to leave, but he had no other choice.

"Don't you dare leave my daughter at that hotel alone, Tre," Sabrina ordered.

"I'll leave her with the hotel concierge. She'll be fine until you arrive. I'm sure they'll give her some free ice cream or something until you get here." Tre hung up the phone.

"Tre! Tre!" Sabrina screamed into the phone, but she heard nothing but a dial tone. Running up the stairs, Sabrina searched the master bedroom for her scattered clothing, but Malcolm turned on the night-stand lamp.

"Sabrina." Malcolm wiped the sleep from his eyes. "What's going on?"

"That bastard is going to leave my child at a hotel alone," Sabrina said as she dressed hurriedly. "Has he not heard of child kidnappings?"

"What?" Malcolm threw the covers back and jumped out of bed. "Why is he leaving early?" he asked. Looking for his briefs on the floor, Malcolm slid them up his legs.

"Apparently, Jasmine behaved poorly and sent Melanie running off to the airport with Tre following behind her like some lost puppy dog."

"And the man can't wait a day to fly back?"

"No!" Sabrina snapped her bra closed. "So he's decided to leave Jasmine at the hotel alone until I arrive."

"I swear I could kill the man," Malcolm said, pulling on a pair of jeans sitting on a nearby ottoman.

"You and me both," Sabrina replied, slipping on her camisole and pulling on her skirt. "You ready?" She glanced over at Malcolm, who was pulling a T-shirt over his head.

"I'm ready now," Malcolm retorted.

Minutes later, they were in his Jaguar, speeding through the streets of Savannah to Tre's hotel. They made it there in record time. Pushing the swinging doors open, they rushed inside. Sabrina headed for the front desk while Malcolm glanced around searching for Jasmine. Sabrina was about to speak with the manager when Malcolm caught sight of a tiny head full of ringlets sitting on the lobby couch. "Sabrina, I see her!" Malcolm yelled.

They both rushed over and sure enough they found Jasmine eating a chocolate ice cream cone.

"Jazzy." Sabrina gathered Jasmine in her arms. "Thank God, you are all right. All the way over, all I could think about what was what could happen…" Her voice trailed off.

Malcolm watched relief descend over Sabrina's face at finding Jasmine unharmed.

"I'm okay," Jasmine replied, licking her lips. "Daddy got me a cone before he left."

"Did he?" Sabrina said, giving Malcolm a knowing look. "I'm just so glad to have you all back to myself." Sabrina placed tons of kisses all over Jasmine's face.

"Mommy, stop. We're in public," she said, wiping them away.

Sabrina grinned from ear to ear. She'd missed being called mommy. "I know, and I don't care. I just love you to pieces." Sabrina hugged her close.

"Mom, I can't breathe."

"Sorry, baby." Sabrina released her and stood up. "You ready to come home now?" Sabrina hoped that was the case because she couldn't bear it if they were still at odds.

"Mom, you have no idea."

Sabrina glanced upward and thanked the Lord. Maybe all this craziness with Tre had to happen to make her and Jasmine appreciate each other all the more. Sabrina and Jasmine began walking hand in hand towards the swinging door.

"You coming, Dr. Malcolm?" Jasmine asked, holding out her other free hand. "'Cause I missed you terribly."

Malcolm's mouth curved into a smile as he accepted her tiny hand. He was not alone anymore. He had a family.

Together, the three of them walked out of the hotel and into the chilly night air.

Chapter 20

Malcolm was nervous when he hung up the phone with Tasha. He'd finally scheduled time to meet his nephew Jayden. And he was bringing reinforcements. He'd never really been around children until Jasmine and he had absolutely no idea how to act around a baby. He was hoping having Sabrina there would be a calming effect on him.

Malcolm couldn't remember the last time he was this nervous. Perhaps it was the first time he tested for his medical boards. Or maybe it was the first time he operated on a patient as the lead surgeon, but none of those quite equaled this momentous occasion.

It didn't take him long to finish dictating some

notes for Grace before locking up the clinic and hopping in his Jag. Along the way, he would pick up Sabrina and head out to Hilton Head Island. It was approximately a thirty-five-mile drive from Savannah.

When he arrived, he found the entire Parker clan outside having a barbecue along with a few close friends, including Monique, and the regulars from the diner, Caleb, Corey and Raymond. Malcolm loved how close their family was and he hoped that when he and Sabrina married, it would be the same way.

He knew it was too soon to talk marriage with Sabrina, so soon after her divorce, which was why he hadn't broached the subject. He was content to wait and enjoy each other's company because one day soon they'd be married and have a child of their own right along with Jasmine.

"Are you excited, nervous, scared?" Sabrina asked on their way to Tasha's apartment in Hilton Head.

"All of the above," Malcolm replied, brusquely taking his eyes off the road. His eyes were wide with fear. "Sabrina, this is Michael's child. When we lost him, Dinah and I thought that was it. He was gone, but now he's not. A part of him will live on in his son. I can hardly believe it's possible, but it is."

Sabrina's knew how much this meant to Malcolm. "Neither can I, but I'm happy that you chose me to share in this experience with you." Sabrina squeezed his hand.

"There's no one else I'd want by my side," Malcolm said.

The short drive to Hilton Head went by quickly and Malcolm and Sabrina made it to the Colonial Grand Apartments within an hour. Stepping out of the car, Malcolm looked up at the three-story resort-style apartments. From what he could tell, Tasha and Jayden were in a good neighborhood. He was not only here today to see his nephew, but to inform Tasha that Michael's estate would provide financial support until Jayden reached eighteen and then of course pay for his college education.

His brother had amassed a substantial fortune in his short time on earth and Malcolm had hired an excellent firm to oversee his portfolio. Jayden would be well taken care of. And of course, with Uncle Malcolm and Grandmother Dinah behind him, he would have need of nothing.

"Let's go," Malcolm held out his hand to Sabrina. She accepted and together they ascended the stairs.

When they found apartment 302, they stopped in front of the oak door. Malcolm smiled nervously at Sabrina before knocking. Tasha answered barefoot and wearing a green silk loungewear set. She nearly equaled Malcolm in height. He estimated she was at least five foot ten. Very model-like and statuesque, Tasha was exactly the kind of beauty that Michael would have gone for.

"Malcolm." She smiled and leaned forward to

give him a hug. "It's so good to finally meet you. Please, come in." When she saw Sabrina standing behind him, she said, "And you must be Sabrina, please, come inside."

"Thank you," Malcolm and Sabrina said in unison, entering the apartment.

The apartment was roomy and nicely decorated with contemporary furniture and top-of-the-line electronics. Malcolm was impressed, but what he was most interested in was the playpen in the corner. Slowly, he walked toward it.

"Please, have a seat," Tasha said, indicating Sabrina should sit on her gold leather sofa. Sabrina did as ordered, but Malcolm had already found someone who caught his fancy. Tasha left them for a moment and returned carrying a tray with freshly squeezed lemonade and three glasses. "Lemonade?" She held up the pitcher.

"Yes, please," Sabrina said. She glanced over at Malcolm. He was standing over the playpen, enraptured by his nephew. Sabrina rose to go over to him, but Tasha stopped her.

"Let him be," she said, pouring Sabrina a glass of lemonade and handing it to her.

What Malcolm found in the playpen was the most beautiful child he'd ever seen. Though he adored Jasmine, Jayden was breathtaking. Tasha had dressed him up for the occasion in overalls, a striped T-shirt and baby Nikes. But what caught him completely off guard was how much he favored his late twin.

Jayden had a head full of curly hair, chubby little cheeks and amazing brown eyes with long curly lashes. Michael's eyes. It overwhelmed Malcolm. Tears ran down his face in earnest as he fell to his knees and stared at his amazingly beautiful nephew. Leaning over, Malcolm reached inside and gathered Jayden in his arms. Though a complete stranger, Jayden came to him without fussing. He merely smiled up at Malcolm and chewed on his plastic toy.

"He's teething," Tasha offered from the couch.

Malcolm turned around suddenly as if it had occurred to him that he and Jayden were not the only people in the room.

The light and glow in Malcolm's eyes was a wondrous thing. Sabrina couldn't be happier for him.

"He's beautiful, Tasha," Malcolm finally spoke from across the room.

"Isn't he?" Tasha shook her head. "I've truly been blessed. And now so have you."

"No doubt," Malcolm replied, running his hands through Jayden's hair. After several minutes, he finally rose and brought Jayden over to the couch to introduce him to Sabrina.

"Say hello to your Auntie Sabrina," Malcolm said, placing Jayden in Sabrina's arms.

Sabrina experienced true bliss holding another baby in her arms again. She hadn't held one since Jasmine was a baby and she just loved that baby smell.

"I have a photo album with pictures of Jayden

from the day he was born until now if you'd like to see them," Tasha spoke up.

"I would love to see them." Malcolm smiled.

"I'll go get them." Tasha rose and went over to her bookshelf. She removed a large album labeled Baby's First Year and handed it to Malcolm. Malcolm accepted it eagerly and flipped through the pages. Tasha had a complete photo history of Jayden's life. Pictures in the hospital, at a month old, first tooth, Jayden's first step and much more. "I've got some professional pictures, too. I've put some aside that you can take back with you."

"Thank you, Tasha." Malcolm was very appreciative of Tasha's kindness considering her shaky start with the Winters family. He and Sabrina swapped. He took back his little nephew while she perused Jayden's photo album.

Malcolm moved from the couch to the floor and that was where he and Jayden played for nearly an hour. Sabrina and Tasha used the opportunity to get to know each other better. Sabrina discovered that Tasha modeled and traveled the world extensively before becoming pregnant. She'd met Michael during Fashion Week in New York and the two had continued to see each other on and off for several years. Michael, however, had been unable to commit and the two had split up right before his death.

Tasha had come back home to Hilton Head to have Jayden. She hadn't discovered that Michael was gone until nearly six months after his death and then she'd been scared of the repercussions if his upper-crust family found out, but then she'd realized that was unfair to Jayden. He had a right to know his father's family, so she'd gone to Boston and told Dinah the truth. Being Dinah, however, she'd automatically assumed Tasha was a gold digger out for her son's fortune, until the paternity test had proved beyond a shadow of a doubt that Michael was Jayden's father. Now Dinah was eager to be a part of his life.

Malcolm sat back while he played with Jayden and listened to Tasha's entire story. "I'm sorry for my mother's reaction to your news," Malcolm said.

"It's not your fault," Tasha said. "Neither of you knew that Michael and I were seeing each other, so I'm sure it seemed an implausible story. But that's behind us now. The truth is out and that's that."

"That's very gracious of you," Malcolm replied.

"I want the Winters family to be a big part of Jayden's life and tell him about his father," Tasha replied. "That's all that's important."

"On that note," Malcolm said, standing up and placing Jayden back in his playpen. Jayden fussed a little when he did. "I'll be right back, little man. I promise."

Malcolm walked back over to the women and pulled out an envelope from his breast pocket. He handed the envelope to Tasha and took a seat beside Sabrina. "It's a document on a trust that's been set up in Jayden's name. The trust will provide a monthly stipend until Jayden reaches the age of eighteen. A separate college fund has also been set up for him."

"Malcolm, this is way too generous…" Tasha began.

"Trust me," Malcolm interrupted her. "It's what Michael would have wanted and as the executor of his will and Jayden's uncle, I'm going to see to it that his son is well provided for."

"Thank you so much." Tasha was deeply touched.

"You're more than welcome," Malcolm said, smiling at her, then at Sabrina. "I want you and Jayden to consider yourselves a part of the Winters family. Now and forever."

"You're incredible." Tasha rushed over and gave Malcolm a great big hug. "God bless you."

As Sabrina watched the scene unfolding in front of her, she couldn't be prouder of her man. He was a prince among men.

Chapter 21

It was nearly ten and if he didn't hustle, Malcolm would be late for church. Unable to sleep last night, he'd arisen late, but feeling alive and full of zest for life.

He was finally going to take Sabrina's advice and see if a little religion could heal his wounds and help him regain his faith. He had an ulterior motive for attending, as well; nothing would please him better than to see his two favorite ladies. Everyone in the community frequented the First Baptist Church for Sunday service and he was sure the Parker family was no exception.

Malcolm rushed in the shower and was in and out in ten minutes. Quickly, he brushed his teeth before twisting open his favorite aftershave. A few quick pats to his cheeks and he was ready for the day.

When he arrived late, Malcolm sat in the back of the hall and as he did, the memory of Dinah forcing him and Michael to attend Sunday worship came rushing back to him, reminding him that once upon a time, he'd hated church. He'd never cared for all the whooping and hollering folks did in church. At the time, he'd been much more interested in reading a science book or performing surgery on his stuffed animals.

Malcolm was surprised though when the preacher's sermon hit on some relevant points that he could apply to his everyday life. Like forgiveness. Maybe it was high time he started forgiving himself for Michael's death. He was contemplating the meaning of it all after the service when Sabrina appeared.

A vision in a simple white sheath that fit her petite frame to perfection and a whimsical scarf wrapped lightly around her neck, Sabrina was breathtaking and it rendered Malcolm momentarily speechless.

As Sabrina stood outside the church in the balmy afternoon breeze with her family, she was surprised to see Malcolm approaching.

"Well, well," Felicia commented, turning around to get a better look at Malcolm as he walked over. "Look who's coming."

"Shhh," her mother whispered.

"Why should I shhh," Felicia answered, not backing

down. "My sister has made herself the catch of the century, *again*. I have to admit, little sis," Felicia teased, "you certainly have a way with the pretty boys."

Sabrina opened her mouth for a choice retort, but her mother shook her head. Malcolm was near, looking hot and sexy in a smart gray suit and tie and polished Italian leather shoes that suited his smooth nutmeg complexion and sexy mustache, causing Sabrina to shiver slightly.

"Sabrina." Malcolm smiled at her and leaned down to bestow Jasmine with a kiss on the forehead. "And how's my favorite girl today?"

"Good," Jasmine replied, blushing. "Am I really your favorite girl?" she asked, glancing up at her best friend with large wide eyes.

"Of course you are." Malcolm grinned and pinched her nose, which she quickly pushed away. "You're second only to another special lady," Malcolm finished, all the while never taking his eyes off Sabrina.

"Can we talk?" Malcolm and Sabrina said in unison. "In private?"

"Sure," Sabrina said. "Felicia, could you take Jasmine over to the ice cream truck?" Sabrina asked. She wanted to discuss with Malcolm how he felt about coming to church again.

"Sure, baby." Her sister departed with her niece in the direction of the ice cream truck with the large crowd of children surrounding it.

Sabrina followed behind Malcolm as he walked out of the sun and into the shade under a big maple tree. She didn't want to see the curious glances coming their way. Despite her attempt at privacy, however, they'd still acquired an audience, who were watching them intently from across the grass. Her mother and several of the women's church group were huddled together. And then there was Jasmine with Felicia and her kids, both smiling and giving her the thumbs-up signal.

"I'm surprised to see you," she said. "What made you finally decide to come to church?" She knew how hard it must have been for him to take this difficult step, but Sabrina knew that this was exactly what Malcolm needed to move on.

"To find peace," Malcolm replied.

"And have you found it?" Sabrina inquired.

Staring deep into her eyes, Malcolm stated emphatically. "Yes, I have."

The night of the Sweetheart Dance, Malcolm was as jittery as a rabbit. There was no doubt in his mind that Sabrina was the woman for him and he'd told himself that he would wait until she was ready, but when he'd stopped at the jeweler for a gift for the dance at the First Baptist Church, he hadn't been able to resist purchasing a platinum three-carat diamond solitaire engagement ring. He knew it was way too soon to spring this on her. He and Sabrina hadn't discussed their future yet and, after her miserable divorce, Malcolm wasn't altogether sure if she would be agreeable to the idea. He was just hoping Sabrina might agree to a long engagement. He intended to ask her after the dance, but the ring was burning a hole in his pocket.

After showering and applying Sabrina's favorite aftershave and cologne, he teamed a coral shirt with dark slacks to finish the look. He could deal with his metrosexual side because Sabrina had requested he wear the same color as her dress.

Since she had class, he planned on meeting her at the dance, but when he arrived the parking lot was jam-packed. Malcolm had to park two blocks away and walk over. Several couples were already milling around in the cool night air, soaking up the romantic ambience.

He passed several patients who wished him well, but he was looking for one person and one person only.

Sabrina was already standing outside waiting with a wrap around her shoulders. Dressed in a sexy silk number with a deep V-neck, spaghetti straps and asymmetrical hem with her hair in an updo, Sabrina was a knockout. He was a very lucky man. Without a shadow of a doubt, Malcolm knew what he had to do.

Sabrina warmed when she saw Malcolm walking toward her. Who would have thought six months ago that she would be standing waiting for the man of her dreams? She'd vowed never to fall in love again, but

Malcolm was everything she had waited her whole life to find.

He was nothing like Tre. Malcolm was strong, kind, compassionate, loyal, a great doctor and an extremely fabulous lover. He would make a great uncle and an even better father. Wow! Malcolm as a stepfather for Jasmine? Had their relationship progressed that far in such a short time? The answer was yes, it had.

She'd fallen hard for the enigmatic, charming, reclusive doctor and she wanted nothing more than to be with him. She was just scared of making that commitment again. After Tre, how could she be sure? She'd been wrong once before. She couldn't afford to make another mistake.

Once Malcolm reached her, however, all negative thoughts and fears flew out the window. Sabrina didn't need to fear him. He would never hurt her. At least not intentionally. He would always love and respect her. He would take care of her and Jasmine, even though she now knew how to do it herself. He would never dishonor her by being unfaithful with another woman. She could believe in him. Trust him. Her heart told her he'd never betray her faith in him.

Malcolm held out both hands to her and Sabrina readily accepted them. "You're breathtaking," he whispered, twirling her around.

"Well, you look pretty spectacular yourself." Sabrina smiled up at him.

"You ready to go inside?" he asked, glancing at the

church's door. The smooth strains of a Luther Vandross song could be heard through the swinging birch doors.

Sabrina nodded. Oh yes, she was. She was ready to shout it from the rooftops. To let everyone including the church congregation know that she loved Dr. Malcolm Winters and she didn't care who saw them.

Thankfully, her parents had accepted Malcolm and he'd transitioned easily into the Parker fold. At first her mother had been a little hesitant, but when she'd seen how happy Sabrina was, she couldn't argue. They had never cared for Tre, so it was welcome relief for Sabrina to know that this time around, her family was in her corner.

"Yes, I am," Sabrina answered fervently. "Let's do this."

Malcolm and Sabrina walked hand in hand into the church recreation room that had been trans-formed into a romantic fantasy. The lights were dim, but Sabrina could see hearts and roses and balloons and streamers everywhere. The women's church group had certainly outdone themselves.

Glancing around the room, Sabrina saw her parents, Alton and Danielle and Felicia and Sean all dressed in their finest and seated at a table for eight.

"Is there room for more?" Sabrina inquired.

"Of course," Felicia replied, pulling out a chair. "We saved you both some seats."

"Thanks, sis." Sabrina smiled. She couldn't believe how well they were getting along now. Their relationship had blossomed since her early days back in town. Sabrina was sure the family was happy about that, too. No more bickering at the dinner table.

Sabrina leaned over. "It's good to see you and Sean out tonight."

"Yeah, we've decided that we need a little more time for ourselves from now on," Felicia replied.

"I couldn't agree more." Sabrina squeezed her arm. "You're always with the kids, tending to their every need. It's good that you're catering to each other's needs."

Sabrina noticed Malcolm didn't sit down beside her. Instead, he whispered something in her father's ear and they disappeared through the swinging doors.

Sabrina wondered what was going on. She hoped everything was okay.

"Do you have any idea how bright your eyes shine when you look at him?" Felicia asked. It had been a long time since she and Sean had looked at each other that way. It was why she was trying to get them out more. Felicia hoped to add a dash of romance in her marriage before she, too, ended up in divorce court.

"Do they?"

"Yes, they light up whenever he's around. I'm real happy that you've found a stand-up guy like Malcolm," Felicia replied, squeezing Sabrina's hand.

"Thank you," Sabrina responded. It meant a lot

that Felicia approved of him. Now that he had her sister's stamp of approval, there was no reason not to marry the guy.

Marriage? Did she just think marriage? Sabrina shook her head. She couldn't have. Yes, they were in love, but marriage? She'd barely been divorced for a year. Surely, she couldn't be ready yet to jump into marriage, could she?

Malcolm and her father returned a short time later, her father sat next to her mother while Malcolm walked back to their seats. A huge grin had replaced the nervous look he'd worn since he'd arrived.

"So, have you got your dancing shoes on, Ms. Parker?" Malcolm asked, striding toward her and extending his arm.

"I sure do." Sabrina grabbed hold of it. "Let's do this. See you later," she said to Felicia and Sean over her shoulder.

Holding hands, Malcolm and Sabrina slowly walked onto the crowded dance floor and found an open spot. His strong hands slid sensuously over her as he gathered her close while he brought their entwined hands to his mouth and planted a kiss across them. "Do you have any idea how crazy in love with you I am?" he whispered.

"I do," Sabrina replied. "Because I feel the same way." They stared into each other's eyes for a prolonged moment. His eyes were serenely compelling as always, but this time something was different, this time they were filled with such…such promise. Sabrina finally looked away and rested her head on Malcolm's chest and listened to his rapid heartbeat.

When his favorite Maxwell song, "Fortunate," came on, Malcolm pressed his body even closer and leaned down to place a hot searing kiss on Sabrina's lips. His mouth moved over hers, slowly and thoughtfully, sending shivers of desire racing through her.

"Hmmm," Malcolm moaned. "You taste so good."

"So do you," Sabrina said, bringing her arms up and circling his neck.

"Come with me," he said, taking her by the hand, and leading her off the dance floor. They walked outside onto the porch. The air outside was cool and crisp, so Malcolm did the gentlemanly thing and removed his jacket and draped it over Sabrina's shoulders.

"What's going on?" she asked.

"You'll see soon enough," he said and brought her to the front of the building near the concrete steps. "Sabrina." Malcolm took both her hands in his.

"Yes?" When Sabrina's eyes gleamed in the dark, Malcolm almost lost his courage. Almost.

"Sabrina." Malcolm reached forward and tucked an errant curl that had fallen loose from her updo. "You know how much I love you, right?"

"Of course." She smiled. "Just as much as I love you." She touched his cheek.

"And Jazzy, too. You know I adore her. She's my little munchkin."

Sabrina nodded. Her daughter had loved Dr. Malcolm from the moment they'd met in the park. She couldn't wait for the day when he officially became a part of their family.

"Then you must know that there's no one else I want. No one else I want to be with." Malcolm paused, struggling to find the words to express how deeply he cared for her.

But he didn't need to make Sabrina understand because she knew what he was trying to say and her eyes welled up with tears. "Me, either. There's no one else for me, Malcolm. I am so over Tre. It's not even funny. I hope you know that."

"That's good to hear. Because I want to spend my life with you, Sabrina." Malcolm dropped to one knee and pulled the ring box out of his breast pocket.

Sabrina's heart lurched.

"What I mean to say is this." Malcolm opened the box and produced a platinum, three-carat, diamond solitaire. "Will you marry me?"

"Yes! Yes!" she said, leaping into his arms and nearly knocking him off his feet.

"Did you just say yes?" Malcolm grabbed her face and searched her eyes for any doubt. He found none.

Sabrina nodded. "Yes, I want to marry you, Malcolm. I want to spend the rest of my life with you. Together. Me, you and Jasmine."

"Yes!" Malcolm shouted and lifted Sabrina off her feet, swinging her in the air. Breathless, he put her back down and slipped the ring onto her finger.

"Then it's official. We're engaged." He smiled and bent down to recapture her lips with a searing kiss. It was a kiss of promise, of hope, of family.

When he withdrew his lips, Sabrina asked, "Is that why you and my father disappeared when we arrived?"

"Guilty as charged," said Malcolm. "I asked your father for your hand in marriage."

"You did?" Sabrina asked. "How very old-fashioned of you."

Malcolm grinned. "I can be sometimes. I was just so happy that he said yes."

"And if he hadn't?"

"Then, I would have proposed anyway," Malcolm stated unequivocally.

"Smart man." Sabrina caressed his chest. "Now, let's go tell everyone," Sabrina said excitedly and pulled him inside.

Her family was thrilled at the news. The Parker family thought the world of Malcolm and extended their best wishes and heartfelt congratulations.

As they danced the night away, cheek-to-cheek, Malcolm and Sabrina were the happiest people alive.

"Jasmine's going to be thrilled when we tell her the news," Sabrina said.

"Hmmm, she sure will be," Malcolm commented, his breath hot against her ear while his hands roamed the sides of her petite figure. "But just think how happy we will be when I get you alone later."

"Oh," Sabrina whispered, loving the feel of his arms around her. "You're one bad, bad boy."

"And you love it."

"I sure do."

Remedy for a broken heart: A sexy cardiologist!

NEVER *Say* NEVER

Yarah St. John

Devastated by her recent divorce, single mom
Sabrina Matthews vows never to fall in love again.
But when she meets Malcolm Winters,
a prominent cardiologist, their chemistry
is irresistible. Can Malcolm convince
Sabrina to never say never again?

*Available the first week of January
wherever books are sold.*

KIMANI™
ROMANCE

www.kimanipress.com

KPYSJ0030107